Bound by Flames

Vlad seized me by the shoulders. "You think I'm angry because he groped you?" Harsh laughter grated out of him. "That might be why I killed him, but it's not why I'm furious now."

"Then why?" I shot back. "Because I didn't leave when you *ordered* me to?"

"Because he could have killed you!" If our bedroom hadn't recently been soundproofed, everyone in the ballroom would've heard his bellow.

"I was alone with him for ten seconds," I snapped.

"I could kill you a dozen times over in ten seconds," Vlad retorted, his voice lower now. "All the different ways you could die ran through my mind as I watched you go into that alcove with him. The only reason I didn't explode him immediately was because you were too close."

Some of my anger drained away as I stared into his eyes. They were green with fury, yes, but something else lurked in them. An emotion I rarely saw in Vlad. Fear.

By Jeaniene Frost

Bound by Flames
Up from the Grave
Twice Tempted
Once Burned
One Grave at a Time
This Side of the Grave
Eternal Kiss of Darkness
First Drop of Crimson
Destined for an Early Grave
At Grave's End
One Foot in the Grave
Halfway to the Grave

Also Available

The Beautiful Ashes

Jeaniene Frost

Bound by Flames
A NIGHT PRINCE NOVEL

AVON
An Imprint of HarperCollinsPublishers

This is a work of fiction. Names, characters, places, and incidents are products of the author's imagination or are used fictitiously and are not to be construed as real. Any resemblance to actual events, locales, organizations, or persons, living or dead, is entirely coincidental.

AVON BOOKS
An Imprint of HarperCollins*Publishers*
195 Broadway
New York, New York 10007

Copyright © 2015 by Jeaniene Frost
Excerpts from *Halfway to the Grave; One Foot in the Grave; At Grave's End; Destined for an Early Grave; This Side of the Grave; One Grave at a Time; Up From the Grave* copyright © 2007, 2008, 2009, 2011, 2014 by Jeaniene Frost
ISBN 978-0-06-207608-3
www.avonromance.com

First Avon Books mass market printing: February 2015

Avon Trademark Reg. U.S. Pat. Off. and in Other Countries, Marca Registrada, Hecho en U.S.A.
HarperCollins® is a registered trademark of HarperCollins Publishers.

Printed in the U.S.A.

10 9 8 7 6 5 4 3 2 1

*To Aunt Dottie and Uncle Bob,
with much love, admiration, and thanks.*

Acknowledgments

First and foremost, I have to thank God for gifting me with the job I dreamed about when I was a child. None of this would be possible without Your many blessings, Lord. Of course, I would have had a much harder time writing about romance if not for my husband, Matthew, who has been the love of my life since I was sixteen. Speaking of writing, sincerest thanks go to my wonderful editor, Erika Tsang, for her work on this novel and the many others before it. I haven't made it easy on Erika at times, but she's soldiered through with vampiric-like determination and I couldn't ask for a better editor. Thanks also to my fabulous agent, Nancy Yost, for too many things to list here, and to my dear friends Melissa Marr and Ilona Andrews, who are truly the wind beneath my wings.

I would be remiss if I didn't take the time to thank Tom Egner for another sizzling cover, as well as Pamela Spengler-Jaffee, Jessie Edwards,

Liate Stehlik, Shawn Nicholls, and the rest of the tremendous team at Avon Books for all of their hard work. I'd also be unforgivably remiss if I didn't say a heartfelt thank you to the readers, reviewers and bloggers who've given my books a chance. You could do many other things with your time, and I so appreciate that you've chosen to spend it on one of my stories.

Last but by no means least, I want to say thank you to my family. I don't say this often enough so let me put it in writing—I love all of you, and I'd be a far lesser person without you in my life.

Chapter 1

Hundreds of candles glowed from the ballroom's gothic chandeliers, casting soft amber light onto the guests below. The lack of modern illumination wasn't because this house used to be a medieval stronghold. The owner was a pyrokinetic vampire, so he was rather fond of fire.

I was perched on one of the ceiling's corner rafters, taking a brief rest from my evening's covert activities. A few stories below, all the guests wore masks and costumes, but even without seeing fangs or glowing green eyes, it was easy to determine who was human and who wasn't. Vampires had an inherent grace, making their movements appear as seamless as water rushing over stones. Their mortal counterparts—well, let's just say they lacked that finesse. Not that it was their fault. Unlike vampires, humans didn't have supernatural control over every muscle in their bodies.

Until several weeks ago, neither did I. Changing

into a vampire had had some unexpected side effects in addition to the now-I-drink-blood stuff. Before, I also didn't have my new ability to briefly hold in the electrical currents that had surged through me since touching a downed power line when I was thirteen.

The candles in the chandeliers suddenly blazed brighter, coinciding with a man striding up to the balcony that overlooked the ballroom. If that wasn't enough to announce his presence, his aura flared, too, sending invisible currents rippling through the room. When they hit me, it felt like being engulfed by an electrical field, which, considering my own inner voltage, was ironic. Only a handful of Master vampires in the world could manifest an aura big enough to encompass the gargantuan ballroom. Vlad's was so powerful, it proclaimed his identity more clearly than if he'd been wearing a neon name tag.

That's why his disguise was pointless. Beneath the mask made famous by the movie *V for Vendetta* was a darkly stubbled jaw, high cheekbones, winged eyebrows and burnished-copper eyes ringed with emerald. His black tuxedo elegantly covered Vlad's lean, muscled body, almost daring onlookers to fantasize about what lay beneath *that*. When he held up a hand to silence the musicians, candlelight reflected off his wedding ring, making the twisting bands of gold briefly gleam.

"The unmasking is in one hour," Vlad announced, his cultured voice tinged with a Slavic accent. Then he smiled, radiating charm and challenge at the same time. "Until then, enjoy the mystery of wondering who's beside you, if you haven't already guessed."

Light laughter and applause greeted his statements, but I was alarmed. If the unmasking was an hour away, I was almost out of time.

A flick of Vlad's hand had the musicians playing again, and the dance floor was once again filled with costumed, waltzing couples. I didn't spare them a glance as I leapt onto a nearby ceiling beam, balancing myself instantly on the narrow plank of wood. I could've used reflexes like these back when I was a circus performer, not to mention when I was trying out for the Olympic gymnastics team. Supernatural agility was another perk of becoming a vampire.

Once I'd sprinted back to the network of organ pipes I'd climbed to reach the ceiling, I slid down, landing in the utility space between the walls. Music from the pipes swelled, almost deafening me, but that was the point. Not even vampires with their hyper-elevated senses could hear me above the racket. I crept around until I reached an air-conditioning filter, removing it before squeezing myself into the cramped air duct. Good thing I was wearing a formfitting costume. If I'd dressed as Marie Antoinette, I'd have never made it through.

Finally, I shimmied out of the duct into a closet. Once there, I replaced the filter, brushed the dust from my black costume, and headed into the ballroom to resume my spying. I hadn't made it ten feet inside before a hand landed on my back.

"There you are," a voice with a heavy Hungarian accent said.

I turned. The vampire behind me wore a much fancier version of the Joker's trademark purple suit, and he'd covered what I could see of his naturally pale skin with white greasepaint. His mask came to his lower lip, and the twisted smile etched onto the ceramic upper one made his face look like it was stuck in a perpetually evil grin.

My mask didn't cover any of my mouth, so the vampire could see it when I smiled.

"Here I am," I agreed. I'd made sure to make the Joker's acquaintance earlier because he'd been on my target list tonight, but he'd also been with another woman. That meant I couldn't deploy my secret weapon since it required closer contact than his date would've put up with. She wasn't with him now, though, so I seized my opportunity.

"I hope you're here to ask me to dance," I said, tilting my head invitingly. At least, I hoped it looked that way. The faux-horned headpiece I wore made me feel like a rabbit with two stiff, extended ears.

"But of course," he said, linking his arm through mine.

My full-body suit kept him from feeling the electricity coursing through me. If not for the suit, he'd have known my real identity the moment he touched me. That's why I'd chosen to attend the ball in a Maleficent costume, annoying pointy headpiece or not. The current-repelling rubber covered me from head to toe, leaving only my face bare. The mask took care of any currents radiating from that and my scent would be unfamiliar to anyone who hadn't met me before, which was most of the people here.

Most. As the Joker—yes, I knew his real name, but this suited him better—led me onto the dance floor, I couldn't stop from glancing up at the balcony. The place where Vlad had stood was now empty. Good. The only vampire I was worried about tonight was him.

Once we were among the other dancers, the Joker drew me into his arms, his blue eyes flaring with an inhuman glow of green as they slid over my body. The costume fit me like a glove, leaving few of my curves to the imagination, but he looked like he was imagining anyway. Explicitly.

I suppressed a shudder, glad the head-to-toe rubber also muted the scent of distaste that had to be coming from me. The Joker's silk and cloth attire didn't act as an olfactory barrier. The scent of lust wafting from him practically clogged my nose, and I didn't even breathe anymore. Since I needed information from him, I smiled as we began to dance. I'd learned how to waltz exactly one day ago, but that turned out to be practice enough. The Joker whirled me through steps I easily kept up with. He held me closer than the formal dance dictated, though, and I didn't think it was an accident when his hand grazed my ass.

Once more, I glanced up at the balcony. Thank *God* it was still empty!

"When will you tell me your name, my enticing stranger?" the Joker asked, his hand still trailing low on my hip. "I can tell you've been newly made. Who do you belong to?"

I wasn't surprised that he'd pegged me as a baby vampire. My costume might hold in my electrical currents and scent, but it couldn't contain my aura, and like all new vampires, it was weak. Vlad's guest list contained the biggest and baddest of Eastern Europe's undead society, so under normal circumstances, I'd only be here as a stronger vampire's servant. Being written off as insignificant suited me. Not knowing who I was meant the Joker didn't know about my abilities, and I wasn't about to give him any hints as to my real identity.

I used the next steps of the dance to maneuver his hand away from my ass. Then I smiled with what I hoped was mysterious allure. "Patience. I'll tell you who I am at the unmasking."

"Patience?" he repeated with more than a hint of scorn. Guess my attempt at being mysterious and alluring had failed.

Truth be told, I didn't have a lot of experience with flirting. I'd started electrocuting anyone I touched at thirteen, which put me firmly in the "dateless" column for the next twelve years. Not even vampires were immune to the dangers of skin-to-skin contact with me, and that's when I wasn't even trying to hurt them. Since I needed the Joker to stay close for the next few minutes, I had to keep up my act, poor faux seduction skills or no. Soon, I'd sneak the detachable fingers off my right glove, touch him while holding in my currents, and thus find out his darkest secret.

Lie detector tests had nothing on my ability to discern people's worst sins through a single touch. I'd hated my psychometric abilities until recently, when they had become a necessary tool for keeping me and the people I loved alive.

The Joker smiled, seeming to look past my less-than-suave flirting skills. Or, I realized as he danced us toward one of the ballroom's curtained, secluded alcoves, he had something else in mind.

"Patience is a virtue and I hate virtues," he murmured, using his body to force me into the alcove. "Besides, I don't really care what your name is or who you belong to. All I want to know is how tight you are."

Whoa. Talk about coming on too strong! "I don't think so, my impatient friend," I said, laughing as if he'd told a joke. "Maybe later, but now, let's go back to the dance—"

"Let's not," he interrupted, pulling me flush against him. Then his hand landed on my ass as if I'd begged him to spank me. I gasped, so horrified at what was about to happen, I froze. The Joker's head began to lower, his lips nearing mine—

He screamed as flames shot up his face. His hands flew off me to beat at the fire in an instinctive attempt to smother it. The flames only spread, glowing brighter before I could finish shouting, "Stop!"

I peeked out from the curtains to see Vlad shoving his way through the guests, who'd quit dancing to stare at the screaming, burning man. Vlad's mask was off and his long dark hair swung from his rapid strides. His hands were covered in flames, but unlike the Joker frantically pummeling his own face, the flames didn't burn Vlad. The same power that allowed him to manifest and control fire also kept him safe from its deadly effects.

"Stop?" Vlad's voice whipped through the air, causing the vampires who'd moved toward the Joker to turn and walk away once they realized who'd caused the fire. "Why would I do that?"

Even if those present hadn't figured it out, I wouldn't let a man burn to death just to keep up the pretense.

I came out of the alcove. "Because he didn't know that I'm your wife."

Chapter 2

 I drew off my mask and pulled down my face-framing headpiece. Black hair spilled around my shoulders, but that wasn't my most distinctive feature. The scar running from the right side of my face all the way down to my hand was.

Gasps sounded and I almost pitied the other men I'd danced with. They probably expected to burst into flames next. Vampires were notoriously territorial over what they considered theirs. Add in Vlad being a centuries-old conqueror who'd earned the nickname "the Impaler" when he was human, and you had someone far scarier than Bram Stoker's fictional version.

"Lock the doors. No one leaves," Vlad stated, adding to the newly ominous atmosphere in the ballroom.

A flurry of activity signified his people rushing to obey. Say what you will about Castle Dracula—whether you saw them or not, Vlad's guards were everywhere.

"Stop burning him, you've made your point," I tried again.

Vlad glanced at the screaming man without remorse. "If he valued his life, he shouldn't have ignored your refusal. Even if he didn't know you were my wife, he knew you were my guest."

Did I mention Vlad tended toward the brutal side of archaic? To him, burning the Joker to death for his forceful come-on was a perfectly appropriate response. A modern man would've considered the matter closed after a punch to the face.

I went over to Vlad, slipping my arms around his neck despite his hands still being lit up with flames. His feelings were locked down, keeping me and all the other vampires he'd made from tapping into his emotions like we usually could. Still, he had to be seething. Otherwise, he wouldn't have blown my cover in such a spectacularly violent way.

Then again, he hadn't wanted me to go under-cover tonight in the first place. I'd had to argue for days to get him to agree. Now this. Pleading wouldn't save the Joker—the only word Vlad hated more than *Dracula* was *please*. Instead, I stood on tiptoe, my mouth brushing his ear as I whispered into it.

"I haven't touched him to learn what we need to know, so you can't kill him. You know how hard it is for me to get the information through his bones."

He said nothing and his body continued to feel statuelike in its stiffness. Then, the flames on his hands vanished as he wound them through my hair, pulling it free of the bun that had mostly come undone anyway.

"Do it."

Two clipped words, but his tone was no longer scathing. The flames on the Joker's face extinguished as abruptly as if he'd been blasted with a fire hose.

I waited until the Joker's face returned to normal, if soot-smeared, skin. Supernatural healing was one of the perks of being a vampire. Otherwise, he'd need to wear a mask for the rest of his life.

"Don't move while my wife touches you," Vlad ordered. He didn't need to add a threat. His tone was menacing enough.

"Your wife?" the Joker repeated, appalled. He must have missed that while he was trying to put out his face earlier. Then he glanced at his hand, as if remembering that it had been plastered to my ass only a few minutes ago.

"I'll take that," Vlad said coolly, and ripped the Joker's hand off with a single, brutal twist.

I winced. So he'd seen that, too. I had to act fast, before Vlad yanked something off that wouldn't grow back. I approached the Joker, who clutched his new stump while grunting harshly. He didn't scream, though. Losing a hand must not have hurt as much as getting his face torched.

"I need to touch Khal Drogo, too," I said, referring to the vampire who'd come costumed as the warlord from *Game of Thrones*. No need for me to be stealthy about copping a feel from anyone now. I gave a frustrated glance at the silent, costumed crowd. This was exactly the way I hadn't wanted tonight to go.

What did you expect? my hated inner voice whispered. *Everything you do ends in failure.*

I tried to ignore my nasty internal critic—and the hundreds of people staring at me—as I touched the Joker with my bare right hand. He jerked at the currents that flowed into him since I didn't bother to hold back my voltage. Why waste the strength? Everyone now knew who I was, so they knew what I could do. Vlad's oldest enemy, Mihaly Szilagyi, had made sure of that.

As soon as I touched him, colorless images flooded my mind, morphing the ballroom into a farmhouse and me into the Joker.

I kicked open the wooden door, taking in the single room with one glance. Two pallets lay on the floor closest to the hearth, the blankets thin and frayed from repeated use. Something bubbled in the earthen pot above the fire and a stack of wood looked like it had been hastily dropped. I smiled. The small farmhouse appeared to be empty, but it wasn't.

It didn't take long to find the trapdoor beneath the single table in the room. The screaming started before I opened it, making me smile wider. I liked it when they screamed. Liked it when they fought, too. The two girls I hauled out of the crawl space were too young and skinny to put up much of a fight, but I'd take what I could get . . .

His hand had grown back by the time I came out of the memory. I stared at it while I fought the urge to vomit or tear my skin off, whichever made me feel cleaner faster. Reliving peoples' worst sins as though I were the one committing them frequently disgusted me. Sometimes, like this, it was worse. When my psychic abilities first developed, all the darkness I experienced drove me to a suicide attempt. Now, I focused until I channeled my anger and repugnance into more useful emotions.

"Rip his clothes off," I stated.

Vlad's guards rushed to obey. As I was his wife, they'd do whatever I told them unless Vlad countermanded it, and he knew why I needed bare skin for what I was going to do next.

When the Joker was wearing only his scorched mask, I ran my right hand over him, starting with his shoulders. I didn't relive his worst sin again; thankfully, that only happened the first time I touched someone. However, essence trails flared beneath my fingertips, marking the invisible imprints from people who'd left emotional impressions on his skin. Many were from former victims of his violent tendencies, though some were affectionate, reminding me that even monsters had people who loved them. After I'd touched his shoulders, neck, arms, and legs, I dropped my hand. I'd felt dozens of essence trails on the Joker, but none of them had been familiar.

"I can't find any trace of Szilagyi," I finally said.

The Joker sagged with relief. I was about to tell Vlad to burn him to death anyway, after what I'd seen of his worst sin, but before I could say anything, the Joker exploded.

I leapt away from the burning remains of the vampire. When I glanced at Vlad, he was still smiling in a friendly way. If I'd have caught that before, I would've known to beat a hasty retreat. Vlad was never more dangerous than when he flashed his relaxed, genial grin. It aimed my way next and I stiffened. Yeah, he was still pissed. His grin plus the fact that he hadn't waited to detonate the Joker before I was out of the splatter path told me that.

"You'll get a lot of 'no' RSVPs to your next party," I said, brushing the smoldering bits from my costume.

His smile only widened. "This isn't the first party I've thrown where fewer guests left than arrived."

No, it wasn't. Most of what history had recorded about Vlad Basarab Dracul, a.k.a. Dracula or Vlad "Tepesh," meaning "the Impaler" was wrong, but some things weren't, such as the infamous dinner in the fourteen hundreds where he slaughtered his nobles sometime between the main course and dessert. Like the Joker, those guests had had it coming, too.

I didn't know if the Khal-Drogo-themed vampire did, but I was about to find out. Three of Vlad's guards hustled him in front of me, not letting go because he was struggling too hard. After what had happened to the last guy I touched, I couldn't blame him. At least I didn't need to order that he be stripped. His upper body was mostly bare anyway.

I ignored his protests as I laid my right hand on his meaty arm. As usual, colorless images from his worst sin overtook me, proving yet again that there was nothing wrong with *that* aspect of my abilities. Once I was mentally back in the present, I started searching him as I had the Joker, whose remains were still smoldering on the alcove's marble floor.

This time, I recognized one of the essence trails marking the vampire's body. I glanced at Vlad and gave him a single, grim nod. Either the costumed Khal Drogo translated that or Vlad's new smile terrified him, because he began to sputter out a denial.

"I knew him long ago, before everyone believed that he'd been killed. I haven't seen him in centuries, I promise!"

Lies. The essence thread I'd felt hadn't been faint from age. It had nearly jumped out at me from its vibrancy. I stepped away, but not to avoid another blast zone. To keep from being jostled as Samir, the new head of Vlad's guards, immediately began to drag the vampire away. Vlad wouldn't kill the costumed Khal Drogo for conspiring with his most dangerous enemy. No, he'd suffer a much worse fate.

"Who else?"

Vlad's glacier tone cut through the flash of sympathy I felt for the vampire being hauled away to the dungeon. Right, I had more work to do.

After I psychically felt up four more vampires to see if they were in league with Szilagyi (they weren't), it was time to call it a night. Or morning, as dawn was only a couple hours away. Once the sun rose, I'd be out of commission whether I wanted to be or not. Vampires didn't burn in sunlight as legend claimed, but new vamps like me passed out at sunrise and stayed out until almost dusk. That gave Vlad plenty of time to see if our duplicitous guest knew Szilagyi's location. I hoped so, yet I doubted it. Vlad's oldest enemy hadn't told any of his conspirators where he was, so unless the costumed Khal Drogo proved to be the exception, we were back to square one.

I was sick of square one, hence my talking Vlad into letting me do some psychic spying tonight. If I'd had the *rest* of my abilities, like seeing the future or tracking someone by following their essence trail back to their location, we might have caught Szilagyi already. But turning into a vampire had caused me to lose those, and no one knew if their loss was permanent. Right now, my psychic abilities were limited to reliving people's worst sins and recognizing essence trails. Sounded exotic, but the former was only good for giving me nightmares and the latter wouldn't lead us to the vampire who'd proven almost impossible to kill. Finding out who Szilagyi was in collusion with only showed how far his reach had grown, and wow, had that man been busy in the three hundred years he'd been pretending to be dead.

"Anyone else?" I asked, wiping my right hand against my leg. No matter how many times I did that, it still felt like the vile images I'd seen were stuck to me.

Vlad's gaze swept the crowd. Nothing but blank expressions stared back at him. If anyone quailed or showed fear, they'd be guaranteeing themselves a turn under my hand.

"No, that will do," he finally said. "Bid our remaining guests good night, Leila. I'll escort you to our room."

I bristled at his dismissive tone. Yes, he had gruesome plans for the rest of the evening, and no, I didn't join in on interrogations, but he was sending me to bed like a child?

"I'm staying," I said, my brow arching in challenge.

For a second, his shields cracked, searing me with his emotions before that invisible wall slammed down again. I wasn't the only vampire he'd made who took a step back after getting hit with that maelstrom of rage. On the outside, Vlad looked like the very picture of self-control, but inside, he was Mount Vesuvius right before it blew.

"Then again, I'm tired," I muttered. Obviously, we were destined for a fight, and I didn't want to have it out with Vlad in front of hundreds of strangers.

Vlad grasped my arm and began to propel me out of the ballroom. Our guests gave us a wide berth, no doubt glad to have his attention directed away from them. I didn't bother bidding anyone good night. After Vlad slammed the ballroom door behind us, it would have been redundant anyway.

Chapter 3

 "What the hell were you thinking?" Vlad demanded as soon as we entered the privacy of our bedroom.

"Which time?" I asked, refusing to back down now that we were alone. Playing dead worked when confronted with an angry grizzly, but Vlad was more like a dragon. You either fought back or you got your ass burned off while you ran away.

His gaze turned to emerald as it raked over me. "When you allowed yourself to be alone with another vampire."

He'd already toasted the Joker; wouldn't he be over the ass-grab by now? "I needed him to stick around until I could sneak my glove off and touch him. I didn't think he'd come on so strong with hundreds of people only a curtain's width away—"

Vlad seized me by the shoulders, his hands so hot I half expected my bodysuit to melt beneath them.

"You think I'm angry because he groped you?"

Harsh laughter grated out of him. "That might be why I killed him, but it's not why I'm furious now."

"Then why?" I shot back. "Because I didn't leave when you *ordered* me to?"

"Because he could have killed you!" If our bedroom hadn't recently been soundproofed, everyone in the ballroom would've heard his bellow. "I agreed to let you try your tricks tonight because you promised never to be alone with anyone, yet you went behind a curtain with a vampire I told you was ruthless enough to be in league with Szilagyi. You're lucky he only tried to fuck you instead of stab you through the heart with silver!"

"I was alone with him for ten seconds," I snapped.

"I could kill you a dozen times over in ten seconds," Vlad retorted, his voice lower now. "All the different ways you could die ran through my mind as I watched you go into that alcove with him. The only reason I didn't explode him immediately was because you were too close."

Some of my anger drained away as I stared into his eyes. They were green with fury, yes, but something else lurked in them. An emotion I rarely saw in Vlad. Fear.

He'd honestly thought my life had been in danger. Oh, Vlad knew I would've fought back if the Joker had made a lethal move, but he also knew the horrible pain of losing someone he loved. Vlad's guilt over his former wife's suicide was the sin I saw when I first touched him. Plus, he did have a point. I shouldn't have let the Joker draw me into a secluded alcove. I'd been in disguise, but a disguise wasn't foolproof and Vlad's enemies had tried to kill me before. One of them had even succeeded. Vlad changing me into a vampire after I'd bled out in his arms was the only reason I was still here, arguing with him.

"I should have been more careful," I acknowledged, letting out a sigh. "Wanting to catch Szilagyi sooner rather than later made me careless. Aside from the hell he's put you and me through, my sister and father have to stay in hiding until this is over. We might have all the time in the world to take Szilagyi down, but they're human, so they don't."

"I don't care," he said with brutal honesty. "If they wish, I can replace every minute your family loses while in hiding, but I cannot replace you."

How like Vlad to say something sweet and infuriating at the same time. Yes, if my family drank enough of his blood, he could add decades to their life span. My sister Gretchen might want that, if our hunt for Szilagyi took a long time, but my father wouldn't. He hadn't even spoken to me since he found out I was no longer human.

"Hopefully we won't need that, but either way, next time, I'll be more careful. Promise." I brushed his face, my touch feather light compared to the grip he still had on my shoulders. "I told you before, you won't lose me—"

"You're right, I won't," he muttered, his mouth cutting off the rest of what I was going to say.

I didn't have time to be surprised by his abrupt change in mood. Vlad backed me against the nearest wall, ripping away his emotional shields along with the front of my costume. Rage, lust and love tore through my subconscious, mixing with my feelings until I couldn't tell which were mine and which were his. Not that it mattered. I loved him with the same crazed intensity, craved him more than the blood I now needed to survive—and no one maddened me more than Vlad. We had that in common, too.

His whiplash transition from fury to passion might've frightened me months ago, but now, I could feel all the things he wouldn't allow himself to say. He needed to touch me, taste me, to ease the hated fear he'd felt when he thought I was in danger. His actions might seem more brutal than sensual, but if I pushed him away, he'd stop. Yet with every emotion that seethed through mine, he was urging me not to. Instead, he dared me to respond with the same unbridled intensity, and to free my inhibitions the way he'd freed his previously untouchable heart.

I took that dare, gripping his hair and using those long dark strands to pull him closer. His mouth was hard yet sensual as it bruised and tantalized mine, until not even moans could make it past my lips. He kissed me as though he wanted to punish me with pleasure, and when he ripped his tuxedo open and his bare flesh touched mine, I shuddered. Vlad's dangerous powers had their own unexpected benefits, such as making his body feel like molten steel when his abilities, or desire, flared to life.

My hands left his hair to pull away the remaining pieces of his shirt. Hot, muscled flesh seared my breasts as he crushed me closer. A growl of dark carnality left him when my hand traveled down his taut stomach and into his pants. He wrapped my legs around his waist, using his body to pin me to the wall while he tore at the lower half of my costume.

My fangs scored his tongue, flavoring our kiss with the coppery taste of his blood. I sucked it from his tongue while rubbing myself against the hard length that jutted along my thigh. His grip tightened, and when he pulled my hips hard against his, I arched upward in blind, blatant need.

His first thrust made me cry out at the rapturous burn within. The sensations were so intense; I would've called them pain if I didn't claw at his back for more. The rest of the cries I made were of pure ecstasy, and they went on until dawn stole my consciousness away.

The bedroom drapes were open when I awoke, showing the rosy shades of a late afternoon Romanian sky. At least it wasn't all the way dark yet. My progress fighting against the anesthetic effects of the sun was improving.

The side of the bed where Vlad slept was empty, of course. He'd beaten the sun's control over him centuries ago. Usually, he made a point to be in the bedroom when I woke up, but not today. With a new prisoner in the dungeons, I couldn't say I was surprised. Vlad might doubt that the Khal Drogo-clad vampire knew where Szilagyi was, but he'd still burn him within an inch of his life to find out. Due diligence, he'd once called it.

A covered mug was on the nightstand closest to me, the warm, rich scent of blood emanating from it. I forced myself to grasp it slowly instead of snatching it up like I wanted to. For one, I was trying to get full control over my hunger, so fall-ing on it like an animal would defeat the purpose. For another, I'd smash the mug to smithereens if I didn't treat it with utmost gentleness and I wanted to *drink* the blood. Not wear it.

After I finished my liquid breakfast, something shiny caught my eye on the nightstand. Right, my wedding ring. I'd taken it off the night before because the wide gold band with its jeweled dragon would've outed me immediately as Leila Dalton Dracul. This was the ring Vlad had worn when he was prince of Wallachia, now called Romania. I'd thought it was the most romantic thing he'd done by resizing the an-cient royal heirloom to be my wedding ring, but when I reached out to put it back on my hand, I stiffened.

I ran my right hand over the ring until the jewels that made up the tiny dragon cut my fingers, yet nothing changed. The ring felt like cold, lifeless metal, and it shouldn't have. Three out of the four Wallachian princes it had belonged to had been murdered while wearing it, so the ring should've throbbed with essence imprints, yet I felt nothing. It was as if the ancient heirloom were dead.

Only one thing would make an object feel that way after I touched it with my right hand. I was already sure, but I went over to the fireplace and rammed my hand into a glowing log anyway. The fire caressed my skin instead of burning it—the way it would to only one other vampire in the world.

Shock gave way to anger, then anger to fury. At some point since I left the ballroom last night, Vlad must have coated me with a massive dose of his aura. I hadn't noticed him doing that, of course, just like I hadn't noticed when he did it the first time. Back then, I'd been focused on a mountain exploding all around me. This time, passion had claimed my full attention.

It couldn't have been accidental. Not with the incredible control Vlad had over his power. He hadn't made love to me until daybreak merely because he'd been overwhelmed by desire. He'd also done it to *distract* me!

That knowledge wiped away my warm memories of the previous evening as thoroughly as the ring felt wiped of its former wearers' essences. As we both knew, coating me in his aura wouldn't only render me fireproof; it would also render me psychic-proof. Now I couldn't do anything to help him track down Szilagyi or his associates. With one imperious move, Vlad had made a Magic 8 Ball more supernaturally intuitive than me.

"Damn you!" I yelled, betrayal making my voice echo throughout the bedroom. "*Why?*"

"You know why," his calm voice said from behind me.

I whirled, seeing Vlad in the farthest corner of the bedroom. He stood so still that he almost blended into the tall furniture next to him. For a moment, I wondered if he'd been there the whole time, then I noticed the bedroom door slowly closing behind him.

"Despite your promise, you won't be more careful next time," he went on, his burnished copper gaze unwavering. "In many ways, you are wise beyond your years, but your impatience makes you reckless. You already died once when an enemy used your recklessness and overconfidence in your abilities against you. I won't allow the same thing to happen again."

I went over to him, anger causing sparks to shoot from my right hand. No matter what happened, nothing seemed to be able to smother *that* ability.

"I know I screwed up last night, but you can't just decide to strip me of my psychic powers, Vlad!

They've saved my life and yours before, plus in the twenty-first century, *husband* is no longer synonymous with *master*."

When I'd almost reached him, he grabbed my hands, the currents that were so dangerous to everyone else absorbing harmlessly into his skin. Being fireproof had more than one advantage.

"I'm very aware that I'm not your master. If one of my people disobeyed me the way you did, they'd spend a month on the pole learning to regret it."

Anger gave way to incredulity. "Are you threatening to *impale* me?"

He yanked me closer, his iron grip in stark contrast to the brush of his lips against my forehead.

"On the contrary, I'm reminding you that it will never happen." I tried to wrench away and his other hand snapped up, tightening on my hair until I couldn't look away from his relentlessly piercing gaze. "I would never harm you, but until you've learned to use your abilities wisely, I will continue to strip you of them as fast as they return."

"You have no right."

Something other than anger sharpened my words. Deep down, I was also afraid. Didn't he see that he was crippling our marriage? We already had different backgrounds and a six-hundred-year age difference to overcome; how did he think we'd make it if he kept insisting that my opinion didn't matter about my own *life*? I might have put myself in hypothetical danger last night, but with all his enemies, Vlad put himself in real danger every time he left the house, yet you didn't see me expecting him to become a recluse. And sure, as a former prince Vlad was used to being obeyed, but I thought he'd learned how to compromise in our relationship—

"You gave me the right," he breathed against my lips, "when you made me admit that I loved you."

At those words, I remembered what Maximus had said the last time I saw him. *I love Vlad and I'd gladly die for him. But whenever he loves something, he ends up destroying it. He can't help it. It's just his nature.*

At the same time, my hated inner voice crowed, *I TOLD you it would never work between you two!*

Vlad released me, walking out of our room without another word. I let him go, fighting to get control over my wildly swinging emotions. I wanted to go after him, but he'd made it clear that he wouldn't change his mind and he wasn't even close to being sorry, so what was the point?

After he left, I stared at the wedding ring on my hand, refusing to believe I'd made a mistake. Despite his infuriating act, I still loved Vlad and he loved me. Not so long ago, that was all I wanted out of life. Now that I had it, I needed to make it work without surrendering my will, identity *or* abilities.

It wouldn't be easy. Vlad had survived for hundreds of years by being ruthless and calculating. No wonder he treated our marriage like a war he had to win. Guess I should've expected what he'd done, not that I intended to stand for it. My abilities were part of me, and Vlad couldn't just decide to rip out the parts of me he didn't like. I couldn't do the same to him, which was why both of us would have to compromise if we wanted our marriage to last.

Still, how did you show the world's biggest control freak that the secret to lasting love meant giving up control? I didn't know, but I intended to find out.

Chapter 4

 I sat next to Vlad in his luxurious private aircraft. Instead of holding his hand to make sure I didn't accidentally short-circuit the plane's electrical system, I wore specialized rubber gloves. We hadn't touched at all since his domineering stunt three days ago. Compromise Lesson One: Pull a dick move, and your dick gets denied. Every woman knew that, and now, so did the vampire sitting next to me.

If his new abstinence was bothering him, he didn't show it. In fact, it might be messing with my emotions more than his. I'd gone to bed the past three nights in the ugliest pajamas I could find; Vlad walked naked from the shower, and with the size of his bedroom, that walk was longer than a model's runway. It gave me plenty of time to see the steam rising from his hard, heated flesh as the drops clinging to him evaporated, plus see how his hair looked wilder and darker when wet, and don't get me started on the way he'd look at me as he slid into bed. If my ugly pajamas were a proclamation of "you can't touch this," his challenging, sensual gaze practically screamed "you know you want to touch *this*."

Yeah, I did, but I had to focus on the big picture. If Vlad thought a few days of flashing his skin—glistening when wet, highlighting those ripped muscles, hollows and sinews while that steam reminded me of how hot he felt deep inside . . . dammit, focus!—would be enough to make me forget what he'd done, he was wrong. Abstinence was merely the first step in my plan. Compromise Lesson Two involved Vlad doing something he didn't like for the greater good of our marriage. I didn't know what yet, but I'd figure it out.

Hopefully soon, because Lesson One sucked.

In Romanian, the pilots announced that we were about to land. I glanced out the window, seeing mostly darkness below. Wasn't Paris called the city of lights?

"Why the sudden trip to Paris?" I asked in a casual tone, as if I hadn't been wondering this for the past few hours.

"Not Paris, Payns," he said, enunciating the word more clearly than he had when he first told me we were going to France. "I'm looking for someone and I believe this is where he is."

"Szilagyi?" I guessed before logic told me it couldn't be.

An eye roll preceded his response. "If I thought *he* were here, would I have brought you?"

No, of course not. If he thought I was too reckless to search for Szilagyi's people among his self-proclaimed allies, Vlad certainly wouldn't bring me to his long-awaited showdown with his enemy. I stifled a snort. It's like he'd forgotten all about the times I'd saved my own butt through my abilities, starting with how we'd met.

After a bumpy landing, the plane taxied to a stop. When the door opened, I was surprised to see we were in a small clearing in the middle of a field. Payns must not have an airport, but wasn't there somewhere else we could have landed? When the pilots immediately switched the plane's lights off, I understood. Vlad didn't want anyone, even a local control tower, to learn about his visit tonight.

"Stay here," Vlad told the pilots as he descended the steps built into the plane's door. I followed after him, not speaking until we were too far away for the pilots to hear.

"Who are you trying to find?"

Vlad's didn't look my way, nor did his long strides falter, but I caught a glimpse of a quick, hard smile. "Maximus."

"Maximus?" I repeated, disbelief raising my voice an octave. "Why? And why here?" I added in a softer tone, looking at the farmlands surrounding us.

Now Vlad did turn toward me, his smile becoming jaded. "This is where he's from. He's been thrown out of my line and most of his friends won't speak to him out of fear of angering me. When people have nowhere else to go, they usually go home."

He hadn't answered my first question. With Vlad, that wasn't an oversight. I shivered. Maximus had been his oldest friend, yet months ago, he'd betrayed Vlad by repeatedly lying to him. Worse, he'd done it over me. The only reason Maximus wasn't a pile of bones was because I'd extracted a promise from Vlad not to kill him, then used Maximus's freedom as my "bride price."

If Vlad was looking for him, he still thought they had unfinished business, and that didn't bode well. My only hope was that Maximus was nowhere near this rural slice of France—

"What are *you* doing here?" a harsh voice demanded.

Ha! my inner voice sneered. *You lose again!*

I turned around, seeing a tall, thickly muscled man next to the river that ran along the edge of the crops. Maximus's blond hair was shorter, but the rest of him looked the same. The wariness in his gray gaze was certainly familiar. He'd given me the same look the last time I saw him, when he predicted doom for my marriage.

"I had an insatiable craving for turnips," Vlad replied mockingly. So that was the field we were in. Then his voice hardened. "I came to see you, of course."

Maximus glanced down at himself and let out a short laugh. "I suppose if you were here to kill me, I'd already be on fire."

"Yes," Vlad almost purred. "But I made her a promise. She's here to witness that I can keep it."

Some of the chill left my body. Vlad was known for keeping his word, but I couldn't imagine why he'd want to seek Maximus out. He'd barely been able to keep himself from killing him the last time he saw him. Then again, that might have been because Maximus had told him we'd had sex. We hadn't, but Vlad hadn't known that. What he had known was that Maximus kept telling me he thought Vlad had been behind an attempt on my life, and thus I shouldn't tell him I'd survived the gas line explosion.

You know. That old bro spat.

"I guess I should invite you inside, then," Maximus said, sweeping his hand toward a ramshackle structure near the river's edge. I'd call it a stone barn, except it smelled like old fish instead of hay.

I kept my nose from wrinkling out of sheer will. "You live here?" I asked carefully.

Maximus threw me a sardonic smile. "Not as nice as what you're used to, I know."

My chin rose. "I lived in an old RV with a fellow carnie for years, remember? Vlad's the billionaire, not me."

Vlad let out a derisive noise. "This hovel and her RV are palaces compared to some of the places I've lived, so if we're finished with the poverty pissing contest, I have business to discuss."

Maximus held open the door and we entered. Inside, it was slightly less decrepit, though the floor had patches of dirt poking through the stone near the front. Water was visible through the back, but that looked to be deliberate, as if part of the house had been built on top of the river. Maybe this used to be the caretaker's home for an ancient water wheel. Since it looked as old as Maximus, it was possible.

"No wonder you're not answering cell messages or e-mails," Vlad commented. "I doubt there's service here."

Maximus shrugged. "There might be. I didn't bring anything electronic, so I don't know."

The interior room had a table, but there was only one chair. Both men seemed to expect me to take it. I remained standing, still racking my brain to figure out why we were here.

Vlad didn't waste time revealing it. "I want you to infiltrate Szilagyi's operation to spy for me."

I don't know who looked more shocked, me or Maximus. "Him? Why?" I sputtered.

Vlad's coolly appraising gaze never left the blond vampire across from him. "Szilagyi has managed to stay one step ahead of me because he keeps surprising me. I never expected him to successfully fake his own death, let alone wait three hundred years to exact his revenge, yet here we are. Quite frankly, he's outwitted me because he's using my knowledge of him against me."

A muscle twitched in Maximus's jaw. "And you think you can do the same to him with me?"

Vlad smiled with the same friendliness that usually meant someone was about to die. "Everyone knows I would never forgive someone who betrayed me, and every time I've cut someone off from my life, it's been permanent. Who then would believe I'd offer forgiveness and reinstatement to the man who lied to me while attempting to seduce my wife?" An elegant snort. "No one, especially not the enemy who knows me so well, he's been able to predict most of my actions before this point."

I had to admit, *I* had a hard time believing it. Vlad's arrogance went hand in hand with his actions—case in point, the current strain in our marriage—but in offering this to Maximus, Vlad was murdering his own ego. He was right: Szilagyi would *never* suspect that of him. He knew Vlad too well.

My hopes began to lift. Maybe, Vlad was closer to learning how to compromise than I realized. This was practically him completing Step Two, in fact.

But still . . . "How will Maximus find Szilagyi? We sure haven't been able to. Plus, even if he does, why would Szilagyi let Maximus close enough to learn anything useful, even if he doesn't suspect him of being a traitor?"

"All my enemies are rooting for Szilagyi," Vlad said shortly. "There will be plenty of people for Maximus to express his interest to, and one of them will relay it to Szilagyi. Since he recently lost his two best spies, he'll be keen to recruit someone who knows my operations as well as Maximus."

Okay, true, but that left the other thing no one seemed to want to talk about. "If he gets caught, Szilagyi will kill him."

Vlad glanced at the ruined structure around us. "And how tragic it would be for Maximus to leave all this behind."

"This isn't all I have," Maximus said, his expression changing from shock to defensiveness.

"Yes, but you aren't touching the rest of it, are you?" was Vlad's instant response. "Instead, you're punishing yourself by staying in the same pile of rocks you went off to war to avoid when you were human. I'm offering you a better way to atone for your betrayal."

"Why?" The word was so soft, I almost didn't hear it. "You could find another way to defeat Szilagyi. Why are you really offering me this?"

Vlad said nothing for a long moment. At last, he shrugged. "Because of my promise to Leila, I can't kill you, so I may as well get some use out of you being alive."

I sighed at the ruthless assessment. Maximus

didn't share my dismay. Instead, his mouth twitched into a shadow of a smile.

"*Now* I believe your offer is real."

"And are you accepting it?" Vlad asked, his emerald-ringed gaze never leaving his former friend's.

Maximus let that twitch slide into a smile that looked anticipatory and relieved at the same time.

"Oh, yes."

Chapter 5

 Gretchen slid her plate away with a groan. "For creatures that only drink blood, your people can *cook*," she told Vlad. "It's their fault I've gained five pounds since I've been here."

"Nine," he replied blandly.

Gretchen's eyes narrowed. "Mind reader," she muttered.

I suppressed my smile. Vlad didn't. He flashed a wicked grin at Gretchen.

"Right. That's how I knew."

"How's Dad?" I asked to change the subject.

My sister gave a final glower at Vlad before she answered. "His knee's been bothering him, but he refuses to let anyone look at it. Says he'll wait until we're home and he can see a *living* doctor, which is stupid, right?"

She raised her voice until she was yelling the last few words. I winced, both at the assault on my supernaturally sensitive hearing and the reason behind it. Gretchen had run out to see us when we arrived at the lovely Tuscan house Vlad had hidden them in, but my father stayed in his room. He didn't join us for dinner, either, yet he was listening. Gretchen didn't need super senses to know that and neither did I.

Vlad caught my gaze, his brow rising. I shook my head. No, I didn't want him to forcibly heal my father's knee, just like I refused to use my new mesmerizing powers to make him forget how much he hated my turning into a vampire. Hugh Dalton would have to come to terms with that on his own. If that meant we didn't speak for a while . . . well. It wouldn't be the first time my father and I had been estranged.

"How much longer do we have to hide out here?" Gretchen asked, giving up on my dad coming out and answering her taunt. "This place is better than Romania, but one day, I'd like to quit playing hide-and-seek and get on with my life."

I winced hearing her give voice to my guilt over their circumstances. "I know, and I'm sorry. We're working on it."

She blew out a sigh and then gave Vlad a speculative look. "It's Szilagyi, isn't it? He's not dead after all."

"Why would you say that?" Vlad asked, his tone dangerously silky. We hadn't told her. Had one of his staff been loose lipped?

She huffed. "You're Dracula, so everyone knows your enemies don't live long, but my dad and I are still locked up, so whoever's yanking your chain must be the king of badasses. The only person I know who fits that description is the same old vampire you couldn't kill before."

Vlad's nostrils flared while I stared at my sister in disbelief. First calling him Dracula, then bringing up Szilagyi successfully faking his death twice? The nine pounds Gretchen had gained must've come from her new brass balls.

"You are correct," Vlad said, the words barely a hiss. "That is why staying hidden is your only hope. If I've had trouble killing Szilagyi, what do you think your survival chances are without my protection?"

"Zero," she said with a sigh. Then her mouth quirked as she looked at me. "Guess it's a good thing you're already dead, sis. Harder to kill you a second time, right?"

"Right," I said, my voice catching as Vlad's feelings briefly crashed through his shields, searing my subconscious with echoes of rage and a darker, stronger emotion. To say he didn't like remembering how I'd died was an understatement.

To punctuate that point, Vlad stood. "I'm sure you would enjoy time alone with your sister before we leave in the morning. Gretchen"—a brief nod—"good night."

I stared at Vlad as he left. Part of me wanted to go after him, but I hadn't seen my sister in weeks and who knew when I'd get to spend time with her again? Our trip to Payns gave us an opportunity to swing by Tuscany, but I couldn't visit often. We had to make sure Szilagyi didn't get a hint of my family's location, plus, with their war heating up, Vlad would rather I never left the lavish fortress he called home.

Besides, when Vlad was in a mood, sometimes it was better to leave him alone. At least for a little while.

I forced a smile as I turned back to Gretchen. "Let's finish catching up over dessert. I think I smell someone hand-firing crème brûlées in the kitchen . . ."

Vlad's Tuscan house was small compared to his Romanian castle, but it still had six bedrooms and a servants' wing. After a couple hours chatting, Gretchen went to bed because she couldn't contain her yawns. Unlike me, she wasn't used to being awake all night. It was easy to figure out which of the remaining rooms Vlad was in. Even if I couldn't tell by scent, I could feel him. His aura filled the house, the power he gave off ominous in its potency even when it also felt relaxed.

Like a sleeping dragon, I thought, spying him through the half-open door at the end of the hall. Vlad was in a chair, his long legs stretched out on a nearby ottoman. He didn't stir as I came inside the room. He must have fallen asleep while using his tablet. It was still open on his lap, his hands resting on the attachable magnetic keyboard as if he'd drifted off in the middle of typing something.

I stared at him in silence. With the sun rendering me unconscious from dawn to dusk, I hadn't seen him sleep since he'd changed me into a vampire. Even before that, it had been a rarity. Was it my new, super-sharp vision or did he look a little different with his features relaxed in slumber? Sure, those winged brows were just as prominent, but his lips were parted instead of curled into the sardonic half smile he usually wore. Dark stubble clung to the lower half of his face, but his jaw wasn't set in its normal, unyielding lines. Closed eyelids hid the penetrating stare he so often leveled at others and for a few moments, the changes let me imagine that I could see hints of the innocence Vlad must have had, once upon a time when he was human.

I came closer, wondering what he'd been like before the brutalities of his life had hardened him into the complex, lethal man I'd fallen in love with. Did he have any happy memories from his childhood? Or had the dangerous political circumstances he'd been born into stolen that from him? As a child, had he ever been afraid of the dark? I leaned down, wanting to touch him but not wanting him to wake up yet—

Flames blasted into me. I screamed, throwing up my arms in instinctive defense before I remembered that I was currently fireproof. In the next instant, I was seized in a viselike grip, Vlad's hard

chest almost bruising my cheek from how force-
fully he yanked me to him. Worse, the emotions
that tore through my subconscious were so fren-
zied, I couldn't tell if he was alarmed, enraged, or
a seething combination of both.

Szilagyi must have found us! I braced for the
next attack, wondering why Vlad wasn't moving.
Was he hurt? I tried to push him away to look, but
he didn't budge. Then water hit us, soaking our
clothes and filling me with fresh panic.

"Vlad, what is it?" I almost screamed.

Shouts from his guards echoed my urgency. Just
as abruptly, he let me go, barking out an order in
Romanian that caused the guards rushing down
the hallway to skid to a stop.

That's when I saw what we were being soaked
with. Ceiling sprinklers, activated by the fire that
must have come from . . . Vlad, I realized as I
glanced around the room. No one was in here with
us and no one was attacking from outside. So why
had he unleashed a fireball that reduced the area
where he'd been sitting to smoldering ruins?

"Gretchen, Leila!" My father's bellow cut
through the guards' confused replies. "Are you all
right?"

"I'm fine," came Gretchen's response, followed
by a glimpse of my dad through the half-open
door. He was trying to shoulder his way past the
five vampire guards who looked as perplexed as I
did over what had just happened.

"I'm fine, too," I said, not adding "But still undead" only because I was too shocked to remind my dad this was the first time he'd spoken to me since he found out I'd become a vampire.

Vlad said something in Romanian that I loosely translated as "back to your stations" before he shut the bedroom door on everyone in the hallway. A door slammed on his emotions, too, cutting off the geyser that had erupted out of him almost as violently as those flames had.

The sprinklers, however, kept dousing us with water. I wiped some off my face before asking "What happened?" in as calm a tone as I could manage.

Vlad turned to me. His expression was closed off, but his features were sharpened with so much tension, I couldn't believe I'd imagined that he looked innocent minutes before.

"Bad dream," he said shortly.

"You flash-fried a ten-foot radius because of a *dream*?" Only the sounds from a nearby heartbeat, indicating my father's lingering presence in the hallway kept me from raising my voice in disbelief.

His reply came out through gritted teeth. "Yes."

I glanced at the ruined carpet, chair and laptop before returning my gaze to him. "Does this, ah, happen a lot?"

"No."

Another one-word answer, as if his tone wasn't already conveying that he didn't want to talk about it. Well, if you give your wife a flaming facial; she's not going to drop the subject.

"What was the dream?" I persisted.

His mouth twisted into a smile that was part annoyed, part challenging. "Are you certain you want to know?"

"I told you before, your secrets don't scare me," I replied, holding his burnished copper gaze. "Besides, I'm not tired anymore and clearly, neither are you."

This time, his smile held shades of darkness that still didn't warn me away. Pandora must've felt the same way when she couldn't stop herself from opening that infamous box.

"Not here. We've given my people enough to wonder about as it is."

He pulled me to him. In two strides, we were at the window, and then he was flying me through it.

Chapter 6

Tuscany was beautiful at night. Of course, I hadn't seen it during the day, but the quiet that draped over the picturesque countryside and old-world architecture made flying over towns such as Casole d'Elsa and Cetona feel romantic despite the circumstances. Eventually, Vlad set us down at the edge of a vineyard, leading me beneath a gnarled tree that might have been as old as he was, judging from its height and girth.

Vlad left me by that thick trunk to pace a few feet away. I didn't say anything. He'd brought me out here, so he'd tell me what was bothering him when he was ready.

"I've been imprisoned twice in my life," he began, his crisp words belying the surge I felt as he dropped his walls and let me back into his feelings. "Once as a boy when my father bartered me in exchange for political security, and again two decades later when Mihaly Szilagyi compelled the king of Hungary to incarcerate me after I first lost my throne."

"I know," I said, remembering the only time he'd spoken of his childhood captivity. *That man wouldn't have survived years of beatings and rape as a boy because sheer hatred kept him from breaking* . . .

He shot me a look, as if he knew what I'd been thinking. "The second time was worse, though I was only starved instead of tortured and raped. Do you know why it was more unbearable?"

"No," I whispered. How could anything be worse than that?

His gaze filled with a terrible knowledge while his irises changed from copper to brilliant green.

"Because love cuts deeper than the sharpest blade, cripples more than shattered bones, and leaves scars that can never fade. Szilagyi held my son's life over me the entire time I was his captive, and being helpless to protect my child was worse torment than anything my previous captors had done. After my wife killed herself, I swore I'd never love another woman. When Szilagyi later had my son murdered, I didn't want to care about anyone again, ever. Love had broken me, so I replaced it with revenge, ruthlessness, and the determination not to be at anyone's mercy, be they enemy, lover or friend. It's why I've protected my people as a whole, yet refused to value one person more than the other, and also why I've had few lovers and even fewer friends. For over five hundred years, I structured my life to keep my vow never to let anyone touch my heart again."

I couldn't stop the tear that slid down my cheek as his emotions changed from bitter remembrance to something richer, deeper, and at the same time, even more fierce. Vlad touched the trail my tear made and smiled with fleeting, jaded amusement.

"Too late to weep for my lost vow, Leila. You're the one who forced me to break it."

"I'm not sorry," I said softly, turning my head to kiss his palm. "I can't be. Not when I love you more than anything, too."

He stroked my face, then dropped his hand. "Long ago, I used to dream that I was back in prison. My rage over my helplessness would sometimes cause me to wake up with my hands on fire. Those dreams went away with time, but another one never did. It's the same thing I dreamt earlier: I'm by the river, holding my wife's dead body and screaming . . ."

I closed my eyes. He'd asked me if I really wanted to know what he'd dreamed and I'd said yes. How would I have guessed that it would hurt me, too? Vlad didn't have to tell me how much he had loved his former wife. I'd felt it when I relived that day by the river the first time I touched him. His guilt over her suicide was the sin he held closest to his skin.

" . . . only this time, when I pushed her hair back, I didn't see Clara's face," Vlad went on, his newly harsh tone snapping my eyes open. "I saw yours."

I drew in a breath out of shock. His smile was a grim slash while his gaze burned into mine.

"Thinking I'd lost you is why I nearly blew up the bedroom in my sleep. I know I . . . overreacted by smothering your abilities. It was wrong of me, but I can't say I'm sorry. I am at war with an enemy who is smart, powerful, and ruthless, but Szilagyi doesn't need to strike me down to win. You aren't just my weakness, Leila." Vlad drew me next to him, one hand sliding along my jaw while the other caressed my back. "You are my destruction, because if I were to lose you, it would finish me."

He kissed me then, deep and passionate, while his emotions swirled with equal intensity through mine. They reaffirmed that he wasn't sorry about what he'd done, would in fact do it again, but they also whispered something else amidst the violent determination that said he'd do anything to protect me.

Forgive me.

I felt drowned by the feelings he continued to pour into me while his mouth devastated me in different ways. The sensations were overwhelming, yet I wrapped my arms around him and pulled him closer. He thought I was his destruction, but he was wrong. Vlad was the fire that would inevitably consume me, and even though I knew that, I wasn't backing away. Instead, I'd become the phoenix that kept rising from the ashes because I would not, could not, let him go.

I broke our kiss to whisper two words that meant more than ending our weeklong abstinence.

They also meant I'd give up trying to fight Szilagyi through my abilities, when they finally returned. Instead, I'd fight him by taking myself out of the battle, allowing Vlad to arm himself with the knowledge that I was safe. Maybe that was worth more to him than all my psychic abilities combined.

"You're forgiven."

I didn't expect that my vow would be tested so soon, but only a month later, Vlad received a text from a burner phone with the numbers 1088 making up the entirety of the message. That meant it was from Maximus, and he'd left a handwritten message for Vlad containing important information in one of their three prearranged locations. Just conveying the information via text, e-mail, or a phone call would've been far quicker, but those also left a permanent trail that Szilagyi could find. Even if Maximus's text had been intercepted and read by someone else, only Vlad knew the significance of the numbers 1088: the year Maximus was born, as specific as a signature.

Of course, personally retrieving what Maximus left for him was also far more dangerous. Vlad wasn't taking bodyguards, for the same reason he insisted on retrieving the message himself: He wanted no one to know that Maximus was spying for him. I didn't think Maximus would willingly betray Vlad, but I still worried that Vlad might be walking into an ambush. What if Maximus made contact with Szilagyi, and then was followed when he made the message drop? What if Szilagyi had found Maximus out and had forced him to lure Vlad into a trap?

I tried to ignore the ominous scenarios my mind kept coming up with as I asked, "How long will you be gone?" in as neutral a tone as I could manage.

"Perhaps a few days, perhaps a week," he replied.

His vagueness only inflamed my morbidly spinning thoughts. *Unless Maximus's information allows him to attack Szilagyi. Then, he's not coming back until one of them is dead.*

I touched his arm, wishing I could feel something aside from the thick, smooth fabric of his coat, but my abilities were still buried beneath who-knew-how-many layers of Vlad's aura.

"Be careful."

His smile reminded me that I was admonishing one of the world's most powerful vampires as if he was a kid about to cross the street. I flashed him an answering, rueful grin.

"I can't help it," I said, slipping my arms around his neck. "I love you, so I worry."

Hard arms encircled me and he bent until his mouth was a velvet brand against my ear.

"I understand completely, which is why I'm clearing all nonessential staff out of the house. I won't risk another wolf in sheep's clothing around you, and if someone here so much as gives you an uneasy vibe, have them thrown into the dungeon. I'll sort it out once I return."

Laughter choked in my throat. And I thought *I* was being paranoid. If Vlad truly thought any of the people in this house were a threat, they'd already be decorating a long wooden pole.

"Dungeon. Got it." *Hey, if it made him feel better . . .*

His mouth claimed mine in a kiss that suffused my whole body with slow, delicious heat. When he let me go, a knowing smile curled his lips.

"That should ensure you'll miss me," he said with his usual arrogance, "but this will help the time pass more pleasantly."

I was still shaking my head when he turned me around to face the massive front doors. They opened, revealing a four-foot-tall vampire with black hair and bushy sideburns.

"Marty!" I said, both surprised and delighted.

My best friend grinned at me. "Come here, kid."

I left Vlad's arms to throw mine around Marty when I reached him. He hugged me back, bracing at the voltage he absorbed because I wasn't wearing my gloves. I seldom did when I was with Vlad. I made a mental note to put them back on now that Vlad was leaving and gave Marty a final pat with my left hand.

"I'm so glad to see you, but what are you doing here?"

"You're giving me grief for swinging by to see you while I was in Europe?" he replied with mock reprimand.

"Of course not," I said, but inwardly, I wasn't buying it. The only time Marty liked to travel was when he was performing on the carnival circuit. Plus, he hated Europe. He'd told me years ago that he didn't understand why so many people went there to see a bunch of "old stuff." The irony of a hundred-and-thirty-something-year-old vampire making that statement was lost on him, but it had amused me to no end.

I let the reason behind his visit drop because I only had moments left with Vlad. Besides, I wouldn't interrogate Marty as soon as he walked through the door. I'd wait until after dinner.

Vlad was already behind me when I turned around. He exchanged polite if somewhat brisk hellos with Marty and then slipped something into my pocket.

"I won't always have my regular mobile on me, but in case of emergency, push the red button on this. It's programmed to a mobile I will always carry."

"Okay." I gave him a final kiss and stopped myself before telling him to be careful again. "You know where to reach me," I joked instead. Then I became serious. "You haven't told me not to go anywhere—big progress for you—but so you know, I won't. So don't worry about me. Just do what you need to do."

I felt the warm brush of his hand on my face, then he left without a backward glance. I told myself it was my imagination that the doors seemed to close with ominous finality behind him.

He'll be fine, I mentally reassured myself. Even if this *was* a setup, if Vlad caught a glimpse of Szilagyi, he could burn him into ash before Szilagyi even had a chance to scream.

I turned to Marty, giving him a smile that felt forced despite how happy I was to see him.

"You hungry? I am, and Vlad has plenty of live-in human blood donors to help with that, so let's go downstairs and say hi to my friends with pulses."

Chapter 7

 The next few days dragged even though I slept through half of them. Try as I might, I still couldn't wake up much before dusk. Plus, it soon became clear that something was bothering Marty. He tried to pass off that he was his normal, jovial self, but beneath all his smiles, jokes and genuine happiness to see me, I kept catching glimpses of something else. Annoyance, I would've expected. Vlad must've insisted that Marty come here to play babysitter, and no one liked being ordered around, especially by someone who'd once tortured you. Yet I didn't sense any annoyance from Marty during the rare moments he let his guard down. Instead, it was an odd sort of . . . sadness.

I was determined to find out why.

On the fourth night, Marty and I were walking around the exterior of Vlad's castle, enjoying the coolness of the predawn summer morning. We were well within sight of the guards on the surrounding wall and towers, but two more followed us on foot, although Dorian and Alexandru stayed a polite distance behind.

"If Szilagyi wasn't on the loose, you'd be wrapping up carnival season right now," I said, thinking of how different my life was compared to a year ago. Had I never met Vlad, I would've been at the carnivals with Marty, hiding my abilities and identity behind my stage name, the Fantastic Frankie.

Nothing changed in Marty's expression, but his scent soured as he said "No big deal," in a tone filled with false pleasantness.

I stopped so suddenly that the guards trailing us looked around in alarm.

"Spill it," I told Marty. "Something big has been eating at you, and it's not just because Vlad must've insisted that you babysit me—although my apologies for that. Sometimes, he forgets that he's not a medieval warlord anymore."

Marty snorted. "Vlad will always be a medieval warlord. *You're* the only one who keeps forgetting that about him."

"Don't change the subject," I said, although he probably had a point. "What's going on, and if you say 'nothing' one more time, I'm going to electrocute you."

Marty stared at me, not speaking for so long, I was about to zap him to show him I meant business. At last, he spoke.

"I'm out of the circuit," he said, his shrug seeming to add, *Shit happens, what are you gonna do?*

Guilt pricked me. "I'm sorry you have to miss this season, but Szilagyi went after you before. Once we catch him—"

"It's not Szilagyi," he cut me off. "It's Vlad, and it's not just for this season. I'm off the carnival circuit forever."

"*What?*"

His smile was lopsided. "Vlad knows you think of me as a second father, and he knows Szilagyi won't be his only enemy who tries to use me because of it. Since there's no way to guard every carnival I go to, he ordered me to stop performing. Said he'd double whatever I used to make and give me another job—"

"He can't expect you to quit," I whispered, stunned.

Marty's smile faded. "He can and he did. He knows I'm in no position to refuse. If I did, he'd cut me off from you, which would hurt worse than quitting the circuit since I love you like my own daughter. Plus, then he'd be pissed, and I already experienced what Vlad does to people when he's not mad."

"But being a carnie is more than your job, it's your life!" I said, as if I was telling him something he didn't know.

"Told you, kid," he said lightly. "You're the only one still in denial about who you married."

I was about to say that Vlad had no idea who *he'd* married if he thought I'd let him get away with this when sirens started blaring from the castle. Before I could react, Marty threw me over his shoulder, rushing back toward the house with Vlad's guards running ahead of him like two fanged linebackers.

Those alarms kept me from arguing about Marty flinging me over his shoulder as if I was a sack of potatoes. Thanks to my trip to the communications room a couple months ago, I knew what they meant. The invisible security grid that extended like a huge bubble around the castle and grounds had been breached.

"Incoming air strike!" one of the guards called out in heavily accented English.

Air strike? Szilagyi had gotten his hands on *missiles*? I shoved away from Marty, landing on my feet in the grand hallway, only to be swept up by more guards as they hustled me to the stairway behind the indoor garden.

"Madame, we need you belowground," Samir said. Then the black-haired head of Vlad's guards pinched his collar and muttered something into the wire concealed there. Another spurt of Romanian came through the same device, then Samir and the rest of them were almost shoving me down the staircase.

"Wait, where's Marty?" I called out, not seeing him through the sea of guards that had surrounded me.

"Go on, I'll catch up!" I heard Marty yell before more communications from the guards' wires and multiple footsteps on the stone staircase drowned out his voice.

"To the dungeon!" Samir said, shooting me an apologetic look as he added, "it's the deepest underground part of the castle, so the surrounding rock will protect you."

Did he really think I'd pick *now* to be snooty about my accommodations? "Will it be big enough to fit everyone?"

Samir wasn't the only one who looked at me like I was crazy. "We stay above to fight," the blond named Christian said.

I put on the brakes at that, but it had as much effect as a leaf trying to stop the raging river it was floating in. "I'm not huddling below while the rest of you risk your lives!"

They kept propelling me down the narrow passageway as if I hadn't spoken, moving so fast that I barely saw us being waved through the first two security doors that led to the dungeon. When we reached the third, I tore my gloves off. Light suffused my right hand, casting a bright glow in the unlit tunnel.

"Stop!" I demanded.

They ran even faster, ushering me through the foot-thick metal door that was the entrance to the dungeon. Frustration made my hand spark. *Vlad.* He must've threatened them with something awful if they didn't get me to a safe place in the event of an emergency. Either I hurt them for their obedience—which I couldn't do—or I switched tactics. They wouldn't let me fight, but maybe I could protect some of them another way.

I pulled my right hand tight to my body and put all the command I could muster into my voice. "Send all the humans in the house down here with me. They can't help in the fight and they could, um, get in the way if they stay up there."

"Get them," Samir said, and one of the guards ran back through the dungeon's entrance. I sighed in relief, then nearly choked at the odor that seemed to shoot up my nose. I'd forgotten how this place reeked, as if the dungeon's oppressive atmosphere, manacles, and other gruesome devices weren't unpleasant enough.

Samir barked more orders at the guards, who half dragged, half carried me past the stone monolith that marked the first section of the dungeon. Then I was whisked past the various "information extraction" devices in the second, larger section before we came to the third, where the roof abruptly sloped and the walls shrank until the passageway was as tight as the narrow staircase leading down here.

It was also so dark I had to squint despite my supernaturally enhanced vision. Cells lined the cold stone walls, their height maxing out at four feet, restricting their unlucky occupants to a permanent stoop. The last time I'd been here, Maximus had been the dungeon's only prisoner, and he'd been in one of the regular-sized cells at the end of this row. This time, the squat cells around me weren't empty.

Since we were now at the end of the dungeon, the guards finally stopped shoving/carrying me. As my eyes adjusted, I saw Shrapnel, Vlad's former third-in-command, in the cell to my left. He'd been down here ever since he got busted for betraying Vlad to an associate of Szilagyi's, not to mention the part where he drove me off a cliff trying to kill me. Thick silver chains hung from Shrapnel's wrists and ankles, their length secured into the stone floor with a large clamp. I met his dark eyes and felt a flash of pity as he looked from me to the cell across the hall from his. It was the only other occupied one in this section of the dungeon, and in it was the woman Shrapnel had betrayed Vlad for. I doubted it was an accident that Shrapnel's cell was positioned so that he had an unrestricted view of her.

Something soot-smeared flung itself against that cell's bars as I neared it, then grunting sounds emerged from a mouth filled with a spiked ball-gag of silver. If I didn't already know who it had to be, I wouldn't have recognized Vlad's former girlfriend, Cynthiana. She looked even more terrible than the last time I'd seen her, and Vlad had been torching information out of her back then.

Cynthiana's long, lustrous brown hair was gone,

replaced by a bald skull that was as soot covered as the rest of her. She couldn't speak past the hideous gag that kept her from uttering spells like the one that had killed me, but her glare conveyed her hatred. She was tiny compared to her tall, heavily muscled lover, yet Cynthiana had more shackles than Shrapnel. Every part of her was bound with silver chain, leaving only her fingers free. Even in her pitiful condition, she wasn't cowed. Two middle fingers shot up at me as we stared at each other.

Alexandru began to rebuke Cynthiana, as if that would do any good. Out of all the crimes that had landed Vlad's former girlfriend in the worst part of his dungeon, cowardice hadn't been among them. She glared at him, twisting her fingers in such a way that the clear translation was *Fuck you in the ass!*

If the situation hadn't been so ominous, I might've made a mental note of how she did that. Instead, being in the dungeon's deepest, darkest— and thus safest—region only highlighted the fact that something terrible was about to happen.

"Alexandru, Petre, Dorian, stay here," Samir said, leaving the corridor of cells at a run. "Protejati-o cu vietile voastre!"

I knew what that last sentence meant because I'd heard Vlad say it many times. *Protect her with your lives.* My gut twisted. I might be safe with the guards and the half mile of rock between me and the impending attack, but what about Marty and everyone else? The only person who could contain the fiery fallout from an air strike wasn't home at the moment!

All at once, I remembered the phone Vlad had left me. If this didn't count as an emergency, nothing did. I shoved my gloves back on despite the entire phone being encased in thick rubber, then pressed the big red button on the front of it. It glowed, and I didn't even hear a ring before Vlad answered.

"Leila."

"We're being attacked," I began.

"I know, my people called," he interrupted. "I'm on my way, but I'm far. I've summoned my closest allies to assist, but you need to stay below until *I* get there. Do you understand?"

"Yes," I said reluctantly.

Playing the cowering princess went against every instinct I had, yet I couldn't distract Vlad's people by forcing them to drag me back down here if I tried to join them in the fight, and drag me they would. They'd already proven that.

"Good." Relief edged the word before his tone hardened into deadly implacableness again. "It's no coincidence that Szilagyi is attacking now, so remember what I told you when I left."

I glanced at Alexandru, Dorian, and Petre. All three were at the entrance to the third section of the dungeon, their stances bow-tight, as if expecting Szilagyi to leap out of a dark corner. They looked like the loyal, fierce guards they were supposed to be, but I also didn't believe in coincidences. Someone had tipped Szilagyi off to Vlad's absence, and for all I knew, it was one of the men down here with me.

"Got it," I said, holding the phone in the crook of my shoulder as I looked at my right hand, my most effective weapon.

"I love you."

Growled just before I heard a click, then the phone's single red button stopped glowing. He'd hung up on me, probably to make more calls rallying his allies. I put the phone back in my jeans and glanced at my left hand, too. I might need all the voltage I could transmit, even down here where it was supposed to be safe.

"This way," I heard Samir shout, then a stampede of echoes sounded in the front part of the dungeon. From the multitude of heartbeats, Samir had followed through on my order to bring the human inhabitants of the castle down here.

I was friends with a few of them, so after a brief argument with my guards, they agreed to let me go to the dungeon's front section to see them. I also wanted to check if Marty had come down with them. He'd promised to be right behind me.

I made it to the second section of the dungeon when the floor suddenly heaved with such force, I was knocked off my feet. Then the walls shook so violently that long cracks appeared in the stone. I grabbed the nearest sturdy object—a modernized version of an ancient rack—and fell again as the ground pitched and heaved like a boat being tossed in high seas.

Alexandru and Petre rushed over, but the next violent heave knocked them to their knees, too. Then a thunderous crash boomed through the dungeon, sending a cloud of stone dust rushing into our section. Amidst the screams, I heard an eruption of Romanian from the guards' communication devices. Most of it was too rapid to translate, but I understood three chilling words.

Explosion. Foundation. Collapse.

Szilagyi hadn't launched an attack from above. Somehow, he'd blown up the foundations that the castle rested on.

Chapter 8

The three of us staggered to the front section of the dungeon, the ground pitching and rolling beneath us the entire time. Once we reached it, I looked around in disbelief. The huge stone monolith in the center of the room had toppled over, crushing several people beneath it. A few were still alive, but trapped by the massive rock formation.

"Help me!" I said, running over to the massive oblong stone. While the dungeon continued to shudder as if in its death throes, Alexandru, Dorian, and I lifted the monolith so that Petre and Samir could yank out the survivors. My friend Sandra was one of them, and I saw with relief that only her lower leg had been crushed. Vampire blood would heal that, as it would heal the other living peoples' injuries—

A tremendous *boom!* sounded, followed by the most horrific screams I had ever heard. Not even the distance between the dungeon and the castle muted sounds that curdled my blood and filled me with an instinctive panic. *What* was happening?

"Napalm!" came through the guards' devices, followed by more crashing sounds and that awful, high-pitched screaming. "It's being dropped from helicopters—!"

That transmission cut off with terrifying abruptness, but more screams came through the lines. I caught the word "trapped" several times, and a sickening picture began to form in my mind. Szilagyi had managed to blow up the house's foundations, causing large parts of the house to collapse. Then, he'd dropped napalm on the trapped survivors, burning them to death before they could free themselves from the rubble.

"Block the door and stay here!" Samir shouted, shoving past the terrified people still trying to spill into the dungeon. He slammed the door behind him, the instant mechanical screech indicating that he'd locked it.

I stared at the door in shock. Samir did *not* just lock out people trying to get to the only safe area in the house! Yet he had, and Alexandru, Petre, and Dorian rushed to heave the stone monolith in front of the door, almost crushing a few people who didn't move quickly enough out of their path.

I shook myself out of my temporary paralysis. "You can't let him lock those people out. They'll burn!"

To punctuate my point, screams leaked through

the thick metal door. A glance around showed that only half the house's human residents had made it into the dungeon. The rest were on the other side of that door, and even if the collapsing house and napalm didn't kill them, the poisonous smoke would. Plus, any vampires who'd freed themselves from the rubble needed to get underground to avoid the merciless fire, but now they couldn't get down here, either.

"We need to move that block and open the door," I said more strongly, heading toward the stone monolith.

Dorian yanked me back so hard, he broke my arm. "Napalm cannot burn through stone, but if you remove the barrier and open the door, it could flood this area and kill us. We need to wait. Help is on the way."

My arm had already healed by the time he stopped speaking, and if my heart still worked, it would have been hammering. Another shudder rocked the dungeon, followed by more crashing noises above us. I looked into Dorian's flinty blue gaze and saw that he really would let everyone on the other side of that door die, all to obey orders. Yes, help was on the way, but by the time Vlad's allies arrived, most of the people in the house would be crushed or burned to death.

I couldn't live with myself if I let that happen. Marty was up there, not to mention all the guards who were fighting for their lives and ours. Yes, we *might* be in danger if we removed that barrier and opened the door, but those people *would* die if we didn't. With a choice like that, there was no choice.

Besides, I thought, steeling myself for what came next, stone wasn't the only thing that was immune to fire. Thanks to Vlad smothering me in his aura, at the moment, so was I.

"Dorian," I said in an even voice. "I'm sorry."

Then I laid my right hand on him and blasted him with enough voltage to send him crashing into the wall behind us. Alexandru started toward me, but stopped when I held the same hand out, a line of dazzling white now dangling from it.

"If you make me, I *will* do it," I said, snapping the electric whip I'd formed. I meant it, too. Countless lives hung in the balance, my best friend's among them.

Alexandru must've sensed that I wasn't bluffing. He nodded and gestured at the huge rock in front of me.

"It will go faster with both of us."

I waved him forward, keeping a wary eye out for any sudden, duplicitous movements as we grasped either end of the rock. Then we heaved, and even with our combined supernatural strength, I felt like I'd burst a spleen by the time we rolled the monolith aside to reveal the door.

"Open it," I ordered. When he hesitated, I snapped, "Samir didn't lock us down here without any keys, so open it!"

"Don't," Dorian gasped out, crawling toward us. "Samir will kill you for disobeying, and if he doesn't, Vlad will."

Alexandru glanced at my glowing whip, at Dorian, and then dropped to his knees. "I can't," he whispered.

My whip glowed brighter as the sounds behind the door grew more desperate. Yes, Vlad had ordered them to keep me safe, but he wouldn't want scores of his people burned alive when all that was needed to save them was to *open a damn door*!

"Get back," I yelled as loud as I could. "Nobody touch the door, it's about to blow!" Then, with a quick prayer that I wouldn't kill the people on the other side, I brought that sizzling electric whip down onto the thick metal door.

A hunk blew off near the lock, the voltage electrifying the highly conductive metal. I brought the whip down again, channeling more energy into it. The entire door became suffused with an eerie white glow before another piece hurtled off.

"No!" Dorian shouted.

A rush of wind warned me of his charge. I pivoted just in time, causing him to smash into the door instead of me. Electricity still coursed through the metal, making his whole body shudder with the voltage he absorbed. Seizing my chance, I yanked him off with my left hand and then kicked him out of my way before aiming another strike at the door.

That final, crackling whip cut through the locks, causing the door to sag open. Grief flooded me as I saw two of Vlad's human blood donors stuck to the other side of the door, their bodies still convulsing from all the electricity they'd absorbed. I didn't get a chance to check them for pulses before the door flung all the way open from the rush of people nearly trampling one another to get inside. In the next instant, a tremendous explosion shook the dungeon, knocking me out.

When I came to moments later, I could barely see through the blood, soot, and stony dust in my eyes. Then I could see with dazzling, horrifying clarity because the pitch-black dungeon was suddenly lit by countless rays of moonlight . . . and flames.

The side of the mountain where the second and third sections of the dungeon were located was gone. A gaping hole was all that was left, and flaming debris from the house rained down in front of it. I couldn't believe what I was seeing, yet that didn't stop the moans, crashing noises, and screams that came from around and above me. Szilagyi wasn't just destroying the house; he was bringing down the entire mountain, just as he'd planned to do months ago when he was laying a trap for Vlad. I didn't know how he'd managed to pull off his stunningly successful attack, but it didn't matter.

Vlad's allies would arrive too late. So would he. We were all going to die.

I knew that, yet I heaved myself up from the rubble anyway. Vlad had spent hundreds of years hardening his heart so he'd never experience loss again, and I'd rammed through his barriers to make him admit that he loved me. Even if it was pointless, I'd fight until the bloody, bitter end. I owed him that.

Besides, I thought, forcing myself through the sea of people still pouring into the dungeon despite more than half of it being destroyed, I owed Szilagyi, too. He hadn't just attacked Vlad; these were *my* house, *my* friends, and *my* people, too!

If Szilagyi had come with his people to admire the destruction he'd wrought, I intended to make it the last sight he ever saw.

Chapter 9

 It took several minutes to get from the staircase to the main level of the house. Between fighting my way through the panicked flood of people, I also had to clear out heavy pieces of debris. The second metal door had been shaken right off its frame, forcing those on the stairwell to climb over it until I leaned it against the wall to make more room. The third door was nowhere to be found, probably because that section had crumbled completely, revealing a deep crevasse where the door used to be.

I ended up backtracking to carry the second door over to the crevasse, laying it over the open space to allow the group of traumatized humans on the other side to use it as a makeshift bridge. The dungeon might be blown half to bits, but it was still safer than the rest of the house. I left them with assurances that help was on the way, and then I continued going up.

Once I reached the basement, I had to climb

through a charred hole in the ceiling to get to the main level of the house. The hallway ahead had completely caved in, and I tried not to wonder if any of the body parts I glimpsed in the rubble belonged to Marty. When I scrambled up the pile of wreckage and the main floor came into view, my mind froze for a second. This flaming ruin could *not* be the magnificent grand hall that had so dazzled me the first time I saw it.

The frescoed ceilings were gone, replaced with huge holes that revealed the sky. Napalm continued to eat through debris piles that were all that remained of the upper floors. Whatever wasn't being destroyed by fire was collapsing as the house continued to pancake under its own weight. When the debris pile next to me began to slide in an ominous manner, I ran through what looked like a charred tunnel, grief and anger quickening my steps. The last time I'd seen Marty, he'd been in the main hall. Now, all that was left here was destruction and death.

Please, let him be alive, I found myself praying.

I cleared the tunnel and found myself standing on what used to be the fancy covered portico. Outside, the full damage from Szilagyi's attack was revealed.

More than half of the house had collapsed, reducing it to barely more than one story on the north and east ends before the southern side rose up in seeming defiance against the assault that still raged on.

Three out of the four towering turrets had been leveled, leaving only holes where black smoke spewed into the lightening predawn sky. The tunnel I'd run through turned out to be the grand entranceway, which now looked like a giant had punched a flaming fist through the debris. Stone chimneys stuck up like lone sentries amid the blackened remains where napalm had eaten through all the wood, concrete, and plaster from the collapsed house. The stone gate was mostly intact, but the manned towers had been reduced to crumbling ruins. From the heavy artillery and anti-aircraft weapons now lying like broken toys on the scorched ground, Szilagyi must have made sure to take the towers out first in his assault.

With their most effective weapons out of commission, the surviving guards were reduced to throwing pieces of the stone ruins at the helicopters that hovered like mechanical demons over the house, spraying fire onto its remains. As I watched, one of them managed to hit a chopper, causing it to careen into the nearby tree line. Savage exultation filled me as I saw black smoke billowing up from the crash site moments later.

Now I knew what I needed to do to help. I started running toward the section of the house where the largest number of survivors had gathered, probably because it had a big pile of stone statues that had broken free when the house crumpled. Then, a sudden blast behind me pitched me forward. I landed face-first in a pile of burnt metal objects that I dimly recognized as coming from the Weapons Room.

Screams jerked my head up. An attack helicopter roared over me, spraying deadly lines of orange at the group of guards ahead. They ran, but not fast enough. At least four of them were coated with that horrible, clinging fire that ate through whatever it touched like a ravenous monster. Before I made it to my feet, they were already dead, their blackened bodies breaking apart over the stones they'd tried to use as weapons.

Rage infused me with fresh strength. I ran toward a pile of large stone pieces, but before I got there, another chopper swooped in, positioning itself between me and the only things I could use to bring it down.

Despite the smoke and thick glass covering the pilot's cockpit, I could see that his eyes were glowing, vampire green. Then the helicopter's long cylinders pointed their deadly payload right at me. I braced—and fire blasted into me with the force of a tidal wave. The sheer velocity knocked me over. Cracking, popping, and breaking sounds joined the roar of flames, but the only pain I felt was from landing on something hard as the floor collapsed beneath me. When I opened my eyes, I was looking up at a smoking, glowing hole, napalm still clinging and burning everything it touched.

Except me. I brushed the smoldering remains

of falling debris from me and stood up. My jeans and top were ripped, but not burnt. Vlad's aura protected me just as it did with him. Even my hair whipped around in its usual long, black waves, not a single end singed. Vlad's aura was still intact, but I didn't know for how long. It had worn off the last time I'd been exposed to repeated, high-intensity flames.

I jumped out of the hole, noting grimly that the remaining three assault choppers were chasing the surviving guards. I ran over to the pile of fallen stone, choosing the largest, sturdiest piece, which happened to be a gargoyle statue. The pilots didn't see me when I ran toward where they hovered because none of their helicopters were pointed my way. Why would they be? They thought they'd eliminated the danger on this end of the ruined castle.

I planted my feet and used all the supernatural strength I had to chuck the snarling stone gargoyle at the back of the closest helicopter. It smashed into the main rotors, causing the chopper to violently dip to the right, then roll and crash with a satisfying explosion into the ruined east side of the house.

That got the attention of the remaining two choppers. They swung around, shooting flaming arcs in my direction. I dove under the nearest pile of stone, using that as a barrier against the worst of the flames. My body felt like it was in a microwave from the heat, but Vlad's aura held, keeping the fire from scorching the flesh right off me. When that orange blast stopped, I was already hefting up a large piece of stone.

The helicopter's abrupt shift to the right wasn't enough. The pillar I threw tore through the cockpit, slamming into the pilot and causing the chopper to drop like, well, a stone. I didn't have time to run away from the fire that blasted out as the helicopter exploded. Instead of being afraid of Vlad's aura dissolving, for a few moments, I found myself savoring the flames as they skipped over me.

That's for everyone you murdered today! I thought, filled with vengeful satisfaction at the destruction of the helicopter. Then I began looking for another piece of stone. Only one more chopper remained and I needed to stop it before anyone else was killed.

When the last helicopter swung back around, I had a large piece of rock ready to go. Before I could throw it, multiple firecrackers went off and something hard smashed into me. Somehow, I was looking at the sky instead of at my final target.

"Leila!" someone yelled. More firecrackers sounded, cutting that person's voice off. I tried to get up but couldn't. That's when I finally looked down.

At least I'm not in pain, was my first, stupid thought, as if that made me any less riddled with bullets. The pilot must've switched his weapons when he saw that fire didn't work on me.

Spoke too soon, my hated inner voice mocked as pain roared through me with such intensity, it was as though it was trying to make up for those first agony-free seconds. I heard the helicopter closing in, tried again to get up, and was immediately strafed with a fresh barrage of bullets. Now I couldn't even turn my head, so when the helicopter hovered right above me, I was completely helpless to save myself.

Something big dropped out of it. I couldn't see what because my vision was blurry and red tinged. As if regular time had been replaced with slow motion, I watched the dark blur fall toward me. *This is it*, I thought, the macabre part of my mind wondering what the instrument of my death would be. A missile? Napalm bomb? The fire might not burn me, but the resulting explosion would blow me to kingdom come—

The thing dropped next to me and scooped me into his arms. "Leila," a familiar voice said.

Even more shocking was the next voice I heard, also familiar—and despised.

"Get away from her, Maximus," Szilagyi ordered.

My vision cleared enough to see Vlad's worst enemy striding toward us. Gray still clung to his temples before streaking through his dark hair. His strong jaw and athlete's build also added to his air of seasoned command. I'd described him as distinguished-looking when I first saw him in a psychic vision, and Mihaly Szilagyi still fit that bill.

Of course, he was also the most evil person I'd ever met, in person or through my abilities.

"Maximus, run," I whispered. How he'd gotten here, I had no idea, but he needed to leave. Maybe Maximus had been one of the "nearby allies" Vlad had sent to help—

"I told you, she's worth more to you alive," Maximus replied, his harsh voice breaking through the pain that fought to cloud my mind with senseless agony.

Szilagyi smiled at me with icy expectation. "I disagree."

Realization hit me, as devastating to my emotions as the silver bullets had been to my body. Maximus hadn't been sent by Vlad to help us. He'd come *with* Szilagyi to destroy us! If I could've moved, I would have shoved away from him, but all the silver burning inside me stole my strength.

"Killing his wife almost finished Vlad the last time I did it," Szilagyi continued. "Perhaps this time, the guilt will be enough to finally crush him."

"What?" I rasped, stunned into replying. "You didn't kill Clara. She committed suicide."

Szilagyi came closer, until only a few feet separated us. "Clara didn't jump to her death—I pushed her off that roof, then erased everyone's memory of my presence afterward. This time, though, Vlad will know exactly who killed his wife, and why."

Maximus's thick arms tightened around me. "Don't be a fool," he said in a flat tone. "The closest you've ever come to defeating Vlad was when you held Leila hostage, and that was *before* he married her. Kill her now; you'll upset him for a few months. Take her with you, and Vlad will be so determined to get her back, he'll make a lethal, reckless mistake—"

I couldn't push myself out of his grip, but my right hand had been creeping toward Maximus the entire time he spoke. When it reached his thigh, I channeled all my remaining voltage into him. With a satisfying crack, he was blown out of my line of sight, hopefully now in pieces.

Then I mustered up a smile at Szilagyi. "No matter what you do, you'll never win against Vlad."

Szilagyi squatted down until his dark brown gaze was almost level with mine. "I will really enjoy killing you," he said, his tone so pleasant it belied the sinister words. "But I can always do that later. For now, I'll see if Maximus is right and you're the straw that ends up breaking Vlad's back."

I didn't want to die, but I didn't want to be the cause of Vlad's death, either. Besides, with the pain increasing until it felt like I was being napalmed on the inside, I might not last long enough for Szilagyi to kill me "later."

"Touch me. See how it works out," I said, letting out a harsh laugh.

Szilagyi glanced past me, where unfortunately,

I could hear Maximus moaning. Damn. I hadn't killed him.

"I don't need to do anything but wait," he said, sounding so confident that I managed another gasping laugh. Didn't he know that Vlad's allies would be here any minute—?

A blaze of light hit my eyes as the first rays of dawn touched the ruined, smoking castle. Before I could finish my thought, I was already unconscious.

Chapter 10

 My hated inner voice awoke before the rest of me did. Its taunting whisper of "What is this? The fourth time?" acted as an alarm clock to my subconscious. If I never woke up as someone's captive again, it would be too soon.

Then, like the other times, I began to assess my situation while pretending to still be unconscious. No more searing pain, so someone had taken the silver out of me. Arms completely immobile, check. Legs immobile, check. Right hand encased in something rubbery, check. No gag, though, and the lack of pitching or vibration meant I wasn't on a boat, car, train or plane. Whether that was good or bad, I'd soon find out.

" . . . telling you, this is the best way to prevent her from using her abilities to link to Vlad," Maximus was saying. "Even if she managed to get her hand free, she'd run up against a clean slate instead of an essence map."

When my eyes opened, the first thing I saw was

Maximus standing at the far end of the room. Szilagyi was with him, looking intrigued by whatever Maximus had proposed. A tripod camera was set up a few feet from me, and in a corner, a fair-haired vampire bent over a table as if he had no interest in anything except its contents. The room itself didn't tell me anything useful. The walls, floor and ceiling were stone, so we were underground . . . somewhere. If I'd stayed out until dusk like I usually did, we might not even be on the same continent anymore.

I fought against the despair that tried to poison my emotions. One of the advantages to being a repeat captive was the knowledge that there was always a way out of a tough situation. You just had to keep looking until you found it.

Then the platinum blond vampire moved enough to reveal the objects on his table, and my stomach felt like it tried to crawl into my spine to hide. The worst part about being a repeat captive? Knowing firsthand how excruciating torture was.

I must have made a noise, or maybe my scent changed with dread, because Maximus and Szilagyi quit talking to stare at me.

"Hello, Leila," Szilagyi said. The two words purred with luxuriant menace. "What do you think of my taking you now?"

Begging would be useless. So would making threats or trying to negotiate. You didn't capture your worst enemy's wife and chain her in an underground room with a table full of sharp instruments because you cared about anything she had to say.

"I think getting a fresh cup of blood is probably out of the question," I settled on.

Being a smartass was the only option I had left. Besides, maybe a little false bravado would help me endure what was about to happen. Fake it until you make it, as the saying went.

Szilagyi smiled with what looked like genuine amusement. "I'm starting to see why Vlad and Maximus have fallen for you."

"I'd blush if I wasn't undead," I muttered. What was that curved knife with the partial loop on the handle for?

Szilagyi caught what I was looking at and his smile widened. "I intended to let Harold torture you the way he normally does, but Maximus just told me how you really kept slipping through my nets the other times I'd captured you. I knew you could link to Vlad through essence imprints on objects or other people, but I didn't know you could also link to him through the imprints he left on your skin."

I swung a hate-filled glare toward Maximus. Despite what he'd done, Vlad had given him a second chance and I had trusted him again, too. Was there no end his backstabbing?

His gray eyes didn't waver. "I don't have a choice, Leila."

"Yes, you do," I spat. "You could die with some dignity, like I intend to do."

"Oh, you're not going to die," Szilagyi said, sounding a bit disappointed this time. "I've agreed to let Maximus keep you, if he's right and you bring about Vlad's demise. Never let it be said that I don't reward loyalty among my people."

"Is that why you did it?" I asked Maximus, incredulous. "You're still holding on to the fantasy that if Vlad was out of the picture, I'd be with you?"

"Something like that." Then his rugged features hardened. "Don't give yourself all the credit. I was loyal to Vlad for over five hundred years, yet he threw me out of his line after one mistake. Would've killed me, too, if not for the promise you forced out of him. In one month, Szilagyi's treated me better than Vlad did in centuries."

"Thank you," Szilagyi said mildly.

Bitterness made my voice vibrate. "I so regret stopping Vlad from killing you, and I hope you get the same reward Shrapnel and Cynthiana got for their *loyalty*. Or didn't you know that Szilagyi blew them up when he took out the lower dungeon?"

"Whose idea do you think that was?" Szilagyi interjected, actually managing to sound offended. "Cynthiana knew what would happen if Vlad ever caught her, so she wanted an insurance policy that doubled as vengeance. She's the one who had

Shrapnel set charges around the house's foundations *and* the dungeon, then spelled both of them so they couldn't admit to it under torture. I agreed not to blow the charges unless they were captured, which, after weeks of not hearing from her, became obvious. Bringing down Vlad's house serves me little purpose otherwise. I couldn't do it while he was there or he'd turn the fire right back around on my people, and I expected you to be traveling with him." A taunting smile. "How happy I was to be mistaken."

And I would have been traveling with Vlad, if he hadn't been so determined to keep me safe that he'd left me behind. More irony: if I'd stayed in the "safest" section of the dungeon like he'd told me to, I would've been blown to bits along with Shrapnel and Cynthiana. Looked like this time, playing it safe had been the most dangerous choice to make.

Cynthiana. Clever bitch knew if Vlad ever captured her, her only escape would be death. If she'd have guessed that her backup plan would result in my capture, she would have been laughing instead of flipping me off the last time I saw her.

Maximus only shrugged. "You hate me now, but eventually, you'll realize that I'll treat you better than Vlad would've, once this business is finished with."

"Yes, back to business," Szilagyi said, his gaze raking over me with palpable coldness. "With all the essence imprints Vlad must have left on you, your skin is as dangerous as your right hand. Harold, take care of both, would you?"

The blond vampire came toward me, holding the knife I'd been wondering about. Now, with sickening certainty, I knew what it was. A skinning blade. I pulled at my restraints, but of course, they didn't budge. I wanted to tell Szilagyi that my abilities didn't work because they'd been smothered by Vlad's aura, but his expression said that it wouldn't matter. He wasn't just doing this for precautions. He *wanted* to hurt me.

"And turn the camera on," Szilagyi added, the relish in his tone hammering home that nothing I said was going to stop this. "We don't want Vlad to miss a moment."

Hours later, after they left me to start the delivery chain for their grisly mementos, I stared at my right arm. The scar that had stretched from my fingers all the way up to my temple was gone. I never thought I'd miss the tangible reminder of touching that downed power line over a dozen years ago, but I did. Now, my scar-free, gleaming pale skin would forever be a reminder of another life-altering event.

I'd experienced many horrible things through my abilities, not to mention being tortured once before. This . . . was different. It wasn't the pain that made me feel shattered inside. Being shot full of silver had hurt worse, but when you didn't have *yourself* anymore, who were you supposed to depend on?

I'd once told Vlad that everyone held their sins close to their skin. A person's past was there, too, essence traces recording memories that would never fade with time. When he had me skinned, Szilagyi didn't just slice off every imprint Vlad had left on me; he'd also taken away the last links I had to my mother, my sister when we were children . . . every moment in my life that had been important enough to leave an imprint was now gone, leaving me in what felt like a stranger's body.

That's what I couldn't deal with. I could handle captivity, pain, fear, uncertainty, but my body was now Szilagyi's tapestry of revenge, each inch of new skin a mocking reminder of what he'd done to me. They'd left me naked except for my restraints, but instead of feeling exposed, every time I looked at myself, I felt like I was watching a replay of the skinning video Szilagyi had shot with such gleeful malevolence. They'd taken that video and packaged it with all my old skin and the final coup de grâce—my right arm.

Szilagyi had ripped that off himself, marveling over how it still sparked with electricity for several minutes afterward. Then his delight knew no bounds when the arm that grew back only had the same amount of voltage as the rest of my body. He hadn't intended to, but with that one, savage pull, Szilagyi had torn my most dangerous weapon out of me, and with it, my hope for escape.

Even when Vlad had smothered my aura, my right hand had still remained lethally charged. Now, I couldn't free myself by overloading that hand until electricity punched through my restraints, nor could I use that same hand to manifest a whip that would cut down anyone who tried to stop me from escaping. Even after Vlad's aura faded, I probably wouldn't be able to discern psychic impressions, either. It wasn't mine anymore. It was another one of Szilagyi's leftovers.

I'd screamed when they cut my flesh from me, despite my best attempts not to. I'd also hurled threats at Maximus, Harold, and Szilagyi even though that had only amused two out of three of them. I'd tried to tell Vlad not to lose it the way they wanted him to when he saw this video, but Szilagyi had silenced me by shoving a handful of my discarded skin into my mouth. Now that I was alone and they'd taken the camera with them, I finally allowed myself to do the one thing I hadn't done during the excruciating, soul-crushing experience.

I cried.

Chapter II

 My cell had no windows, so I measured the time by my cycle of consciousness versus unconsciousness. When I abruptly passed out, that meant dawn. When I awoke, dusk. From that, I knew that five days had passed since the castle attack. Oddly enough, my jailers had left me alone during the time. To keep from drowning in despair over Vlad, my circumstances, and wondering if Marty had made it out alive, I occupied myself by doing two things: testing my manacles and eavesdropping.

The former turned out to be a bust. Not surprisingly, Szilagyi was a pro at knowing how to restrain a vampire. The thick clamps on my upper arms, elbows, and wrists were embedded so solidly into the rock wall behind me that the wall had to have been reinforced. The clamp around my waist meant that I couldn't wriggle down to get any traction, and my legs were bolted to the wall in no fewer than four places.

In short, I could give myself a really good case of rock burn by repeated squirming, but I couldn't get free. I could, however, tell a few things about my surrounding from listening.

First, though his guards spoke Romanian when they talked among themselves, Szilagyi only spoke to them in Old Novgorod, an ancient, dead language that I couldn't understand a word of. Second, I doubted that wherever we were was his main hideaway. Szilagyi had just returned after being gone for three days, and that was too long to be away from home base when he was playing a winner-take-all game with Vlad the Impaler.

Three, whatever this place was, it was *definitely* underground. The lack of natural or urban background sounds confirmed that. Szilagyi had a penchant for subterranean lairs, considering his last hiding place had been below the castle that Vlad had lived in when he was human. This one didn't have as many people, so it must be smaller. It was possible the guards Szilagyi had brought with him were just very quiet, but from the number of heartbeats I counted, there weren't enough humans to feed more than a dozen vampires.

I certainly wasn't dipping into that supply. I hadn't been given a drop of blood, as my ever-stronger hunger pangs could attest. Not that I expected any different. Starvation was one of the first things you did with a captive. I supposed I should be happy that they hadn't gone for the other, sure-fire way to weaken an undead captive—silver poisoning. Maybe skinning and dismembering me had been brutal enough for Szilagyi's first attempt to rattle Vlad into making a reckless move.

As I found out the next evening, I'd given Szilagyi too much credit by thinking that.

Shouts woke me. From how leaden my whole body felt, I'd risen earlier than I ever had before. Maybe it was still even sunny out. Before I could celebrate that small victory, I caught some of the heated argument between Maximus and Szilagyi.

" . . . not going to let you do that to her. This is going too far," Maximus said, sounding furious.

" . . . need something more drastic to be effective . . ." I caught before Szilagyi's voice lowered to where I couldn't hear him.

"Think of something *else*!" was Maximus's shouted reply.

Ice blossomed from my stomach to my leaden limbs. Maximus had given Szilagyi the idea to skin me. If he was appalled by what Szilagyi wanted to do now, it must be truly horrendous.

"Careful, Maximus," Szilagyi said. He didn't shout, but I could hear him clearly because they were right outside my cell now. "I value your place in my operation, but I am the one who makes the decisions. Not you."

Maximus said nothing, apparently not willing to jeopardize his position by further argument. The manacles that bound me to the wall felt like they tightened even though it was only my imagination. My heart didn't beat, but it felt like it was being squeezed from the panic I tried to fight back. If I could, I'd be sweating. What was Szilagyi going to do to me this time?

"Then let it be me," Maximus said, now speaking so softly I could barely hear him through the thick wall. "If you're going for maximum rage effect, it's better that way anyway."

"How?" Szilagyi sounded doubtful.

Maximus's next words sliced through my emotions as if they were razors. "Because six weeks ago, Vlad sent me to spy on you. He didn't think you'd suspect me because he'd thrown me out of his line, but part of you must've wondered. Vlad thought I wanted back in his good graces, but all I want is Leila. That's why I wasn't lying when I joined you, and it might enrage Vlad to watch his worst enemy fuck his wife, but it won't drive him mad like it will to watch the man who twice betrayed him do it."

I sucked in a horrified breath. They were arguing over who was going to *rape* me? I began pulling at my restraints for all I was worth. Maximus kept talking, sounding amused now.

"You'll also never have to doubt my loyalty after this. Vlad would invent new ways to torture me for it, so I'll need him dead now even more than you will. Besides, women can forgive a lot, but Leila would hate me forever if I went along with you raping her. If it's me . . . well, let's just say that I don't think she'll entirely mind."

"I'll kill you myself!" I shouted.

Blood began to drip from the metal restraints as I tore open my skin faster than it could heal trying to get free of the clamps. Szilagyi's burst of laughter covered my roiling dread with a flash of rage. My right hand tingled, but it still didn't manifest so much as a spark. I'd never needed my abilities as much as I did now, and instead, I was completely helpless.

"Then again, she might need a little warming up," Maximus muttered, opening the stone door. "Bring me some lubricant."

"We don't have that here," Szilagyi said as he followed Maximus into the room. He had the tripod camera, and the sight of it slammed home that what was about to happen was going to be videoed and sent to Vlad.

"Twelve guys, no women, and they're not allowed to leave?" Maximus's snort was scornful. "*Someone's* got lube."

Szilagyi shrugged, disappearing briefly to shout something in Old Novgorod at his guards. By the time an abashed guard returned with a small bottle, causing Maximus to arch a knowing brow, Szilagyi was done setting up the camera.

And I was in a frenzy to find some way, anyway, to stop this.

"You're wrong, I *will* hate you forever if you do this," I rasped. "You sided with Szilagyi to be with me? You're about to destroy any chance you had of that."

He already had no chance, but maybe if he believed that . . .

Maximus came closer and the wall cut into my back from how I pressed against it in a futile attempt to move away. I hadn't felt naked before in my new skin, but I did now. Oh, I did now.

"Better me than him, Leila," he said, throwing a "sorry, bro" type of glance at Szilagyi, who grunted. "I'll be gentle, whereas he would take out all of his anger against Vlad on you."

"True," Szilagyi in a casual tone.

Hatred swelled until I was shaking from it. "You're right, Vlad *will* invent new ways to torture you, and that's only after I'm done making both of you the sorriest people on earth!"

Szilagyi laughed. "Oh, she does have spirit. I'll enjoy watching this."

"You're leaving," Maximus said, not taking his eyes off me. "I've waited a long time to be with her. I don't mind the camera, but I'm not going to have an audience."

Szilagyi sighed. "Very well. As I said, I always reward loyalty among my people, but don't take too long. I want the video on its way to Vlad by dawn."

Maximus let out a low laugh that had me yanking on my restraints until I felt my bones snap. "Don't worry, you'll have it well before then."

"You disgust me," I spat, my fangs splitting my lip from how hard I was clenching my jaw.

"Oh, before you go, have someone bring me some duct tape, too," Maximus added, glancing at the blood that leaked out from my lip. "Something tells me she's a biter."

With another laugh, Szilagyi left. Maximus went over to the camera and flicked a button. The light still glowed green, indicating that it was filming.

I looked directly into it and said, "Don't give them what they want, Vlad. You have to be colder than you've ever been. Knowing they won't break you is how I'll get through this."

"We'll need to edit that out, won't we?" Szilagyi said, returning with the duct tape.

I looked away from the camera, blinking hard as fury mingled with bitter despair inside me. Of course they'd take that out. There was nothing I could do except endure whatever they chose to do to me. With blistering clarity, I understood how his former helplessness had caused Vlad to wake up in a fiery rage for decades. I wanted to kill everyone here, yet I couldn't even stop them from laughing at me.

Szilagyi gave Maximus a final wink as he handed him the duct tape and then closed the stone door. Maximus began to take off his clothes. I closed my eyes, promising myself that, like before when they'd skinned me, I wouldn't cry in front of them. I couldn't stop what was about to happen, but I could keep myself from breaking down . . . at least, until I was alone again. For days, I'd felt like this wasn't my body. Now, I realized that essence-filled or blank, weaponized or weak, it was.

And every bit of my new skin crawled when I felt Maximus walk toward me.

Chapter 12

 The sound of tape being torn into several strips made me flinch. I didn't want to look at Maximus, but not seeing what was going on made me feel even more helpless. If someone had told me a week ago that Maximus would be responsible for my being skinned alive and raped, I would've called that person a liar. How had I not sensed how cruel he was during the time we spent on the run together? How had I ever trusted him?

You knew what he was, my hated inner voice whispered with its usual venom. *You relived his worst sin, so you of* all *people should have known!*

Maybe I should have, I acknowledged bleakly. Instead, I'd chosen to believe him when said that his worst sin had also been his epiphany that made him change his life. More the fool, me.

From the sounds, Maximus kept ripping off new pieces of tape, but he hadn't put any over my mouth yet. He was near enough to; I could feel his aura bridging the scant distance between us, making my skin crawl even more. With how much he was tearing off, he must be making a ball gag with the tape, or was it something worse? Unable to help it, I opened my eyes—

His hand clapped over my mouth before it could fall open in disbelief. As dreaded, Maximus was stark naked. What I didn't expect was the duct tape that plastered his cock against his lower abdomen.

"Don't fight me, Leila, it'll only make it worse," he said in a stern tone, then mouthed the words *Bite me*.

I wasn't sure what was going on, but I didn't hesitate. The vicious chomp released only the tiniest part of my rage, but it left him snatching back his hand while a big piece of it was still in my mouth. I spat it at him, watching with satisfaction as the glop hit him in the chest.

He seized my newly smooth scalp and wrapped a long strip of tape across my mouth.

"I *was* going to unchain you so you'd be more comfortable, but now I'm only freeing one leg," he all but snarled into my face. "This is your fault, Leila. I didn't want it this way."

So sorry raping me isn't romantic for you! I would've snarled back, except I could only grunt. Besides, a fearful hope was starting to grow. Why would Maximus tape his genitals down? Talk about defeating the purpose of his intentions.

With his back still to the camera, Maximus released the clamps on my right leg. Then, holding the lube bottle like it was a trophy, he slathered some onto his palm before reaching between my legs. What the camera would've seen was me kicking in a futile attempt to deny him access and him using his knees to force my legs open. What I felt rather than saw was him securing a piece of tape across the most intimate part of me, then dropping the bottle and gripping my thigh to his waist.

"I've wanted this for so long," he said, burying his face into my neck and arching against me with a loud groan.

My eyes clamped shut to keep the tears at bay, but this time, they were of confused hope. Maximus ground his hips into mine in a graphic mime of penetration, but the tape covering both of us made that impossible. All it did was embarrass me to the extreme, and considering what I'd been through the past week, that was worlds better than I had dared to hope for.

"They're listening," Maximus whispered so low that I could barely hear him even though his lips were pressed to my ear.

I grunted at the next hard arch against my center, turning my head as if I couldn't bear to face the camera. In reality, I was trying to press my ear closer to Maximus's mouth.

"I swear, I didn't know what Szilagyi was going to do that day." Whispered in anguish as Maximus groaned again and gripped my hip in feigned lust. "By the time he flew us to the castle, I couldn't stop the attack. I could only watch him destroy everything."

I wanted to believe him, but what if this was another lie? If Maximus really had sided with Szilagyi for the reasons he'd given him, he knew he couldn't rape me without earning my undying hatred—although how he could rationalize that I'd forgive him for killing Vlad, I had no idea. Once again, I pulled at my restraints until I felt blood slick my skin.

In a normal voice, Maximus said, "Stop it, Leila! You're only hurting yourself." In that too-soft whisper, he said, "You're doing it wrong. You can't pull free that way, but if you use enough force, you can break your bones and then slide your arms from the restraints. Once your hands are free, you can unlock the rest of them."

I stiffened, finally allowing myself to hope that Maximus was still on our side. Unlike faking a rape so I wouldn't hate him, he had no ulterior reason to tell me how to free myself unless he really was doing everything he could for Vlad and me, even under these awful circumstances.

My rush of gratitude turned to more severe embarrassment at the rhythmic way he began to move. Then he groaned gutturally and his free hand squeezed its way from my breast to my ass and back again. Instinctively, I jerked hard against my restraints, but he flattened me against the wall before kissing my neck with a hunger that didn't quite feel feigned.

"Not now," he growled low. "Later, when Vlad comes. You'll need to be free to protect yourself from the guards. They're ordered to kill you at the first sign of attack."

I froze for a second, hope giving way to a surge of excitement. Had Maximus told Vlad where we were?

My head began to bang against the stone wall as he moved faster, his groans sounding more urgent.

"I'm sorry," he whispered raggedly. "If I don't make it look real, Szilagyi will brutalize you himself later. I can't let that happen, for your sake as well as Vlad's."

Relief and gratitude mixed with shame and awkwardness, forming a toxic emotional brew. If my arms were free, I would have hugged Maximus for risking his life to save me from such an awful fate. At the same time, I couldn't stop myself from thrashing in futile attempts to get away from him. He gripped my free thigh hard enough to hurt, but I realized that the way he had my limb positioned also kept the camera from viewing an angle that would reveal this was all an act.

Then he shattered my new hopes by whispering, "I'm watched too closely to reach Vlad to tell him where we are. You need to link to him and let him know that you're underneath the old Sukhumi train station in Abkhazia."

I turned my head to give him a stunned glare. Did he forget something important, like how my abilities were smothered even before he'd made sure that I had been *skinned*?

"Doesn't this feel even a little good, baby?" he said loud enough for our eavesdroppers, then began to move faster. This might not be real, but it was so graphic and intimate that I couldn't even look at him anymore. If I was still human, my pelvic area would need an ice pack after being repeatedly beaten by a certain blunt object, taped down or no.

"Szilagyi doesn't know it, but he sliced Vlad's aura off when he took your skin." A whisper that seemed to sear me when I realized its implications. "And you don't need to touch anything to link to Vlad. You can reach him through your dreams. He taunted me with that when he held me prisoner."

I couldn't stop the tear that slid past my tightly clenched eyelids. I'd thought that Maximus had talked Szilagyi into skinning me to keep me from using my abilities. Instead, he'd done it to reactivate them. Maybe, I didn't need anything more than what I already had to save myself.

Even as that hope rose, my vicious inner voice tried to quash it. *You haven't been able to link to anyone since you became a vampire, and Vlad can't hear your thoughts anymore, so how will you tell him where you are even if you do link to him?*

I shoved that nasty little voice back down.

Twenty minutes ago, I'd thought I was helpless. Right now, Maximus had reminded me that I wasn't, all while risking his life in order to *not* rape me. I didn't need him to explain how pissed Szilagyi would be if he found out that his new video was only R-rated instead of X, and even if Vlad knew that, he still might kill him for what Maximus was doing to me.

I pushed that thought back. I'd link to Vlad and I'd find a way to make him hear me, period. Maximus had given me my location. All I needed to do was relay it. It had to be possible. Vlad had told me that Mencheres, the vampire that Vlad often referred to as his "honorary" sire, could speak directly into other vampire's minds, and Mencheres didn't have the sire/offspring connection to Vlad that I did.

Maximus let out a sharp sound, half groan, half shout, as he shuddered against me. Something moist hit my inner thigh, and beneath his new moan, I heard a rip of tape. Then I felt the sting of it being torn from my own delicate flesh. Not having any hair grow back on my new skin yet was suddenly a good thing.

When Maximus moved away, letting the camera get its first unhindered view of us, he was tapeless and erect while I had semen coating my inner thighs and pubis mound. Martin Scorsese couldn't have directed a more convincing scene.

I knew why Maximus had gone with the

"method" approach—anything less would have roused too much suspicion—but this was still traumatizing. I wanted to bathe with boiling water, yet I couldn't even wipe the smears away.

"Sorry it had to be this way, baby. Next time, it will be better," Maximus said, ripping the tape away from my mouth and adding it to the pile he'd concealed in his fist.

Next time. Would he need to repeat this ruse to ensure that Szilagyi had enough filthy videos to send to Vlad? I couldn't suppress a revolted shudder at the thought.

I'd find a way to reach Vlad. I had to. Besides, despair might have made me oblivious to it before, but now, I realized a very important thing about the camera in the corner of my cell.

It had a cord that was plugged into an electrical socket.

Chapter 13

It felt like I broke my brain trying to mentally link to Vlad over the next two days. So far, I might have struck out in my progress with that, but I did have a breakthrough in another area: the stranglehold of the sun.

Dawn still hit me like a boulder to the head, but I awoke earlier each passing day. My willpower was growing from the ugliness of my circumstances, but in the meantime, my body was getting frighteningly weak. Being skinned had made me lose most of the blood I'd had in me at my capture and I hadn't been given a drop since. Before, I'd listened to the heartbeats here in an effort to figure out how many people were in this hideout. Now, I had to fight *not* to listen to them because they inflamed my hunger to the point where I could barely concentrate enough to attempt linking to Vlad.

I need blood, I'd mouthed to Maximus during his heavily guarded visit the second day after my not-rape. He hadn't brought the tripod camera with him for a repeat, thank God, but instead, he came with a bucket and a washcloth. It was beyond humiliating to have him give me a sponge bath with four smirking guards watching, but at least their trading comments about my anatomy kept them from focusing on my mouth, so they didn't see my wordless message. Maximus did, and his single nod said he'd do the best he could.

Maybe feeding would help me to push past the barriers to my abilities. My link to Vlad *had* to still be there. We hadn't just exchanged blood; he'd turned me into a vampire, so every cell in my body must have an intrinsic connection to him. I just needed to reactivate those connections and follow them to their source.

I tried for the rest of the night. When dawn finally hit me with its usual knockout blow, I was still trying.

Vlad's castle wasn't burning anymore. That wasn't the only change since the last time I'd seen it. The sections where it had collapsed had been cleared out, revealing cratered spaces that went down as far as the basement in some places. Huge debris piles were lined up outside what was left of the stone walls. Cranes and bulldozers were lessening those piles by hefting loads into nearby steel shipping containers. The castle had looked almost deserted before, but now it was crawling with people involved in clean-up activity.

The north and east ends of the house looked

*like a fallen soufflé with how concave they were.
The west side had fared better, but it had been reduced to one story. By comparison, the southern
side towered over the ruins, all four stories intact
and the turret in defiant relief against the clear afternoon sky.*

*That's where Vlad was, hands clasped behind
his back while he looked down on the progress.
Mencheres was there, too, seated on a couch next
to a computer table. The couch I recognized; the
computer area was new. Even if I didn't remember
what the room had looked like before, the metal
table didn't fit with the sumptuous furnishings
that, like the turret and the rest of the south wing,
had somehow survived Szilagyi's two-pronged
attack.*

*I didn't know if this was real or a dream. That
didn't stop me from staring at Vlad with a hunger
that eclipsed the one that ravaged me now. I'd tried
not to dwell on how much I had missed him, but
seeing him destroyed the emotional defense I'd
built up. I ached to touch him, yet I couldn't. The
other times I'd linked to Vlad in my sleep, I'd had
a ghostly version of a body. This time, I had nothing. Maybe I really was dreaming.*

*If so, I'd dreamed him into looking more di-
sheveled than I'd ever seen him. His dark hair was
matted and his clothes were streaked with so much
soot, dirt, and blood, I couldn't tell what their real
color was. A thick layer of hair shadowed his jaw,*

making it more beard than sensual stubble, and his shoes had pieces of charred flesh stuck to them. Despite this, his posture was regally erect, as if he were garbed in spotless royal robes instead of his filthy attire.

"Come," Vlad said in Romanian.

Marty walked into the room, causing a wave of joy to crash over me. He'd survived the attack! Thank God! Then, just as quickly, my joy was replaced with concern.

Marty looked almost as bad as Vlad. Both sideburns were gone and he only had a few patches of black hair remaining on his head. His face was also covered in blood, and it took me a moment to realize why.

"This was mailed to one of your people, like the last video," Marty said, his hoarse voice catching on the next words. "I watched it on the way here. It's definitely her."

Vlad held out his hand, but the rest of his body stayed in that perfect, statuesque stillness. I looked at the envelope and the scarlet tears streaking Marty's cheeks, then a chill of dread went through me. No. Don't let it be that tape—

"You don't want to see it," Marty rasped, confirming my suspicions. "I wish I hadn't. She's still alive at the end. That's all you need to—"

"Give it to me." Four snarled words that made me recoil from the violence seething from them.

Mencheres didn't wait for Marty's response. An

invisible force yanked the envelope out of Marty's hand and floated it over to Vlad. Then Mencheres's power propelled Marty out of the room. Once that manila envelope touched Vlad, he was a blur of motion, streaking over to the computer table. Then he put the DVD into the laptop and clicked "play." Now I was praying that this was only a dream. Just in case it wasn't, I began screaming at him with my thoughts.

Don't watch it, Vlad! Listen to my voice instead. I know where I am, and all you need to do is listen so I can tell you—

Fire erupted from his hands when the screen filled with the image of me, naked and struggling so fiercely against my restraints that blood ran beneath my clamps. Then it showed Maximus's naked ass as he walked toward me holding a bottle of lube and several strips of duct tape. I was so upset that Vlad was watching this; it took a few moments to realize that the recording had no sound, which surprised me until I remembered Maximus flicking a button before he took off his clothes. Smart, the sound could have been isolated and amplified until you could hear what he had been whispering to me, and I had no doubt that Szilagyi had watched this before sending it to Vlad.

No wonder Szilagyi hadn't suspected a thing, *I thought, feeling sick as I watched Maximus begin the mime of my rape. Maximus must have been a director in his former life, because he had an uncanny sense of camera angles. Not once did I glimpse the tape he'd applied to me or himself as he rocked and thrust against me as if out of control with lust. I tried to focus on Vlad instead of the graphic images, willing him to hear the words I kept mentally roaring at him.*

It's not real, it's not real, stop watching it! Listen to me, I'm right here and I know where I am!

Either I really was dreaming or I wasn't getting through, because not once did Vlad take his eyes off the screen. The video ended with Maximus leaving me manacled to the wall with his semen still coating me in pink smears. Vlad didn't move and nothing changed in his granite expression, but the flames on his hands grew until they encompassed his entire body. Soon, I couldn't see him beneath the layers of red, orange, and blue, and when fire kept pouring from him like water gushing out of a geyser, Mencheres rose.

"*Vlad,*" *he began.*

A wall of flames hurled the Egyptian vampire across the room. Mencheres didn't try to talk to Vlad again. He ran, shouting in Romanian and English for everyone else to leave.

Over the next several minutes, I watched in agonized disbelief as the people who'd been working to repair the house ran from the rage-fueled inferno that continued to spill out of Vlad until it covered every inch of the castle. The ones that didn't move fast enough were thrown to safety by Mencheres's telekinesis, until it looked like the house was hurtling people away from it while writhing in its death throes. Even the napalm attack hadn't been this destructive. In a shocking display of power, Vlad's fire burned until nothing remained except him amidst a sea of flames, crumpled stone, and swirling embers.

Chapter 14

Despite Maximus's repeated cajoling, Szilagyi refused to lift his ban on my starvation. After the "dream" that I strongly suspected was a psychic vision, I'd do anything to strengthen myself enough to make Vlad hear me the next time I was able to link to him. Anything.

Szilagyi had accomplished his goal of driving Vlad into a psychotic rage, since he burned down the house he'd lived in for centuries, not to mention almost killed dozens of his own people in the process. I didn't know what Vlad would do next, and that terrified me. Since my "dream," I hadn't been able to reach him again. No great stretch to figure out why. Linking to people took a lot out of me, and with starvation continuing to deplete my strength, I was like a car that had run out of gas.

That's why, when I heard Maximus negotiate a non-videoed "conjugal" visit, I knew it must really be a mask for him to sneak me some blood. I hated the thought of repeating the fake assault, but this was the only thing that Szilagyi had agreed to, so it was our only shot. I still wasn't sure how Maximus would do it. Hide a tube of blood in his pants and pretend that the bulge was just him looking forward to Round Two?

"If you don't want to be filmed this time, you strip out here and the door stays open and manned by a guard," I heard Szilagyi order, and my spirits sank. Now what? "Not that I don't trust you, Maximus," Szilagyi went on in a friendlier tone, "but women can be very persuasive, especially when you're in love with one of them."

"Aww, I knew you were a romantic at heart," Maximus replied flippantly, then the two of them shared a laugh as though they weren't discussing an impending rape. Well, I wasn't really about to be raped, but Szilagyi didn't know that. Anger at my helplessness burned through me again, fueling my determination to get the blood any way I could. With it, I wouldn't remain Szilagyi's little torture trophy for much longer.

"You need a whole roll of that?" Szilagyi asked, his tone taunting now. "Is she that bad of a biter?"

Something small thumped right outside the door. "Just this," Maximus said. "I don't mind the bites, but I could do without all the bitching."

A snort of laughter was Szilagyi's response, and a few moments later, the stone door opened and Maximus came in. I averted my eyes because, as ordered, he was naked. Then I glanced back at him with a sense of foreboding.

He was *totally* naked and only holding two small pieces of duct tape. Neither one of them would be enough to cover his necessary assets, let alone mine, too.

"I know, you'll hate me forever for this," Maximus said, walking over and pressing one of the pieces of tape to my mouth. "But you don't know how long forever really is. A thousand years later, I've got an idea, and let me assure you, Leila, things change."

Over his broad shoulders, I saw the guard lean in to check out what was happening. Maximus must have sensed him, too, because he turned around, keeping the other piece of tape concealed behind him.

"Szilagyi said to man the door. He didn't say come inside to oversee, and if I wanted an audience, I would've invited everyone," Maximus said, his tone harder than granite.

The guard muttered an apology and left, though the door stayed wide open.

I kept my eyes glued to that space as Maximus put the single remaining piece of tape on me. Not looking at him when he did that created a false sense of distance, as if I could separate my mind from my body. I couldn't, of course, and the grimly determined scent emanating from Maximus reminded me that he wasn't acting of his own free will, either. We were both forced into this awful situation, and for what? *Damn* Szilagyi! He'd made sure that Maximus couldn't hide any blood on him, so now we'd have to go through this embarrassing, shameful ruse for nothing.

When Maximus's hands moved from my most intimate spot to my shoulders and he touched his forehead to mine, a slow sigh seemed to slip from my soul. Neither of us wanted to be here, but right at this moment, I felt . . . oddly safe. For the next several minutes, I knew that no one would hurt me because Maximus wouldn't let them. When you could be tortured at any moment, the assurance of safety, no matter how brief, was precious, and I had it because of him.

As if he sensed my need amidst my dread over what was to happen next, he stroked my head and my face with light, comforting touches.

"It's okay," he murmured, his gray gaze conveying all the support and encouragement that he couldn't say out loud with our multiple eavesdroppers. Then, in a normal voice, he said, "I've wanted this for days, Leila."

My restraints creaked as I strained against them, though it was more for sound effects than revulsion when the length of his body pressed against mine. He didn't immediately begin to act out what Szilagyi and everyone else thought he was here to do. Instead, with a quick glance over his shoulder, he held his hips away from mine and then hugged me as much as my many manacles would allow.

"Don't worry," he whispered. "I'll give you what you need."

Then he began to mime what the single piece of tape prevented him from actually doing. Awkwardness washed over me, yet it wasn't as extreme as last time. The survivalist in me was already running through the list of all the ways this could be worse. Besides, Maximus was stuck faking this because it would look odd if he said he wasn't in the mood after he'd gotten the green light from Szilagyi, and with the open door, anyone could peep in to make sure that he was here for his stated intentions.

He did what he could to make it easier on me, though. Like keeping his hands on my hips or shoulders instead of letting them roam as he had the last time when we'd been filmed. In the strangest way, it reminded me of months ago, when Vlad and I were broken up and I'd checked Maximus for incriminating essence trails under the guise of making out with him. Then, like now, his touch didn't elicit any desire like Vlad's always did, but his light grip on my shoulders was almost soothing, a reminder that we were in this together. I didn't want to be with him like this and I was sure he'd rather be anywhere else than fake-raping me, but everything Maximus was doing was a testament to his loyalty and bravery. Amidst my brutal, dangerous circumstances, having a friend like him was a godsend.

Maximus paused in his movements, glancing over his shoulder once again to assure himself that no one was peeking in. Then he pulled the tape off my mouth and his lips covered mine.

I stiffened in confusion. No one was watching us, so why was he doing this? I really tensed when his mouth opened and slanted to form a seal, but right as I was wondering what the hell he was thinking, warm liquid rushed into my throat.

It was blood. Sweet, glorious blood. Relief made me sag in my restraints. He *had* found a way to get it to me, even when he'd been forced to strip to the skin!

Then hunger took over and I swallowed that crimson ambrosia so fast, I would've choked if I still breathed. The tiny part of me that was still human found the nature-tested method of him feeding me disgusting, but the starved vampire in me bulldozed over that. I hadn't realized how deep my deprivation ran until the blood caused my whole body to burn the way it had the first week I'd been changed over. Without conscious thought, I ground my mouth against Maximus's, desperate to get more of that pain-killing ambrosia. When another stream of blood filled me, feeding frenzy took over and nothing else mattered.

I didn't care that the naked man pressed next to me wasn't my husband. Had no concerns over how I strained against my restraints to get closer to him, and the very *last* thing on my mind was how I'd explain any of this to Vlad if I ever saw him again.

* * *

After it was over and Maximus had left, my emotions were in such turmoil that I was glad he'd arranged for his "visit" close to dawn so I couldn't attempt to link to Vlad until the next dusk. On one hand, I was beyond grateful to Maximus. If he'd gotten caught sneaking me blood, let alone caught in the act of *not* raping me, he'd be killed. He knew that and so did I, yet he continued to help me even though if I was successful and Vlad managed to rescue me, the first thing he'd do was kill Maximus. I probably wouldn't even have time to tell Vlad that the video had been a fake before he toasted him to kingdom come. Besides, even if Vlad knew that the tape wasn't real, he might kill Maximus anyway. He'd killed the Joker for far, far less than what Maximus had done to me.

On the other hand, after what had happened during my feeding frenzy, I was so disgusted with myself that I almost wished I'd gotten skinned again instead. Due to the roughly three pints of blood that Maximus had managed to sneak into me, my mind felt clear, my body felt rejuvenated, and my focus was back. No wonder starvation was second only to silver poisoning as the most effective way to keep a vampire captive weak and docile. However, that also meant that I had a crystal clear recollection of everything I'd done while gripped by that insatiable, conscienceless hunger. If Vlad ever found out . . . Maximus might not be the only one he killed.

Despite my guilt and misgivings, as soon as I awoke the next evening, I channeled all of my new energy into my attempt to link to Vlad. He never needed to know what had happened with me and Maximus earlier, and after what I'd done to get that blood, I wasn't about to waste it. When over half the night went by but nothing happened, my frustration grew. Why could I reach him in my sleep while starved and weak, yet not be able to connect to him while I was awake and stronger?

Because you didn't link to him before, it was only a dream! my inner voice taunted me.

My jaw clenched. I don't care if it officially made me a schizophrenic; one day I was going to kill that bitch.

I forced back my anger to concentrate again, searching for those internal essence traces that had to be there. More time went by, and all that happened was I overheard Szilagyi telling Maximus that he needed to accompany him on a "scouting" mission over the next few days. That fueled my desperation. No Maximus meant no more blood, plus I figured the only reason the guards hadn't taken advantage of my unconscious state each morning was because they knew that Maximus would kill them if they tried anything. If he wasn't there and they didn't think Szilagyi would mind . . .

As the minutes continued to slip by without any progress, I began to despair that my inner voice had been right. Maybe it really had been a dream last time. Otherwise, I was doing something in my sleep that I wasn't doing now, and for the life of me, I couldn't imagine what. I couldn't be more focused on finding the link, whereas when I was asleep, I wasn't even looking for it. All I did was miss Vlad with a ferocity I didn't allow myself to dwell on when I was awake—

He strode through a dense forest with Mencheres at his side. Sunlight peeked through the trees, reflecting off of a piece of metal about a hundred yards ahead.

"Why the bloody hell did you bring him *here?"* *an English voice demanded, then a dark-haired man stepped out from behind a tree, his silver knife still glinting in the sun.*

"Because you're not the only vampire he values as family," *Vlad replied, his tone equally harsh.* *"I don't have time for our usual insults, Bones, so take me to Cat. Now."*

The image dissolved, leaving me staring at my stone prison with a mixture of shock, excitement and determination. That hadn't been a dream, so my abilities *were* back! At once, I tried to reestablish the link, but almost an hour later, I was still running up against a metaphysical wall.

Frustration made me want to scream. I was doing exactly what I'd done before, yet it wasn't working! My psychic abilities were there, so why couldn't I control them? Or were they unreliable now, like a cell phone with a bad signal?

Vlad. Even that small glimpse made me bang my head against the wall to combat the stronger ache inside. He hadn't been dressed in filthy clothes, but his expression had held the same wildness as when he'd burned down the remains of his castle—

"I lost days searching the ruins of my house until I realized that Leila wasn't buried beneath the rubble. Then you cost me more time because you couldn't be bothered to check your messages," Vlad was saying in a blistering tone as he, Bones, and Mencheres walked out of the woods. *"If you'd returned Mencheres's calls immediately, I might have been able to prevent the worst of my wife's suffering."*

"Your wife?" Bones asked in surprise.

Vlad shot him a look. "I'll explain when I see Cat."

The vision slipped away and a strangled sob escaped me as I finally realized what I'd been doing wrong. All this time, I'd been focusing on finding my *link* to Vlad, not on Vlad himself. I'd had it backward. Vlad was my link, not some hidden essence trail within me. That's why I'd been able to reach him in my dreams, both recently and back when I'd been hiding from him months ago. Once free of my willpower, my subconscious had zeroed in on him, forming its own link.

I closed my eyes and dropped the emotional shields I'd erected to protect myself from the pain of thinking about him. At once, memories began to rip through me. *His scent, like cinnamon mixed with wood smoke. The emerald rings around his copper-colored eyes. How thick his hair felt in my hands. The heat that radiated from his skin, and the stubble on his jaw that gently rasped me every time we kissed . . .*

Dark gray walls fell away, revealing the panorama of a deep blue sky. I let the vision take me, until I wasn't in the dank, depressing cell anymore.

I stood like an invisible shadow next to Vlad. He, Mencheres, Bones, and Cat were in front of a large, luxurious-looking farmhouse. Trees surrounded it on three sides, and I didn't see any other houses along the long gravel road that disappeared over the hill behind it.

"Tell the child to come out, I already know she's in there," Vlad was saying to the beautiful redheaded vampire.

Cat swung an accusing glare at Mencheres. "You told him?"

Bones also glowered at him, but Mencheres lifted one shoulder in a shrug. "I didn't."

Now that I felt centered in the vision, I started yelling at Vlad with my thoughts, but he didn't appear to hear me.

"As if he needed to," Vlad replied curtly. "You forget that I know several of your secrets, Cat, such as your being best friends with a demon-branded shapeshifter. As soon as I heard you'd secluded yourself in grief after the Law Guard-

ians 'killed' your daughter, I knew what had really happened."

"Then you also know we'd do anything to protect our child from those who'd harm her if they knew she was still alive," Bones said, recovering from his surprise quicker than Cat.

Vlad smiled for the first time. "Oh, I'm counting on it."

"What do you want?" Cat asked in a low voice.

"To call in every favor you owe me," Vlad responded bluntly. "Since I don't expect that to be enough, I'm also offering your daughter honorary status in my line. I know why you hid her survival from me and you were correct. Under extreme circumstances, I would choose my people over her despite our friendship, but if she's an honorary part of my line, you don't have to worry about that anymore. When she wearies of hiding herself away— and that day will come—you'll have yet another powerful ally in your fight to keep her alive."

Wondering why people would want to kill a little girl made me pause in my mental attempts to get Vlad's attention. Then I redoubled my efforts. I had a solid link to him. All I had to do was make him hear me.

"In exchange for what?" Bones asked, his tone steely.

"Grave power," Vlad stated, and from their reactions, they knew what that meant even if I didn't.

"No," Bones said at once.

Vlad ignored him, staring at Cat. She glanced back at the house twice before she replied.

"I'm sorry, Vlad. To do that, I'd have to leave with you for who knows how long, plus that could expose me to the same people we're hiding from. I know you're at war, but—"

"Have you ever seen an animal skinned?" Vlad interrupted, his voice icily pleasant. "It's a bloody, brutal business under normal circumstances, but imagine if the animal were alive and screaming. Then imagine that it wasn't an animal, but the person you loved being repeatedly slashed and hacked so that their skin could be ripped away faster than it could heal."

Cat gasped, her hand flying to her mouth. Vlad seized her by the shoulders, his tone sharpening into razor wire.

"That's the first tape Szilagyi sent me to prove that he had captured Leila during his attack on my home. The second showed my oldest friend raping her while she was manacled to a wall. Now, ask yourself if you'd rather have my undying gratitude and promised support for helping me save my wife from further suffering, or if you'd rather have me as the merciless enemy I will become *if you refuse.*"

Cat didn't take her eyes off Vlad as she held out a hand to Bones, whom Mencheres had needed to restrain as soon as Vlad grabbed Cat. Then her gaze started to shine with green.

"I didn't know that Leila had been taken captive. I'm so sorry, but what you want me to do . . . it's too risky to do more than once, so you need to decide if you want it for her, or for the vampire responsible for everything that's happened to her."

Vlad's mouth twisted. *"Do you really need to ask?"*

Cat smiled back with equal coldness. *"Good choice."*

Vlad let her go and she turned toward the house, raising her voice. *"It's okay, Tate and Mom, you can put the guns down now. Katie, come on out and meet your Uncle Vlad—"*

"Sleeping already?" Szilagyi asked, crashing into my vision like an unwelcome visitor. My eyes snapped open and I released my link. Szilagyi was in front of me, his head cocked as he stared at me. I'd been so deep in the vision, I hadn't felt him come in. What if he could tell that I'd been linking to Vlad?

"I can only play I Spy With My Little Eye so many times before it gets boring," I replied, attempting to throw him off. "Or maybe I was ignoring you because I really, really hate you."

Szilagyi smiled, letting his gaze slide over me in a way that made my skin ripple as if it were trying to scoot away. I listened for Maximus, but I didn't hear him anymore. *Please, don't let him have left already,* I found myself thinking.

"I never would have expected it, but you are

very similar to Vlad," Szilagyi said at last. "When he was young, nothing I did to him broke him, and I've done quite a bit to you, but you still stare at me with the same defiance in your eyes."

"Why did you hate him so much back then?" I asked, trying to keep him talking instead of looking. "I know why he hated you, but what made you single him out even when he was human?"

Szilagyi's scoff was instant. "*I* had helped build Hungary to unprecedented greatness, *I* had fought in just as many wars, yet when the Church needed a defender against Mehmed's army, they chose Vlad. Later, when our sire turned him into a vampire, Tenoch gave Vlad the remains of his power legacy instead of me."

Jealousy, I realized with amazement. Back then, Vlad had hated Szilagyi for good reasons, like imprisoning him, costing him his throne, and murdering his son, not to mention what he didn't know—that Szilagyi had killed his first wife, too. Yet the other man's resentment stemmed from something as simple as feeling slighted. It would have been laughable if the repercussions hadn't resulted in rivers of spilled blood.

"Yet in the end, it only matters who wins," Szilagyi said, his tone turning silky as he trailed a hand down my stomach. "I had my doubts, but I'm starting to believe that Maximus was right. You're what I need to finally bring Vlad down. Seems he destroyed what was left of his home in a fit of rage the other day. I wonder what made him do that, hmm?"

Szilagyi's taunting smile caused my right hand to tingle as if it was about to spark. It was gloved, but I still didn't dare glance at it out of hope that it *was* refilling with electricity. If so, then I couldn't draw Szilagyi's attention. He'd only rip my arm off again.

"Maybe Vlad just wanted the insurance money so he could offer up a fat reward for your corpse," I replied instead.

Szilagyi let his hand dip below my navel and held it there to emphasize that there was nothing I could do to stop him.

"If there's one thing I can count on after the tapes I've sent him, it's Vlad wanting to murder me himself," he said, moving his hand away at last. Then he smiled, chilling and anticipatory. "What you should hope is that I don't get more creative with new tapes of you in the meantime to madden him into making a reckless mistake that will deliver him right into my hands."

Chapter 15

 I waited as long as I dared after Szilagyi left, worried that he'd come back and somehow sense that I was linking to Vlad. With dawn now only minutes away, I had to try again or wait another twelve hours, and I couldn't do that. Szilagyi would be off with Maximus on his "scouting" mission, but what if he'd arranged for another round of torture in his absence? I couldn't risk losing the scant three pints of blood I'd imbibed, especially now that I didn't know when I'd get my next meal.

So I closed my eyes and let myself feel all the longing, regret, and heartache that came with thinking about Vlad. I loved him more than anything and I wanted to believe we'd get through this, but the dark part of me whispered that it was hopeless. After all, our track record was grim. If I insisted on helping him search for his enemies, I ended up captured and tortured. Agree *not* to help and stay in his stone fortress instead? Get captured and tortured. I'd have been blown up, too, if I'd obeyed Vlad's wishes and not left the lowest level of the dungeon. If I were an outsider, I'd say that fate was giving me a big head's up that this wasn't going to work—

"Don't sit there."

Cat pivoted, lowering herself into the chair across from Vlad instead of the one next to him. In Romanian, the pilots announced that they were taking off. Moments later, the sleek Learjet tilted as it became airborne.

"Sorry," Cat murmured. "Didn't mean to invade your space."

Vlad glanced at the ivory seat to his left, his mouth tightening. "It's not that. This is where Leila normally sits so that I can keep hold of her hand . . ."

He muttered a foul curse and stopped speaking. Cat stared at him, her features creased with empathy.

"She's strong," she said quietly. "She'll get through this."

Vlad's laugh was harsh. "And then what? She'll brace for the next assault? I can't even keep her safe in our own home. Even if I kill Szilagyi and everyone else who hates me, in time I'll make new enemies, all of whom will know that the most effective way to get to me is through her. If I truly wanted to keep her safe, I would never have married her."

The first part was so close to what I'd been thinking that I was stunned. Then Vlad got to the last sentence and I barely heard Cat's reply because of the roar from my own mind.

Don't you dare give up on us! I don't care what will happen later, we'll face it together!

You never learn, *my inner voice instantly mocked.* Are you a special kind of stupid or what?

I was so angry that I had a flash of absolute clarity. As if in a dream within a dream, I saw myself reach into slimy darkness where she lived, yank her up by her tentacles, and rip that fucking bitch to pieces.

You took away my hope when I was a frightened, injured child! *I screamed at her.* You made me believe I'd killed my mother, you talked me into slitting my wrists and you've tried to ruin every bit of happiness I've ever had since, but you are done, hear me? I *will* get out of this and I *will* get back with Vlad and we *will* make it work, and if I hear another word out of you, you're fucking dead! You got that? *DEAD!*

"*Did you just threaten me?*" Vlad asked, his voice flinty.

Cat leaned forward, her gray gaze concerned. "*I said I'd always be there for you. Unless you take that as a threat—*"

"*Shh,*" he interrupted, slowly glancing around the cabin. Then my heart felt like it kick-started when he whispered, "*Leila?*" in a disbelieving voice.

Yes, I'm here! *my thoughts screamed before I could even finish processing that he'd heard me at last. Tears spilled from my eyes as I went on.* I'm here and I love you and I'm underneath the abandoned Sukhumi train station in Abkhazia. Don't attack until dusk. I need to be awake to defend myself.

Cat looked around the cabin, her brows drawing together in confusion. "Vlad, what are—?"

He leapt up, clapping his hand over her mouth. Her eyes bugged and she began to struggle until he snapped, "Quiet. I can't hear her now, but I think Leila was trying to reach me."

He couldn't hear me anymore? I began repeating "Under the Sukhumi train station in Abkhazia!" *but a sudden, bone-numbing lethargy meant the first rays of the sun were breaking. I struggled against the undertow while trying to turn the volume up on a single word, hoping it made the difference.*

Abkhazia, Abkhazia, Abkhazia!

Then the undertow dragged me down into the darkness.

My eyes snapped open with a suddenness that made me surprised to find that I was alone in my cell. I tried not to let the fact that I was still *in* my cell depress me. After all, what had I expected, to wake up in Vlad's arms because he'd heard me and already rescued my while I slept? Nothing had ever come that easily for me.

What had woken me, then? I strained my ears, but didn't hear anything unusual. Just the guards going about whatever tasks Szilagyi had assigned them to, which, I knew, consisted mostly of making sure that no one got near the former Soviet train station and that I didn't get out. Same old, same old . . .

A scream escaped me as a transparent head suddenly appeared next to my own—through the rock behind me! The filmy face frowned and a single ethereal finger appeared over the thing's lips while it—he?—shook his head as if warning me to keep it down. By the time one of the guards ran in to check on me, the head had already disappeared back into the rock.

"What?" the guard demanded in English.

"I, ah, thought I saw a rat," I stammered.

What was I going to say? I'd seen a ghost who had longer facial sideburns than Marty, but who seemed to be missing the rest of his body? I'd call myself crazy if I said it out loud.

The guard, a brunet vampire who looked to be the same age Szilagyi had been when he was changed, gave me another suspicious glare, but then left. As soon as he did, the ghost's head popped back out of the rock again.

"Get ready," he whispered directly into my ear before disappearing.

I didn't feel any breath, but the words, though soft, had been clear. Then, faster than a lightning bolt, rage and ice-cold determination flashed through my emotions before they, too, were gone. Gooseflesh broke out over my skin that wasn't a result of the cell's perpetual chilliness.

Those hadn't been *my* emotions. That meant . . .

I let thoughts of Vlad explode into my mind. Just as quickly, my stone cell faded.

He stood next to Cat, but I wouldn't have rec- ognized either of them if I'd passed them on the street. Both had on incredibly lifelike, full-face masks beneath their wigs, which were a bland shade of brown. They were dressed in equally nondescript clothing, their ragged, long-sleeved T-shirts slouching over jeans that had also seen much better days.

They blended in perfectly with the few other loi- terers who wandered in and out of the abandoned buildings that lined the old train tracks. In fact, the only thing that stood out was the ghost who zoomed up to Cat, although no one but she and Vlad seemed to notice him. As soon as he came to a stop, I realized he was the same one who'd just haunted my cell.

"She's in the southeast corner of the bunker," the ghost stated. "There are thirteen guards and ten humans below, with seven or eight more guards in and around the station above, and that doesn't count the security cameras."

I didn't know what shocked me more: that Vlad was really here, or that he'd sent a ghost to do *reconnaissance—not to mention how efficiently the ghost had done it.*

"You told her to prepare?" Vlad asked.

That transparent head bobbed out a nod. Vlad and Cat exchanged a look, but I didn't wait to see what they did next.

I dropped the link while wild bursts of excitement and fear coursed through me. Even with Vlad's incredible power, if I wasn't free by the time he attacked, the guards would kill me just as Szilagyi had ordered them to. Vlad hadn't brought Mencheres with him, so the telekinetic vampire couldn't freeze everyone in place as he had during a prior ambush with Vlad. I didn't have time to wonder at Vlad's choice of Cat as backup instead. I stretched my arms, using the restraints as a brace. Then, with a deep breath for courage, I threw myself forward with all of the inhuman strength in me.

It took two more times with me biting through my lip to keep from screaming, but I finally felt my bones crush enough to where I could yank my pulpy arms out of the triple restraints. Then I felt something I hadn't felt in weeks; my upper body sagging forward, freed from the clamps.

I waited, clenching my jaw to keep from verbalizing my agony as my pulverized bones began to grow back into their proper shape. At the same time, I listened hard, but the guards didn't seem aware that anything was going on. I glanced at the clamps that fastened around my legs and urgency replaced my former excitement. I didn't have much time.

As soon as I had ripped the glove and tape off my right hand, I bent and started on my ankle restraints. During his faux rapes, I'd paid attention to how Maximus had uncuffed my leg. The locks didn't require a key and the latch was a fairly simple, smaller-case H shape. Once I had it lifted in the right direction and then turned, the clamps on my right ankle opened. Five more clamps later, and I stepped away from the wall at last.

If I'd still been human, I would've fallen to the ground from muscle atrophy, not to mention tissue damage from being in the same cramped position for weeks. As a vampire, my body adjusted almost instantly. I wanted to whoop with victory at finally being free—and good Lord, I wanted some *clothes*!—but I didn't have time for any of that. I needed to recharge so I could fight for my life.

I was halfway across the room to the electrical socket when the alarms went off.

Chapter 16

 Above the screech of sirens, I heard one of the guards yell, "Perimeter breach, unknown vampire." Vlad was attacking now, so the guards would be coming for me! Panicked, I dove toward the socket. My velocity caused my right hand to ram through it, electrocuting me instantly. Voltage surged through my body, the effect similar to my first bellyful of blood after being starved. My eyes rolled back and I began to convulse as my cells felt like they were exploding from the overload of unbridled, delirious energy.

I hadn't pulled electricity from a socket since before I turned into a vampire. Back then, it had felt like a painful shot of adrenaline. Now, it felt like I'd just been struck by a lightning bolt containing pure, ecstatic power.

I couldn't see the guard who ran into the room, but when he grabbed me, I held onto him with my legs, free arm, and teeth, still shuddering from the raw, addictive bliss shooting into my body. The electricity I absorbed like a desert drinking in the rain proved too much for the guard. With it transferring into him from my unbreakable grip, he screamed over and over, now fighting to get away from me instead of trying to harm me.

Then I wasn't just the recipient of the voltage: A wild, unknown part of me started *yanking* it out of the socket in large, greedy gulps that drained the wires in the next few moments. Still, it wasn't enough. Like a vampire rising undead for the first time, I was filled with a mindless, insatiable hunger that nothing except rampant gorging would satisfy.

I threw the guard aside, so consumed with need that I barely noticed him smacking into the wall like a rag doll. Then, my vision hazy, I followed the power I felt pulsating beneath the stone walls outside my room. When I came to the socket in the hallway, I shoved my hand through it, crying out in relief at the new surge of electricity. In moments, however, that dried up, too, and my whole body burned from the pain of denial.

I would have kept mindlessly seeking out the next power source if not for the emotions that blasted over mine. They surpassed even my ravenous need, filling me with rage such as I'd never known. That rage cleared away most of the haze that had filled my vision, and I saw Harold, my torturer, try to run by me. I grabbed him, letting out a howl of vengeance as I unloaded my voltage into him. Part of me didn't want to release the energy; I wanted to hoard it until I was bursting with it, but the frenzy riding my emotions told me I had to kill anything that moved and I had to do it *now*.

When Harold exploded from the force of too much electricity ramming into him, I threw his remains aside and sought out new prey. Screams rang in my ears while freezing shadows seemed to merge with solid shapes around me, making it feel like I was walking through an icy, nightmarish tunnel. The tiny part of my mind that was still rational urged me to hide, not to grab each guard I saw and unleash a dizzying surge of electricity into him, but I had to *kill*. Tear. Rip. Burn. Leila. Leila. Leila.

"Leila!" a hoarse voice shouted behind me.

I whirled, seeing those hideous shadows part to let a far darker, larger figure pass. Fire haloed the form, making it appear demonic, while my emotions flared with a crescendo of relief-soaked rage that was so powerful, it shattered me. I fell, first hitting the wall, then a pain of scalding arms that swept me up against a body that felt like fire encased in stone.

"Go," a feminine voice yelled. "Get her out of here!"

The haze that had descended on my mind lifted enough for me to see as the dark figure flew us through the hallway. The guards that were still alive made no move to stop us. Instead, they were on the ground, their bodies violently contorting as what looked like hellish shadows tore into them and *through* them, all while emitting deafening, high-pitched shrieks.

The rest of my mental haze lifted as the psychotic rage that had filled me abruptly vanished, leaving me with only my own emotions. That's when I fully realized whose arms I was in, and a sob tore past my lips.

Vlad!

I didn't say his name out loud. I couldn't speak past the sobs that kept clogging my throat, but I didn't want to start crying. If I did, I didn't know when I'd be able to stop, and we might not be out of the woods yet.

Somehow, he wrapped a cloak around me while flying us so high up that I had to close my eyes to keep from getting sick. Then, he plummeted down to set us on a hill about a mile away from the train station. With the higher elevation and my enhanced vision, I could still see what was going on, and I watched with disbelief as the grayish figures I'd first thought were shadows tore through the perimeter guards like translucent sharks. More filmy figures sprang up from the ground, joining the gruesome melee. I wasn't surprised when some of the guards stopped moving and the creatures abandoned those now-shriveling bodies for whoever was still alive. I was only shocked that creatures without solid form could be so lethal.

"What are they?" I whispered.

"Remnants," Vlad said, yanking off his mask and wig. Rivers of cruel satisfaction snaked through my emotions before he closed his feelings off again. "They can't be killed because they're already dead, and they feed from energy and pain. That's why not even the strongest vampire is a match for them."

Were the Remnants what Vlad had wanted from Cat? I'd thought he meant "grave power" as a metaphor. As if to reinforce my guess, Cat strode out of the old station and onto the train platform. Not only did the hideous creatures refrain from attacking her, they swayed in a trancelike way as she neared them, reminding me of snakes and a skilled charmer.

"That's . . . that's . . ." Words failed me, but not Vlad.

"An even more excruciating way to die than being burned," he finished, his palm sliding along my smooth, bald head before he cupped my face. "I cannot take back what was done to you, but I will avenge your pain a thousandfold. That, I promise."

I wanted to throw myself into his arms, not because of his vow but because he was there and I could. Before I made a move toward him, however, shame seared me, making it hard for me to even hold his gaze. He was determined to avenge me for what he'd seen, but what about the things he *hadn't* seen? The things that, truth be told, I could have stopped and yet didn't?

"Are we safe here?" I asked, hugging the long cloak around me instead of reaching out to him.

As if he sensed my reluctance, he stepped back until his body no longer brushed mine. "Yes. Even Mencheres couldn't best Cat when she manifests grave power. As I said, it's unstoppable. However, it's also recordable."

With that, multiple small explosions rocked the former station, until black smoke rose up in dozens of places. Just when I was worried about those drawing bystanders, the entire structure exploded in a thunderous detonation that sent a fireball mushrooming into the sky. Cat got pelted with burning debris before she dove out of the way. Then she turned and threw an aggravated look in Vlad's direction.

"That's for not saying yes to me immediately," he muttered without a hint of remorse.

Then he wrapped his arms around me, but not in the embrace I so desperately needed. Instead, he propelled us back into the sky, taking us so high up that once again, I couldn't stand to look. Tears escape my clenched lids as I locked my arms around him. We might be holding each other out of necessity, but his heat still seared me, his scent filled my nose, and his hair was whips I reveled in as strands lashed my cheek from the wind.

I was so overwhelmed by being back in his arms, it took me several minutes to notice that my right hand kept shooting tiny pulses of voltage into him.

Chapter 17

 Vlad flew us through the air faster than I'd known he was capable of, yet it still took almost two hours to reach his plane. He must not have wanted to land anywhere near the station to avoid tipping off Szilagyi's people. With the wind snatching away everything except the loudest shouts, it meant we didn't have a chance to talk. I had a lot to say to him, but none of it seemed the type of thing to scream.

Of course, once we reached his plane, then we had an audience in the two pilots who greeted me with utmost respect while also managing not to look at the long cloak that was my only clothing. Our audience expanded when Cat showed up in time for me to emerge from the bathroom wearing the sweater and pants that Vlad had provided. In private, I'd also drained both big bags of blood that came with the clothes, then spent several minutes fighting my body's response to the blood. Afterward, I tried to clean up, but there was only so much I could do with the small sink and hand soap. When I finally got to take a shower, I didn't plan on coming out for hours.

The plane took off before I made it from the bathroom back to my seat. Clearly, Vlad was taking no chances about anyone coming after us. He waited for me before he sat down, and when he held out his hand as he had so many times before, I had to fight back a fresh surge of tears before I took it.

If he noticed my slight pause, he didn't say anything. In truth, the electricity my right hand currently emitted probably couldn't damage the aircraft, but I savored the simple act of touching him. When I asked where we were going, Cat said to Germany to drop her off. I didn't ask where after that. Wherever it was, it wouldn't be to Vlad's Romania house. That was gone.

Cat sat as close to the pilots as she could, trying to give us as much privacy as the interior allowed. I wasn't sure, but I also thought I glimpsed the same ghost that had warned me about the attack up there with her, too. Then I forgot about them as Vlad drew a blanket over me once I was settled into my chair. How did he know that I wanted as many layers on me as possible after being denied even a single piece of clothing for weeks?

"You should try to sleep, if you can," he said, his voice oddly neutral. "You must be exhausted."

His hand was still curled around mine, but other

than that, he didn't touch me. Aside from vowing vengeance and answering my questions, he also hadn't really spoken to me. I didn't know why and I found myself afraid to ask. Yes, he'd gone batshit with rage over those tapes, but the last thing he'd said to Cat in my vision was that he never should have married me.

What if he hadn't been speaking facetiously in a moment of frustration over my captivity? What if he were still thinking that now? I had no way to know. His face was expressionless and he had his emotions under tight lockdown, which wasn't what I had imagined when I'd dared to envision our reunion.

Maybe he couldn't get past the thought that I'd been raped. In the vampire world, it was the ultimate way Szilagyi could humiliate Vlad, and Vlad's pride was legendary. I'd rather not discuss what had really happened with an audience, but some things couldn't wait until later.

"What you saw on the second tape . . . I need to explain," I began, only to have Vlad's sharp wave cut me off.

"No, you don't." Then he moved nearer and squeezed my hand. "None of that was your doing. You have nothing to explain because Maximus was the culprit, and nothing you could have said or done would have changed what happened."

Instead of comforting me, tears sprang into my eyes as a fresh wave of shame washed over me. I should have known Vlad wouldn't be so shallow as to feel differently about me over what he thought Maximus had done, and he was right. If Maximus *had* raped me, it wouldn't have been my fault. But I had been complicit in what had happened when Maximus gave me blood, and that *would* change Vlad's feelings if he found out about it. At the time, I'd rationalized it as necessary, yet now, I cursed myself for not thinking of another way. How was I supposed to tell Vlad the "rape" he'd witnessed wasn't real, but the other incident he didn't know about was, and I had allowed it?

I couldn't. Not now and maybe not ever.

"That's not what I meant," I said, unable to look him in the eye. "Szilagyi insisted on sending you a rape video, so Maximus had everyone leave, then used duct tape on himself and me so that, ah, nothing penetrated but it looked real. While he was . . . acting, he told me where I was and that he'd had me skinned to remove your aura so I could use my abilities." My voice caught. "It was the first time I felt like I had a chance."

Vlad didn't say anything and his emotions remained locked down. After a moment, I risked a glance at him, then wished I hadn't. His eyes were lasered onto mine like heat-seeking missiles.

"You don't have to lie," he said, that stare compelling me not to look away although I desperately wanted to. "I am the last person to scorn, judge, or revile someone for being raped."

"I know," I choked out, another avalanche of guilt making it hard for me to speak. Yes, he'd survived years of real rape while refusing to let the abuse break him, whereas I had sold out after two weeks of far less harsh captivity. "I'm not lying. Maximus didn't rape me. He risked his life not to, in fact."

My voice strengthened on that last part. I couldn't let Vlad blame Maximus for something he hadn't done. Otherwise, he'd murder him the first chance he got. Then again, as I'd worried, he might anyway.

Maybe he'll kill you, too, once he learns what you did when Maximus gave you blood, my inner voice whispered, breaking her recent silence.

I couldn't stand to think about it anymore. With a muttered, "I need a minute," I got up and went into the bathroom. Then I tried again to scrub away the remains of the past two weeks, but it was useless. I'd hated how my body had felt like a stranger's after I was skinned. Now, it was covered with taunting essence imprints of what I couldn't bring myself to admit to.

At last, I shut the water off. From the barely perceptible whispers I caught, I had been the topic of conversation in my absence.

"She doesn't need an avenging warrior right now," Cat was saying. "She needs her husband, so save the crushing of your enemies to hear the lamentations of their women for later."

I sighed as I wiped up the remains of the water I'd spilled in my attempt to wash away more than the tangible results of my captivity. Then, unable to stall anymore, I left the bathroom.

Cat got up, returning to the front of the plane where, yes, the ghost with the long sideburns was hovering near the cockpit. I returned the ghost's nod, hoping there was no chance that he'd turn into one of the murderous Remnants.

"Leila," Vlad said in a carefully controlled tone when I sat back down. "I've seen enough suffering in my time to know that everyone handles it differently. If you want to talk about what happened, I will listen. If you don't, I won't press you. If you need anything, you will have it. Do you understand?"

I swallowed hard and nodded, getting used to the sting of tears in my eyes. How I wished I could ask for forgiveness, but though that was what I needed most, I didn't have the courage to admit what I'd done. Or worse, how I would have done it again.

"I think I am tired," I said, further proving my cowardice. Then I closed my eyes, wishing he'd pull me against him as he usually did, but though his grip on my hand briefly tightened, he stayed exactly where he was.

Chapter 18

Vlad didn't say where we were headed after we dropped off Cat and the ghost she introduced as Fabian in Munich. I might have faked sleep for a few hours, but I eventually succumbed to the real thing well before dawn hit me with its usual knockout blow. When I awoke to find a crystal chandelier a couple dozen feet above me, I thought that I must be in another of Vlad's extravagant homes.

I couldn't ask because I was alone in the four-poster bed. The large, ornate room was decorated in soothing shades of white and cream with soft maroon accents in the carpet. An open arch with marble columns separated this room from another one, so I got out of bed to see if that's where Vlad was. He wasn't, but the sight of the large marble tub in the gilded bathroom almost made me abandon my search. Then I caught a glimpse of myself in the mirror and stopped in disbelief.

My hair was back! I tugged a black handful,

expecting to feel the give of a wig, but all I felt was the pull on my own scalp. I even had eyebrows again. I tugged them, too, even yanking out a hair for confirmation. Ouch! Yep, real. A glance inside my sweat pants revealed that my hair wasn't back *every*where, but the parts that made me feel like me again were. How, I had no idea, and I was too grateful to care.

I happily finger-combed my hair as I went back through the bedroom to another door that opened into a large marble room with dozens of vases. They looked Grecian, as did many of the other decorative touches including more pillars and columns. If not for the floor-to-ceiling windows that allowed me to glimpse a stunning pool area surrounded by what was clearly a hotel, I would have sworn that this was a former Roman ruler's residence.

"Vlad?" I called out, walking through the vase room into what looked like an elegant pub complete with a lounge, pool table, and a full bar area.

"Here," he called out, sounding faintly surprised.

He met me halfway through the next extravagant room, an outdoor covered patio that faced the pool area. It even had a sunken hot tub, but since Vlad was fully clothed and dry, he hadn't been partaking of that amenity.

"I didn't expect you to be awake yet," he went on, and though his gaze roved over me, he made no move to touch me.

"I've gotten better at waking up earlier," I said, squinting at the late afternoon sunlight that poured over the patio. Then I fingered a lock of hair. "How did you manage this? It's even the same length as . . . before."

I stumbled a little over the last word, not wanting to remember the skinning any more than Vlad probably did.

He looked at my hair from my scalp to where it ended several inches past my shoulders, but once again, only his gaze touched me. His hands stayed almost rigidly at his sides.

"Magic." At my shocked expression, he shrugged. "I don't practice it, but before the Law Guardians outlawed it thousands of years ago, Mencheres had already forgotten more of the dark arts than most living sorcerers will ever learn."

"Mencheres is here?"

A nod. "In the next villa."

"Won't he get into trouble if someone finds out that he did this?" I asked, still trying to come to terms with Vlad outsourcing a spell. He hadn't been a fan of magic *before* he found out Cynthiana had used it to manipulate him for decades, and he'd really hated it when one of her spells had killed me.

His teeth flashed in the briefest of grins. "I won't tell if you won't."

I smiled back a bit tentatively. "Where are we, anyway?"

"Caesar's Palace in Las Vegas."

"Vegas?" Why? He couldn't have had a sudden, uncontrollable urge to gamble.

Vlad shrugged. "Szilagyi could only hope to defeat me with an ambush more powerful than the one that destroyed my home. If he did that in the heart of the Vegas strip, it would result in mass human casualties and enough international attention to rouse the Law Guardians' wrath. He can't afford to fight me as well as them, so even if I announced my presence on a billboard, he couldn't do anything until after we left."

I took comfort in him saying "after we left" instead of "after I left." I wasn't sure where things stood between Vlad and me, but if he did still regret marrying me, at least it didn't sound like he had any immediate plans to leave me.

He will when he finds out what you did, my insidious inner voice whispered.

My jaw ground. *One day*, I promised that voice. *Dead!*

"I have something for you," Vlad said, yanking my attention back to him. His mouth twisted as he pulled a rubber-lined glove out of his pocket. "Seems you already have need of it."

I glanced down to see two tiny sparks emanating from my right hand. Nothing compared to what I used to manifest, but seeing them made me almost as happy as my new head of hair.

"Thanks," I said, sliding the glove onto my hand.

What I really wanted to do was stick my fingers in the nearest light socket. I never again wanted to feel as helpless as I did when I thought that my best means of defense had been literally ripped out of me. Maybe, in order to manifest the deadly voltage that I used to, I'd need to manually recharge now. Or would my electrical abilities, much like the rest of me, just need time to return to the way they were?

Vlad watched me, his humorless half smile telling me nothing of what he was thinking. As for what he was feeling, well, he had that under tighter security than Fort Knox. I wanted to ask him, but since I wasn't able to give him honesty yet, it didn't seem fair to expect the same from him.

"So, I'll, ahem, get cleaned up and see you later," I said, almost tripping over my words at the invisible wall between us.

His look said he knew I was hiding something, but he replied, "Later, then," in a light tone and returned to where he'd been sitting on the patio.

I walked away, guilt making me feel like I carried a huge boulder on my back. I had never been good at lying, nor had I ever wanted to be the type of person who was. Now, I was clinging to a huge lie of omission. Though I was terrified at the thought of losing Vlad, I couldn't keep this up much longer. Plus, he deserved to know *everything* that had happened during my captivity, even the parts that might change his feelings for me.

I'll tell him later tonight, I decided, trying to ignore how my stomach twisted at the thought. In the meantime, I really did want to scrub myself until I'd gotten every last vestige of my former experience off of me, and that would take a while.

Chapter 19

 Vlad stayed out of the bedroom and bathroom the entire time I was in there, which turned out to be over an hour. Despite scouring my flesh, I still didn't feel clean once I emerged from the shower, though I doubted a team of forensic experts could find a single particle on me from my old cell. It must be guilt that made me feel like I was covered with invisible stains.

After my extensive shower, I dressed in a long caftan that I found in the closet, not surprised to see that Vlad had stocked this room with clothes. All new, of course, since everything I owned had burned to the ground along with the rest of Vlad's castle. The long-sleeved ankle-length dress had pretty shell buttons down the front and its pale cream color matched the villa's décor. I left my hair loose after I blew it dry. Feeling it brush my shoulders was a comforting, tangible reminder that I really had it back again.

Vlad wasn't on the patio when I went to look for

him. He wasn't in the vase room or the plush pub, either. I was surprised to find that the villa had two more bedrooms, an indoor movie theater, a library, formal dining room, exercise room, living room, and a grand entryway with a separate elegant lounge. Each room seemed to come with its own guard, too, and I was relieved to see familiar faces like Samir and Petre. I surprised them—and myself—by hugging them. I didn't see Dorian or Alexandru, however, and I was afraid to ask if that was because they'd stayed behind in Romania, or because they hadn't survived the castle attack. To keep from dwelling on that grim thought, I marveled at the villa. It was so large; I couldn't believe we were in a hotel. This could have been one of the wings in Vlad's former castle.

I followed the throb of power in the air to finally find Vlad in a fancy version of a family room. Several people were sitting on couches near him, but they all had their backs to me. Mencheres was easy to pick out, his black hair being as long and straight as mine. Next to him was a blonde, who must have been his wife, Kira. Then a girl with bobbed black hair and a bald man who was so short, all I saw was the top of his head . . .

"Gretchen, Marty," I said in delighted surprise. "I didn't know you were in Vegas, too!"

Marty made it to me first, vaulting over the couch to envelop me in a bear hug. My tears hit the top of his newly bald head as I hugged him back, so happy to see him that I barely noticed the sharp look Vlad gave me.

"The Strip is a constant dull roar, no wonder you didn't hear us slip in," Marty said, letting me go at last. Then he swiped at the front of my dress. "Aw, hell," he said, sounding embarrassed. "Got stains on you."

I glanced at the pink smudges his tears had made and froze. For a moment, all I could see were the stains on my thighs from Maximus, and the memory almost knocked me off my feet. My sister didn't notice my reaction. She gave me a hug next, and if I responded far more woodenly, she didn't comment.

"Aren't these villas the shit?" Gretchen said in glee. "Finally, your husband locks us up somewhere awesome!"

Her reference to being locked up also made me flinch, which was ridiculous. So was my reaction to the pink smears on my dress, yet I couldn't shake the overwhelming sense of suffocation and guilt that suddenly came over me.

"Leila," Vlad said, his low voice cutting through Gretchen's continued, excited comments. "Are you all right?"

Gretchen didn't seem to hear him. Marty did, and he gave me an appraising look as my sister went on about how amazing Vegas was and did I know that Vlad had given her a gambling allowance?

"She doesn't know, does she?" I rasped.

Vlad rose, his stare never wavering. "No. I leave it to you to decide if she can handle it."

"Handle what?" Gretchen said, still not catching on. "My gambling allowance? Hell, yes, I can handle it!"

I looked at my little sister, who hid so much of the pain she'd been through since our mother's death behind a wall of flippancy and sarcasm. She looked happy now, so I'd be damned if I was going to be the one who ruined that.

"Good," I said, trying to pull myself together. "Space out your gambling allowance. Don't blow it all in one day."

"Sure, sis," she said, giving me a quick kiss.

I wanted to touch the spot on my cheek to hold her kiss there. Vlad hadn't been the only person I'd feared I would never see again when Szilagyi had captured me.

"Where's Dad?" I asked, sounding almost normal now.

Gretchen made a disgusted noise. "In the next villa, refusing to come out of his room. He's still pouting about being in hiding, not to mention still pissed that you became a vampire against his wishes."

I shouldn't have expected anything different. Especially if, like Gretchen, Hugh Dalton had no idea of what I'd just been through, but my raw emotional wounds made this more than I could fake nonchalance over. It was foolish for me, a grown woman, to let my father's continued rejection make me feel like a hurt little girl, yet that's exactly how his actions hit me.

"Oh," I said, and though I meant it to sound noncommittal, the single word came out as more of a stifled sob.

"I have had enough," Vlad said in a barely restrained growl, then he thundered, "Hugh!" loud enough for the nearby window panes to tremble. Without waiting for a response, he strode out of the room.

"Vlad, don't," I said, starting after him. He didn't slow and Marty grabbed me, preventing me from going after him.

"Don't, kid," Marty said, something dark lurking in his tone. "Hugh's your dad so Vlad won't kill him, but whatever he *does* do, that man has coming."

Gretchen glanced between me and the open door that Vlad had almost flown through in his anger. "What's going on?"

"Nothing you need to worry about," Marty replied, his gaze pure emerald green as he stared at her.

Gretchen nodded with a new, glazed complacency. I stared at Marty, as shocked by him mesmerizing my sister as I was by the iciness in his expression. He must have been harboring a lot of resentment against my father, and I'd had no idea.

I didn't have to strain my hearing to know when Vlad reached my father. His command of "Sit down, shut up, and don't move" rang out over the other background noise. Then I shuddered when, moments later, I heard my own screams and the far softer sounds of Szilagyi's taunting laughter.

"Don't you dare look away," Vlad said, each word sharper than the lash of a whip. "This is what your seclusion protects you and Gretchen from because this is what happened when Leila fell into my enemy's hands a fortnight ago."

More bloodcurdling screams cut off whatever Vlad said next, followed by my shouted vow that all of them would pay. I clenched my fists as my mind replayed an image of Szilagyi's expression as his fresh burst of laughter echoed from the video.

"At any moment, they could have killed her," Vlad said during a pause in my screams, which would have been when Harold repositioned me to better remove the skin on my back. "You don't know what it's like to lose a child, but I do. When they're gone, every cold word you uttered is a scar on your soul, every missed opportunity with them a pain that will never heal."

The new barrage of screams had me swaying. Marty put his arms around me, murmuring comforting words I didn't hear because I was fighting back the remembered horror of that moment.

"You think me a monster?" Vlad went on when

I could hear him again. "You are worse, for my child never had to plead for the love you so cruelly withhold from Leila. Think on that the next time you tell yourself you're justified in your continued emotional abandonment of your daughter."

My screams ceased, which meant that Vlad had shut off the tape since I knew from awful memory that the skinning had lasted several more minutes. Then I heard a harsh retching sound and tears burned my gaze. Vlad had ordered him to be silent and still, but vampire hypnosis couldn't prevent my father from throwing up over what he'd seen.

"He shouldn't have done that," I whispered, wiping my eyes.

"Yes, he should," Marty said in a steely tone. "Hugh's been a shitty father to you ever since you busted him for cheating on your mother. I only wish I'd had the balls to rub it in his face the way your husband just did."

Gretchen didn't say anything. She still had the same unconcerned look she'd had since Marty told her she didn't need to worry. Without superhuman senses, she probably hadn't heard the tape or Vlad's ruthless commentary, either.

"Everything Vlad said about losing a child is true," Marty went on with a deep sniff. "When I lost Vera, I wanted to die myself. Eighty years later, you gave me the chance to be a father again. I'll never replace your dad, but I love you like you were my own flesh and blood, and I'm so damned grateful you're alive so I can tell you that again."

I got on my knees so I could bury my face in his neck while whispering in a ragged voice that I loved him, too. Then I silently thanked God that Marty had caught me scrounging for food in a carnival Dumpster years ago, when I'd been a frightened, lonely teenager trying to deal with abilities that made me a menace to anyone I touched. If unconditional love counted, the man hugging me *was* my father while the man in the other room was more like a reluctant step-dad.

Then I felt a flash of blindingly intense emotion, gone too fast for me to decipher what it was. I looked over Marty's shoulder and saw Vlad in the doorway, his expression inscrutable as he watched me embracing my oldest friend.

"I'm sorry you overheard that," he said in a deceptively mild tone. "After his continued refusal to see you, either I forced your father to watch that tape or I shoved my tablet down his throat, and that would have had more permanent consequences."

I glanced at the computer Vlad held, images of it sticking cartoonlike out of either end of my father's neck sweeping through my mind. Worse, I didn't think he'd been kidding. After all, he was Vlad the Impaler, not Vlad the Bluffer.

Mencheres rose, speaking for the first time since I'd entered the room. "Kira and I were just about to avail ourselves of the various entertainments in this hotel. We'd be delighted, Marty and Gretchen, if you would join us."

"Sure, sounds great," Marty said, translating the polite version of, "Let's leave Vlad and Leila alone now." My sister didn't respond. She still stared ahead with that cheerful, clueless look on her face.

"Gretchen," Marty said, flashing green in his gaze. "Wake up." After she blinked and the slack look left her, he went on. "Want to party with a former pharaoh who doesn't need to count cards because he can read minds?"

"Oh, hell, yeah!" Gretchen said, almost running to the door in her excitement. "Just give me twenty minutes to look even more fabulous."

Chapter 20

 "Hungry?" Vlad asked in that faux casual tone when everyone cleared out of the villa half an hour later.

I was, but I was also afraid that if I put off admitting my guilt any longer, I'd chicken out for the rest of tonight. Or the rest of my life, which was what I really wanted to do.

"No," I said, steeling myself for what I had to do.

His half smile remained although his gaze narrowed. "You always smell of guilt when you lie to me."

Then I must have stunk up the place since he'd rescued me. "Fine. I *am* hungry, but I want to talk more than I want to eat."

"You can do both," he said, beckoning me to follow as he left the room.

I did, a desperate part of me trying to memorize how he looked. With how he reacted to betrayal, this might be the last time I saw him. Vlad's hair was brushed back in smooth waves and he'd shaved

the excess growth on his jaw until it was that enticing, stubbled shadow again. He wore sand-colored
pants and a white silk shirt, an open button at
the neck showing only the cleft at the base of his
throat. The rest of his body was concealed by the
rich material, which stretched to highlight his muscles as he moved with his usual stalking grace. The
effect was sexier than all the bare-chested men I'd
glimpsed around the pool earlier. Vlad didn't show
off his seething masculinity by wearing fewer
clothes. Instead, he wore more to taunt people with
what he didn't allow them to feast their eyes on.

"Here," he said when we reached the elegant
interior pub and he went behind the bar. Then he
pulled out a bag of blood.

"It's warm," I said in surprise when I accepted it.

"There's an appliance back here that keeps
items at exactly ninety-nine degrees." He gave me
a jaded smile. "We're not the first vampires to stay
in these villas."

Talk about catering to every type of clientele.
The bag even had a spout; how fancy. I unscrewed
it and took a long swig before setting it down in
suspicion.

"You don't think they killed anyone to fill this,
do you?"

Vlad's laugh held notes of contempt. "No.
They're probably overrun with volunteers. This
town stinks of greed and desperation. Becoming

a vampire's blood donor would be a large step up compared to other ways people make money here."

"You really don't like Vegas," I noted, although his answer mollified me into taking another swallow.

"Why would I? 'What happens here, stays here' is a call for people to indulge in their favorite depravities, as if I don't get more than my fill of those through the thoughts I overhear."

I could sympathize with that. I'd kept my right glove on not out of voltage concerns, but because I didn't want to relive any of the essence imprints that these rooms were probably soaked with. And speaking of overhearing things . . .

"Can you, um, send the guards away for a little bit?" I asked, biting my lower lip.

Vlad issued a command in Romanian that had multiple doors opening and closing moments later. Now that we had some privacy, I tried to think up the best way to begin my confession, but as usual, Vlad cut right to the point.

"Why don't you want me to touch you?" he asked, his light tone belying the intended shock of the question.

"I, ah, that's not," I began to stammer.

"At first, I believed you couldn't stand for anyone to do so, which I understood," he went on. "For years after my boyhood captivity, I couldn't tolerate another person's hands on me. In truth, it's why I'm so particular about that to this day, although now I'm only angered instead of disgusted when people touch me without my leave. That's why I honored your obvious aversion before, yet when I saw you embracing Martin and your sister, I realized it was directed only at me."

My mouth remained open while dozens of thoughts swirled around my mind. For once, I wished I wasn't a vampire so he could hear them in their entirety instead of me trying to piece together an explanation that would fall short of my intentions.

"I can't stand the guilt when I touch you," I finally said. See? *Woefully* short.

He rested his arms against the bar and leaned forward. "Why? Because you won't admit that Maximus raped you?"

He still didn't believe me? "I told you; he *didn't*."

Vlad inhaled, green glittering in his eyes. "Remember how I said you smell like guilt when you lie? Leila, my love, every time you speak of what happened with Maximus, you reek of it."

I turned away from the memory—and his hands were suddenly around my face, forcing me to look at him.

"I meant it when I said you don't have to talk about it, but you can't keep lying to me or yourself." His tone was hard, but his fingers caressed me in a way that made me want to lean into him instead of pull way. "It might feel easier now to pretend that someone you trusted, a friend, couldn't do that to you, but in the end, the pretense will destroy you."

I couldn't stop the tears that started to flow, and they flowed even more when he leaned over the bar and kissed them.

"It changes nothing between us," he breathed against my skin. "I love you, Leila, no matter what he or anyone else did."

I closed my eyes, something starved in me soaking up the acceptance he conveyed with his words and every brush of his lips. I wasn't aware that I'd leaned forward until I felt his neck against my cheek. His hands slid down my back, and in one smooth motion, he swept me onto the counter and into his arms. I wanted to stay there forever, but the lie he sensed loomed between us, a wall I couldn't scale. The only way past it was to blow it—and possibly our relationship—to pieces.

"It isn't what Maximus did that's eating me up with guilt," I forced myself to say. "It's what I did. Maximus didn't rape me. He did exactly what I told you, only . . . that's not the only time he did it, and the second time wasn't against my will."

He stiffened and pulled away. The instant chill from the absence of his body struck me almost as much as a physical blow.

"Explain," he bit out.

I hugged my knees for more than better balance on the bar's narrow counter top.

"I lost most of the blood in me when Harold

skinned me, and Szilagyi kept me starved. I got so weak, so hungry that I couldn't concentrate enough to link to you even after I realized that it might work. Maximus was rarely allowed near me and he was watched every time he was, so he couldn't sneak me blood without . . . extreme pretense."

I started to tremble, but now that I'd begun to tell him what happened, I wouldn't allow myself to stop.

"I had told Maximus that I needed blood, so he told Szilagyi he wanted to fuck me again. Szilagyi didn't mind that; he loved how it had driven you to burn your house down. They made Maximus keep the door open and only let him bring in a couple pieces of tape. He put one on my mouth and the other he snuck, um, below. Then h-he did what you saw in the video, only this time, he took the tape off and kissed me to regurgitate the blood he'd just drunk back into me."

Vlad made a low, visceral sound. My trembling increased and I could barely see from the tears flooding my eyes. This was the part I hadn't wanted to remember, let alone ever tell Vlad.

"I was so hungry; it threw me into a feeding frenzy. I sucked on his mouth and-and ground against him and pleaded for more. It was like the blood made my body go nuts from need and I-I didn't care about where I was, who I was with, or what I was doing."

I whispered those last few words, gripped by the

same shame that had plagued me since then. The last thing I wanted to do was to admit what came next, because it was the worst part.

"Maximus played it off like I was getting into his screwing me, which the guard thought was hilarious. When I finally got enough blood that the feeding frenzy lifted and I was back in my right mind, Maximus asked if I-I wanted him to sneak me blood this way again and," I raised my head and looked square at Vlad despite the pain of the admission, "I said yes."

He stared at me, his gaze so green it was as though firelit emeralds had replaced his eyes. "And?"

"And?" I repeated in disbelief. "I said *yes*, didn't you hear me the first time?"

Shame scalded my tone, making the question almost a scream. Vlad waited, giving me a chance to say something else, then he dropped his fists onto the bar, which shook as though it had been hit by twin sledgehammers.

"Unless you are leaving something out, what you're telling me is that you're wracked with guilt over responding to blood the same way every other newly made, starved vampire would."

I stiffened. The last thing I expected was that I'd need to explain why he should be furious with me!

"I agree I wasn't responsible for my initial reaction, but I knew exactly what I was doing when I told Maximus to come back. I knew the blood would probably make me whore-out again. I also knew that Maximus might not be able to use tape on me at all the next time, but I didn't care. All I cared about was getting more blood, even if it meant practically or possibly literally cheating on you to get it. *Now* is it clear?"

He made that low, guttural sound again. The one I'd taken for an overabundance of rage before, but when he let his walls down and his feelings flooded into mine, I was shocked.

"If I hadn't heard the word *Abkhazia* in my mind, Szilagyi would still have you. Cat's ghosts would've searched for you, but it would have taken weeks or months since I didn't even know what side of the world you were on. Szilagyi would have killed you by then, or at least broken you from the horrors he inflicted on you to torment me. Next to that, Leila, I wouldn't care if you fucked Maximus, every guard assigned to watch you, and Szilagyi himself, if the result was you getting the blood you needed in order to tell me your location."

I couldn't speak. Not because of his words, though they vibrated with vehemence, but because of the emotions that continued to surge into mine like waves breaking over rocks. They contained none of the recriminations I'd heaped upon myself. Instead, I felt the most savage sort of pride, as if he'd been hoping that I had it in me to do whatever was necessary to survive, and now he knew that I did.

If I had any lingering doubts, the way he caught

me to him and kissed me put them to rest. When he finally lifted his head, my body throbbed and my lips felt almost blistered from the heat that seemed to pour out of him and into me.

"Besides," he said, his voice rough. "Even if I did feel wronged by your actions, you were more wronged by mine. I insisted you stay at the castle, I smothered your abilities with my aura, and I turned you into a target by marrying you. If I—"

"Don't," I interrupted at once. "Don't ever again say you wish you hadn't married me. Szilagyi brought me into this fight *before* we met, remember? Then later, he knew that you loved me before you did. Whether you had married me or not, we'd still be right where we are now."

He stared at me with such intensity that I had to blink to keep my eyes from feeling burned.

"Perhaps. I will always have enemies, and though I intend to crush them all, I want your word that you will continue to do whatever it takes in order to survive. You can't let yourself be crippled by guilt, fear, or hesitation ever again. Promise me."

"Okay," I said, the word a little ragged because part of me still couldn't believe the way he was taking this. "Survival first, no matter what. Promise."

He smiled while new, much colder emotions began to snake through my own. "Good. Now, since you've proven me utterly wrong for stripping you of your abilities before, why don't you use them to link to Szilagyi so that we can finally kill him?"

Chapter 21

 It felt like a lightbulb turned on over my head. That's right; my abilities were back, *all* of them. I hopped off the counter in my newfound excitement.

"Oh, hell, yes! Why didn't you prod me to link to him the second I set foot on your plane?"

I'd been so weighed down over my actions with Maximus, I hadn't even thought of it. Vlad was right; my guilt had been crippling, and when the stakes were life or death, I couldn't afford those kinds of handicaps.

He came out from behind the bar. "I told you, your survival is my first priority. If you were too emotionally damaged to admit what I believed Maximus had done to you, then you were in no condition to attempt to link to Szilagyi."

I started running my hands beneath my dress, looking for Szilagyi's essence trail. I had lots on me from Maximus and a few from Harold since he'd held me down on my new skin to finish slicing off my old. When I finally found Szilagyi's, I smiled. He'd been so smug about resting his hand near my crotch as he taunted me with my helplessness. Well, look who was smug now?

Vlad saw where my hand had paused. He said nothing, though fury singed my emotions before he closed himself off again. I didn't object. I wanted nothing to distract me while I attempted to link to the man who'd inflicted so much pain on both of us.

I was surprised when I followed Szilagyi's essence trail back to him with much more ease than it had taken me to find Vlad. Our mutual enemy was in a car, driving up a windy, steep road with a startlingly handsome black-haired young man in the passenger seat next to him. *Maybe being well fed really* is *the secret to unlocking my abilities*, I thought as I walked out of the pub and went into the villa's version of a kitchen. Then I pulled a knife out of the chopping block on the counter and swung it at my throat as hard as I could—

Vlad grabbed my arm, stopping me before the blade could complete its lethal arc. I tried to hack at my neck again, but all my muscles suddenly lacked coordination. Vlad wrested the knife away and threw it across the room.

"Let me go, I need to do this," I tried to say, but the words came out unintelligible. Unable to talk, I glared at him. Couldn't he see that I had to cut my head off? Right now?

His response was to slap me so hard, my teeth

ached. The shock of the blow made me lose the last
vestiges of my link to Szilagyi. As if coming out
of a dream, I realized that Vlad had wrestled me
onto the kitchen floor, and the scarlet streaks on
me and him were from the blood that had gushed
out when I'd half decapitated myself. I was pretty
sure I hadn't just experienced a psychotic break,
so I could only come up with one reason for my
sudden, uncontrollable urge to commit suicide.

"Oh, shit," I whispered, able to talk now that
my vocal cords had healed with supernatural swiftness. "Szilagyi must've done the same thing Cynthiana did: booby-trapped himself with a spell so
if I ever linked to him, it would end up killing me."

"For the hundredth time, I feel fine now," I called
out, yet Vlad's response was a derisive snort from
the other room. "Seriously, you can let me out," I
continued.

No response to that, only more sounds of things
being moved around and/or carted out. Well, I
hadn't really thought he'd capitulate. I was dealing
with the trauma of my near suicide by refusing to
dwell on it. Otherwise, the horror of how close I'd
come to killing myself would break the thin control I had over my emotions and I'd fall completely
to pieces. As Vlad had said, survival first. Panic,
self-recriminations, and hysteria later.

Vlad was employing his own coping methods. I
tried to shift into a more comfortable position, but

that was impossible, probably because I was at the bottom of the tub I'd admired, with a grand piano and five marble columns on top of me. I could get out from underneath the massive, weighty barriers, but Vlad would hear my attempts long before I freed a single finger.

And then I'd really be in for it.

Vlad hadn't forgotten that Mencheres was telekinetic when he piled heavy objects onto me so he and Mencheres could clear out any lethal objects from the villa. No, Vlad was sending me a one-ton memo that there would be no more attempts to link to Szilagyi. Yes, I'd reached him easily, and yes, I now knew that Szilagyi was on the move with an unknown young man, but that wasn't enough to tell me where he *was*. Vlad wouldn't consider me trying again, whether I was safely restrained or not.

"You don't know if the spell is set to reactivate as soon as you have another opportunity," he'd ground out as he stacked the weighty objects on top of me. "Szilagyi would be laughing in hell if we found him and killed him, then you celebrated by committing suicide under the lasting directive of his spell."

"Cynthiana's spells always wore off after I dropped my link to her," I'd argued.

"Not before they did lethal damage," had been Vlad's short response. "You're only alive now because you were human and vampire blood kept bringing you back."

"Then let me try linking to Maximus. He left with him, so he might be at whatever place Szilagyi was heading to—"

"After your rescue, he's either dead or similarly spelled," Vlad had responded brutally. "Either way, the answer is no."

He had valid points, and I didn't want to die any more than Vlad wanted me to commit spell-induced suicide. But the idea that Szilagyi was only a psychic link away was as enticing as it was infuriatingly out of reach. After everything he'd done, I wanted that man dead. Truly, permanently dead, but that couldn't happen until we found him, and after my recent rescue, he would have probably gone to ground again. He'd managed to hide himself for hundreds of years before. What if he did it again?

After what felt like hours, Vlad unloaded the tub and let me out. I arched my back to relieve a kink that had been bothering me since the piano had landed on me, then began to dust myself off before I stopped. What was the point? The dress was covered in so much blood; a little dust hardly mattered.

"This is ruined," I said before the ridiculousness of my comment struck me. One trashed dress was quite literally the least of our concerns.

Vlad said nothing. Just watched me with expectant wariness, as if he was ready to pounce on my slightest move.

"I'll return in a few hours," I heard Mencheres call out, then a door closing signified his exit.

"He's going back to gamble with the others?" I asked, more to break the tenseness than because I cared what he was doing.

"No," Vlad said, his unruffled tone not fooling me. "I told you Mencheres was well versed in magic. He should be able to break Szilagyi's spell, once he has the right supplies."

I was stunned. If Mencheres could get this hara-kiri mojo off me, why did he waste time helping Vlad move furniture?

"He can find what he needs in Vegas?" *I love you, Vegas!* I wanted to crow.

"The dark arts are very alive and well here. How else do you explain Cirque De Solei's best tricks?"

Since I hadn't been to one of their shows, I'd never had cause to wonder. "I don't even care. I'm just so relieved Mencheres can break this spell, I can't even tell you."

Vlad's smile had a definite edge to it. "No need to."

Of course not. If there was one person who could understand my relief over this news, it was him.

"While Mencheres is out magic-shopping, I'm going to wash this blood off," I said, giving him a lopsided smile. "Can't hurt myself with a little soap and water, right?"

"Don't."

The single word stopped me before my hand reached the shower door. Good thing, too, because with a blast of heat, the glass began to melt like ice under a blowtorch. I jumped back to avoid the scalding puddle that hit the ground near my feet.

"Why?" I managed.

Vlad didn't spare a glance at the gelatinous blob that, moments ago, had been lovely, frosted glass doors.

"You could have broken them and used one of the shards as a weapon. Now you can't, but best wait until it cools before you step inside the shower. Otherwise, you'll burn your feet."

He could have stayed and watched to make sure I didn't try anything with the glass doors. Instead, he'd melted them into a puddle that fused with the marble floor. If that didn't make me realize that tonight's awful events had pushed him past his limits, nothing would.

"Okay," I said a little shakily. "Guess the mirror's next?"

He bared his teeth in more of a threat than a smile. "You guessed correctly."

His emotions were contained, but his coppery green eyes shone with a wildness I'd only seen when he was in battle. From the way his aura kept coiling like dozens of snakes readying to strike, he was barely able to stop himself from further drastic action. If I'd been through a lot over the past couple weeks, so had he, and this had clearly been his last straw.

I walked over to him, careful not to step in

one of the rivulets that snaked out from the main glass puddle. Then I put my arms around him and leaned my head against his chest. His body felt far hotter than normal, as if he was holding back the fire in him with great effort. Maybe it had done him some good to burn that glass into liquid. A mini-release, of sorts.

Well, I knew another, more effective means of release.

"I didn't like those doors, anyway," I breathed against his chest. "This new, open look is much nicer, if you ask me."

His short exhalation wasn't a real laugh, but it was the closest I'd heard since he'd stormed Szila-gyi's underground train-station lair to rescue me. Then his arms encircled me, and I closed my eyes in bliss at the feel of them.

"The glass won't burn you," I whispered, kissing his chest through his shirt. "And you need a shower, too."

A harsher sound escaped him before he picked me up, leaving footprints in the slowly hardening puddle as he carried me to the shower. Once inside, he turned on the water, sending up clouds of steam where it bounced off us and hit the molten mass on the floor. I tipped my head back, letting it fall beneath the spray to wash the blood from my face and neck. Fingers warmer than the water unbuttoned my dress, then a scalding mouth traced a path from my throat to the front of my bra. That gave way with a slice of fangs, baring my breasts while my dress slid down in a sodden heap around my hips.

I moaned when his mouth closed over my breast, searing it before a graze of teeth had me clutching him closer. He didn't bite me, although I wanted him to. Instead, he lightly scored the tip with his fangs before laving and sucking my nipple until it throbbed with the same intensity as if he *had* bitten it. I tried to pull his head up to kiss him, but his arms clamped around my back, holding me in place. When he moved to my other breast, giving it the same deliberate, passionate attention, I stopped resisting and gave in to the sensations.

The water had washed all the blood off me by the time he lifted his head. Very slowly, he lowered his arms, allowing my body to slide along his until my feet touched the ground. All the while, his mouth dragged from my breasts to my shoulders and up to my neck. When it finally slanted over mine, his kiss was more demanding than sensual, as if his need had long since transcended passion and burned with something far stronger.

I shoved my hands into his hair and opened my mouth to take him in deeper. He tasted like wine-soaked fantasies mixed with dark, unspeakable cravings. It wasn't enough to rake his tongue with mine, or have my head fall back at the bruising intensity of his kiss. I wanted more, and the moan that vibrated in his throat as I pierced his tongue so I could suck his blood only inflamed my need.

Far too soon, he tore away, his grip on my hair keeping me from resuming our kiss. With his other hand, he pulled my dress and underwear off with a single, impatient tug. Now I was only covered in the water that continued to spill over us, and I drew in a sharp breath as his gaze raked me with palpable hunger.

"Vlad."

I said his name more pleadingly than anything else. Gooseflesh broke out on me, as if my skin were finding its own way to beg for his touch. His clothes were soaked but he hadn't taken them off yet. When I started to, he caught my wrists. Then his hands settled around my waist as he knelt in front of me.

"Leila."

My name was a growl that had me shivering before his mouth even touched my stomach. When it slid lower, those shivers turned into shudders. All thought fled at the feel of his tongue probing me. I couldn't even form words as he continued to lick, suck, delve, and sensually torment my flesh. Then I couldn't stop myself from clutching his head, and when he yanked me closer and buried his tongue deeper, my moans turned into sobs of pleasure.

The ecstasy that followed made me feel like the glass he'd melted; one moment I was solid, the next, I'd dissolved into liquid heat. Dimly, I was aware of him holding me up, followed by a rending sound and the slap of wet fabric at my feet. Then he swept me into his arms and carried me out of the shower.

I barely registered the mattress dipping beneath our weight. His mouth covered mine before I could moan his name, and the feel of his hard, naked body was almost too much for my senses. His skin was so hot, I expected steam to replace the water clinging to him, and when he moved between my legs, I arched upward in desperate need.

His mouth absorbed my cry as he cleaved into me while dropping his emotional shields. For a few, dizzying moments, I drowned in an ocean of fierce need and overwhelming pleasure, mine or his, I didn't know. Each new thrust intensified the sensations, until I lost myself in them. Our emotions were so deeply entwined, we didn't feel like separate people anymore.

My nails raked down Vlad's back, and he arched at the sharp bliss of them scoring his skin. He moved deeper inside me, and I shuddered at the rapturous clench of my flesh around him. I urged him to move faster, and he slowed because he needed to hear me beg from pleasure instead of pain.

When he finally released his control, the climax that had him shouting brought me to my own shattering release as well. While I was still shuddering from ecstasy, he rolled me on top of him and brushed my hair out of my face. With our emotions still inexorably entwined, I knew, without a shadow of a doubt, that if Szilagyi had killed me, Vlad would have burned the entire world down if that's what it took to make him pay.

I had never loved him more, yet in that moment, part of me was also afraid of what he'd become if something did happen to me.

Chapter 22

Dawn wasn't far away. I sensed its approach in the lethargy that crept up my limbs, making them harder to move.

Of course, that could also be from over-satiation. Vlad had wanted to hear me plead from passion several times, as it turned out. I'd been drowsily tracing my hand behind his neck when a familiar essence trail flared beneath my fingers, reviving me as if I'd been doused with a bucket of icy water.

"I forgot to tell you something," I said, then cursed at my choice of words, not to mention my lack of tact. *Way to ease into a highly personal, traumatic subject, Leila!*

"What?" he said, and though his tone was normal, his shields went back up.

I closed my eyes, still cursing myself. "First, let me apologize for not telling you sooner. It's not that I forgot, really, it's just . . . well, a lot's happened, as you know, and—"

"What?" he repeated, his tone sharper now.

I opened my eyes, not surprised to find him drilling me with his Interrogation stare. Under that hard, unrelenting gaze, no one in their right mind would give him anything less than the truth, the whole truth, and nothing but the truth, which is what I'd intended to do anyway.

"It's about Clara." When he showed no reaction, I amended, "Your first *wife*, Clara."

That widened his gaze a fraction, though he still didn't blink or look away. "What about her?"

I don't know why, but I touched the spot on the back of his neck before I spoke. The first time I'd felt it, I'd known it was hers. Though faint from age, the essence imprint still pulsed with the kind of love that time could never fully erase.

"When Szilagyi found me during the castle attack, he said he was going to kill me just like he'd killed your first wife."

"Clara wasn't murdered, she jumped to her death," Vlad said, unknowingly echoing the same denial I'd made.

My hand left his neck. "Szilagyi said he erased everyone's memory of him being there so you'd think that. He wanted your guilt over Clara's 'suicide' to crush you, but . . . he told me he pushed her off that roof, and since he'd intended to kill me when he said it, he didn't have any reason to lie."

Vlad said nothing. His emotions were still locked down, but from the new rigidness in his posture, he was now questioning what he'd believed for over five hundred years.

If I were still human, I would have held my breath as I waited for his response. He'd loved Clara so much that his self-appointed culpability in her "suicide" marked his worst sin. Besides, judging from his emotions, Vlad had already been tightrope walking between a justified need for vengeance and a near psychotic obsession to bring Szilagyi down. Would this end up pushing him over the edge?

In hindsight, maybe I shouldn't have told him.

"Even if he had no cause to lie, I can't bring myself to trust Szilagyi's word," Vlad said at last. "At least in this case, I don't need to. Your abilities can discern the truth."

I sucked in a breath of surprise. *Serves you right!* my inner voice jeered. *You just* had *to tell him about his wife. Now you know that he values her vengeance more than your life.*

"Okay," I said, stumbling over the word while I tried to bury my vindictive inner monologue— and my hurt—under a practical mindset. "You've already weapons-proofed the villa, so it should be safe for me to try linking to him again—"

"Not Szilagyi," Vlad interrupted, his shields cracking to spill frustration and fury over my churning emotions. "You are *not* linking to him again, Leila!"

How many times do I have to tell you that? his

glare seemed to add, but instead of feeling chastised, I was relieved. *Suck on that!* I shot back to my hated inner voice.

"I meant Clara," Vlad went on, unaware of the schizophrenic battle going on within me. "You can read a person's death through their bones. Once I've dealt with Szilagyi, I want you to read hers and tell me if she jumped or if he pushed her."

"You kept her bones?" How oddly sentimental of him.

He gave me a look. "No, but I remember where I buried her."

"Okay," I said, wondering why the word came out slurred.

Vlad grasped the blankets we'd kicked to the bottom of the bed and pulled them over me. I would have asked why, but my mouth suddenly didn't work. My vision went dark, too, but I felt it when he pressed his lips to my forehead.

"Sleep well," he murmured.

If he said anything else, I didn't hear it. Oblivion had already claimed me.

My first conscious realization was of chains wrapped around my arms and legs. For a terrifying moment, I thought I was back in my old cell and my rescue had only been a dream. Then my eyes opened and I saw the crystal chandelier above me, and a turn of my head revealed Vlad sitting on the floor a few feet away. Relief that I wasn't back in my former cell turned to confusion. Why was I tied up? And why did the bedroom look so trashed; it was as if coked-up rock stars had been partying here for a week.

"What's going on?"

Vlad rose, nailing me with that hard, almost predatory stare. "You don't remember?"

That didn't sound good, as if waking up chained in a trashed room hadn't been ominous enough. "No," I whispered.

He approached the bed. My restraints wrapped around the four iron posts of the canopy before being nailed into the floor for additional support. His bill for this villa would be astronomical, but that wasn't my biggest concern at the moment.

"If you don't remember, then the spell compelled you to act in your sleep," he said, touching my chains but making no move to undo them. "It makes sense. You're too newly changed to be awake that soon after dawn, let alone with such strength."

I looked at the chains, broken furniture, and deep gashes in the walls with new, shocked understanding. "I did this?"

"Most of it," he said, his gaze never leaving mine. "Some of it I did during our struggle. You were determined to kill anyone who tried to stop you from harming yourself."

My gut constricted so tightly, it hurt. "I tried to kill you." Not a question; a realization, and with it came another clenching that was so strong, I began to dry heave.

His hand went to my stomach at once. "What's wrong?"

"What's wrong?" Crazed laughter slipped out between my gags. "*I tried to kill you*, that's what's wrong, and knowing it is making me *sick!*"

"Leila." His harsh tone snapped my eyes open. I must have closed them in disgust. "I know you'd never harm me of your own volition. It was the spell, so cease your useless guilt. As I told you before, we don't have time for it."

The brusque directive shouldn't have comforted me, but it did. So did his hand on my stomach, his warmth seeping through the thick blanket covering me. I nodded, blinking past the tears that had sprung to my eyes. Then I took some deliberate, deep breaths while I forced my gut to quit its repeated clenching.

"I must have linked to him in my sleep," I said, trying to make sense of what I didn't remember. "I've never done that with anyone but you, but Szilagyi's essence is still on me, and I went to sleep without wearing my gloves."

"That also occurred to me," he said, fingering my chains. "Another reason for these."

I looked at the chains and then the deep gashes in the wall that could only have come from an electrical whip. My right hand wasn't even sparking now, but that lethal power must still be in me. And one lucky strike with that whip could take off Vlad's head. After all, he'd be fighting to restrain me, not kill me, even if I wasn't showing him the same courtesy.

"Don't let me out of these," I said hoarsely. After my captivity, being restrained filled me with panic, but I'd rather freak the hell out than risk trying to harm him again.

"You won't be in them long," Vlad said, his nearness easing my guilt as well as my fear. "Mencheres will break the spell."

I hadn't realized I'd tensed everywhere until his statement caused me to relax with the suddenness of a balloon popping. "Did he get what he needed?"

He glanced toward the door. "Yes, and from the footsteps headed our way, he's awake and ready to begin."

Chapter 23

I didn't want to know what Mencheres put into the pot boiling on the stove. Images of rat's tails and bat's wings danced in my mind, but that was probably because I'd seen too many movies. Besides, I don't think those were the supplies that had taken Mencheres hours to acquire, and the scent coming from the pot was more reminiscent of herbs than rodent stew.

I was glad to be out of my chains, although I still felt that I deserved worse. In addition to wresting the guilt that gnawed at me, I was also fighting to keep my captivity memories at bay. Unlike the other times I'd been in enemies' hands, I wasn't able to shake the post-traumatic stress, and being trussed up had made it worse. Vlad must have sensed that, because he told me he'd only chained me to allow Mencheres a few hours' sleep. Before that, the Egyptian's power had kept me from harming myself, saving Vlad from resorting to violence to accomplish the same thing.

As we waited for Mencheres to finish cooking up his magical brew, Vlad held my right hand in a light grip. I knew it would turn viselike if the spell reared its head again, and that comforted me, but it hadn't escaped my notice that we were the only three people in the villa. It couldn't be concern over my going on another rampage: Vlad alone would be enough to contain me. With Mencheres here, too, I was laughably outgunned. They must not want the guards or anyone else to know what Mencheres was doing, which begged another question.

"If magic is so illegal in the vampire world that this would get all of us in trouble if we were caught, why don't we just tell on Szilagyi for using a spell?"

Mencheres gave me a sidelong glance before resuming his attention to the pot. "The same reason why some humans choose not to call the authorities: the repercussions aren't worth the potential assistance."

Vlad, as usual, was more blunt. "The Law Guardians wouldn't believe your actions were the result of a spell unless they saw you kill yourself as proof."

"But *that* defeats the purpose!" I said, aghast.

Vlad snorted. "Exactly."

Great. The Law Guardians were useless when it came to helping us, but they'd do Szilagyi's job for him if they found out that we were dabbling in magic. No wonder Vlad and Mencheres weren't rushing to call the vampire version of 911.

"Szilagyi knows that, doesn't he?" I guessed, letting out a short laugh. "That's why he hasn't hesitated to use spells against us. He knows we can't do anything about it."

"I wouldn't say that," Vlad replied, his copper gaze turning green. "But before we get to that, we're going to reverse the one he put on you."

"Ready at last," Mencheres said with a final stir of his spoon. Then he poured the brownish mixture into a tall plastic glass. "Drink."

I took the glass with my left hand. Vlad still hadn't released my right one, and from his expression, he wasn't going to. The mixture looked like pureed mud and it smelled earthy and fragrant, as if Mencheres had blended together a forest and a flower garden. Mencheres watched me with the expectant air of a chef as I blew on it to cool it, then took a small sip.

I began to choke after my first swallow, my stomach seizing with more ferocity than when I found out I'd tried to kill Vlad in my sleep. I would have spewed the mixture out, but my lips sealed shut as if they'd been welded by invisible tools.

"Swallow," Mencheres said, his tone suddenly hard. "You must drink all of it in order to break the spell."

My stomach still felt like it was shoving my other organs through an internal wood chipper, but I'd be damned if I let one glass of foul-tasting stuff stand between me and freedom. I nodded, and

Mencheres released his invisible hold on my mouth and I tipped the glass high, chugging its contents. My insides burned as if I drank liquid silver and I had to swallow back my own vomit several times, but finally, the glass was empty.

"That wasn't . . . so bad," I gasped, my sides still heaving from nausea so intense that it was crushing. "Do you think—"

I didn't get the rest out. Agony slammed into every cell at once, blinding me to everything except the pitiless, searing pain. I was still screaming when I came to my senses to find that I'd collapsed onto the kitchen floor. Mencheres was crouched in front of me and Vlad gripped me from behind.

" . . . the hell is she turning blue?" I heard Vlad snarl beneath the last, shrill sound of my scream.

It took a moment for his words to penetrate and for my eyes to refocus enough to note that my arms were indeed turning a brilliant indigo shade. So were my legs, which scissored out from my long dress as if I had been trying to run away from the pain. The shiny, reflective steel surface of the dishwasher confirmed that my face was blue, too. It was as though I'd morphed into a raven-haired version of Mystique, and from Mencheres's expression, that wasn't supposed to have happened.

"This is . . . unexpected," the former pharaoh breathed.

"Elaborate," Vlad said in his most scathing voice.

Mencheres shook his head as though stunned by what he had to admit. "It means that my remedy did not break the spell, which has never happened before. Whoever cast it must have bound it flesh to flesh and blood to blood. Since Leila is a vampire, that is more than magic; it's necromancy, which is beyond even my capabilities."

I couldn't see Vlad's face, but his tone seethed with enough undercurrents to know that he was barely controlling his anger. Or disbelief.

"You yanked wraiths out of the bones of slain men and you summoned the ferryman of the underworld to do your bidding, yet *this* is beyond you?"

Mencheres stared at Vlad, though since he was right above me, it also felt as if he was looking at me, too.

"Yes."

Vlad's hissing sigh blew my hair back where it landed. He didn't say anything for several moments. Neither did Mencheres. Now that the agony had faded, I had a question.

"If you can't break it, can anyone?"

"Only death can break it," Mencheres said, still sounding like he was having a hard time trying to process everything. "Not just your death," he added in a comforting way. "The death of the necromancer should also suffice. Since the cure soured within you, turning your body blue, it proves the spell was set with your flesh and blood as well as the necromancer's, so destruction of either should break it."

Vlad let out a low, vicious sound. "And we know where the necromancer would've gotten her flesh and blood. Explains why Szilagyi didn't send me all of her skin in his first package."

I shuddered. As if the memory of my skinning wasn't bad enough, now I had an image of Vlad piecing my stripped flesh back together enough to know that parts of it had been missing.

"That rules out Cynthiana," I said, trying to force back emotions I couldn't deal with yet. She'd managed to kill me with a spell before, but Szilagyi had blown her to bits in his castle attack, so she couldn't have been responsible for this.

Vlad released me and stood. "Even if she wasn't dead, I'd know it wasn't Cynthiana. It's feat enough to cast a spell that could control a vampire. One that transcends magic into necromancy?" His gaze raked me. "If I hadn't seen it for myself, I would've said it was impossible."

"So would I," Mencheres added with a hint of grimness.

Vlad rubbed his chin, the scars on his hands catching my gaze. I no longer had any scars, and oddly enough, seeing his struck me with inspiration.

"The spell started when I linked to Szilagyi through my skin, so burn it off," I said softly.

Vlad stopped pacing and bent down, laying his palm flat against my lower belly.

"If you're referring to his essence trail, I already did this morning, while you were unconscious."

That explained the charred odor I'd smelled in the bedroom, but it wasn't what I'd meant.

"Not just that." My voice was hoarse. "All of it. The spell's set in flesh and blood, so if we remove my flesh and blood, maybe it will . . . blunt the effects? At least, it would erase all my essence trails of him, then you could cover my new skin with your aura. That way, it would add another layer of protection against the spell and I won't be able to accidentally link to Szilagyi again and make things worse."

A normal man would've sputtered out an indignant refusal. What I was suggesting was as gruesome as what Harold had done to me, and no doubt more painful. Vlad didn't respond with outraged protestations. He just stared at me with those deep, copper-colored eyes while weighing the pros and cons of my proposal.

I already had. Yes, it would be agonizing, but Vlad was more surgical with fire than Harold had been with his knives, and considering I'd tried to kill him once and might do so again, the pain was a cheap price to pay.

Vlad finally looked away from me and raised a brow at Mencheres. *Do you agree with her logic?* the silent query asked.

The admiring yet pitying glance Mencheres gave me was answer enough. Vlad's hand left my stomach and he caressed my face. Then he rose, lifting me to my feet.

"I'll do it after dawn, when you're unconscious," he said, no emotion coloring his tone. "Even still, the pain might wake you. I've seen it happen before."

You mean you've done *it before*, I thought, but didn't say out loud. It hadn't occurred to me to wait until I was unconscious, yet I was all for the change in plans. After the horrors of being skinned, having my flesh burned off was a daunting prospect to say the least, but if it was my best chance for beating this spell, then bring on the barbeque.

I forced a smile to show that I wasn't having second thoughts and tried not to dwell on what was to come.

"Well, we've got our plans for the morning. What do you want to do until then?"

Vlad stared at me, splinters of emotions breaching the walls he'd mostly kept up since he rescued me. At last, a hint of a smile curled his lips.

"The same thing many other people do when they come to Vegas. Get married."

I waited for the punch line. When it didn't come, I was almost stammering in my confusion.

"But we already are . . . oh, okay, not vampire-style, and I would . . . but we can't now. Right?"

Vlad flashed a tolerant look at Mencheres. "Pay this no mind. She always argues with me when I propose to her."

"You're serious?" I got out without sputtering this time.

He rolled his eyes. "Yes, Leila, I'm serious. Need for me to get on my knees again?"

"But I'm blue," I said, stunned into more nonsensicalness.

"The color should fade within the hour," Mencheres offered, backing out of the room to let us handle this ourselves. "Not that any of Vlad's people would dare comment if it didn't."

I stared at Vlad, seeing the raw, steely determination in his gaze.

"You know that I consider you my wife, as do my people, but our previous ceremony was legal by human standards only. In the vampire world, it counted as nothing more than an engagement because you were human and thus unable to swear the required blood oath. You're a vampire now, and I don't want to wait any longer to have everyone know that you have been, and will always be, my wife."

He took my hand, sliding a thick, heavy gold ring onto my finger that I hadn't seen since Szilagyi had captured me.

"Mihaly returned this with your skin to taunt me, but I swore that if you lived, I would see it on your finger again," he said in a deep, resonant voice. "Months ago, you made me ask you if you would marry me. This time, I'm not asking. I'm telling you to say yes, so say it, and be mine for eternity."

I looked at the ring, so moved to be wearing it again that I almost didn't notice the startlingly blue color of my skin. Then I looked at Vlad. His expression was darker with intensity and the grip he had on my hand was both warm and unbreakable.

In some ways, he intimidated me more now than he had the day I'd met him. Vlad loved the same way that he lived—untamable, dangerous, and full throttle, just as he'd warned me. I'd felt the repercussions of that love more than once and I'd feel it again if I said yes, yet like before, I only had one answer.

"Yes. Yesterday, today, forever . . . yes."

Chapter 24

 Our first marriage took place in the ballroom of his castle with over two thousand witnesses cheering us on. The air had been thick with the scent of flowers and beeswax candles, and I'd worn an exquisite white dress while Vlad had been decked out in scarlet and black like a medieval king.

This time, we were in a villa in Vegas and I wore a simple blue dress that thankfully no longer matched my skin tone. As Mencheres promised, my blueberry shade had vanished within an hour. Vlad was dressed in black pants and a black jacket, his white shirt the only contrast to the dark ensemble. Our witnesses consisted of my sister, Marty, Mencheres, Kira, and about two dozen of Vlad's guards. Either Vlad hadn't invited my father or my dad had refused to come, because he wasn't here. Instead of cheering like our witnesses had last time, everyone was almost eerily quiet.

Vlad drew out a knife, the blade cut down

until less than a quarter inch remained. I saw a few raised brows but only I, Vlad, and Mencheres knew why it was so short. I couldn't kill myself with that if I had a solid hour alone with it to try. Even with my hand in his, Vlad still wasn't taking any chances.

The blade might be only the size of a thumb-nail, but it was sharp. With his fingers still curled around mine, he scored a line from one side of his palm to the other, then pressed the cut to the inside of my hand.

"By my blood," he said in a strong, steady voice, "I declare that you, Leila Dalton Dracul, are my wife."

His part was now done, no clergy member, justice of the peace, or notary necessary. What a vampire marriage ceremony lacked in formalities, it made up for in significance. Much like the spell in my skin, only death could break the vow I was about to make.

Even so, I wasn't the slightest bit nervous as I took the knife and scored a line into my own palm. "By my blood, Vladislav Basarab Dracul, I declare that you are my husband," I said in a clear voice before handing the knife back and pressing my bloodied palm to his.

His lips curled with a familiar arrogance, as if he'd never doubted that I would bind myself to him this way. Maybe he hadn't. I wasn't a big believer in fate, but as his mouth sealed over mine in a kiss that rocked me back on my heels, I felt more sure of this than I had of any other decision before it. Call it fate, inevitability, whatever; right now, I knew that I was exactly where I was supposed to be, and my soul felt like it took in a deep breath to remember the moment.

My body wasn't in a meditative mood. As Vlad kissed me, it flared with need so strong, even I could smell the lust that started pouring off me. I'd almost died more times than I cared to count in the past few weeks and our future was still uncertain. *Claim what's yours, don't wait*, something inside me seemed to insist, stamping out embarrassment beneath an ancient, inhuman urge that was raw, powerful—and undeniable. Wasting even a moment seemed almost criminally ungrateful.

From the tightening of his grip and the new, rough carnality in his kiss, Vlad felt the same way. Our guests scattered as he tore away long enough to mutter, "Get out," before backing me against the nearest sturdy object.

I crushed my mouth to his, needing each stroke of his tongue and the hot, bruising pressure of his lips. His clothes were obstacles that I took no pity on. They fell in a ripped heap at our feet in my desperation to feel his skin on mine.

He didn't bother ripping off my dress, just my underwear. Then he shoved the dress up, a dark sound of satisfaction escaping him as his fingers found my wet depths. I moved against his hand, my moans turning harsh as those fingers penetrated deep. His mouth ravaged mine as he began to rub with strong, fast strokes that had inner muscles clenching with an urgency that turned need into unbearable demand.

"You're mine," he breathed against my neck when his lips left mine to travel lower. "Forever. Say it."

"I'm yours," I swore, the words ragged from passion. "Forever. Now, take me and prove it."

His mouth slanted over mine again and he grasped my hips with both hands. A deep, searing thrust tore a cry from me, then another and another as he moved with barely restrained ferocity. His hands were brands on my hips, his body lava contained by rock-hard muscles. Pleasure mixed with sensations that felt too good to be pain, yet before this, only agony had made me aware of every nerve ending with such excruciating intensity. I began to whimper, yet my legs tightened around his hips, and if I clutched his head any tighter as I lost myself in his kiss, I might crush him.

I screamed into his mouth as I climaxed so hard, my body felt splintered from the ecstasy. My arms dropped, my head fell forward, and the strength left me as suddenly as I'd been filled with my burning, uncontrollable lust. I was boneless, held up only by his grip, body, and the sensations that crested inside me like the popping of millions of champagne bubbles.

He pulled my head back, lips curled with primal triumph as he stared at me. Then he dropped to his knees, taking me down with him since I couldn't hold myself up. With a single, lithe movement, he was behind me, one arm locking me to his chest while his free hand slid between my thighs.

The change in position took him deeper inside me. He moved with those powerful strokes that now felt like they split me down the center, yet my climax-induced lethargy vanished. I bit my lip to stifle the cries that built in my throat, then couldn't hold them back as he thrust so deep, it pushed me forward until my forehead touched the pillar in front of us.

Later, I'd be embarrassed at how loud I shouted. Every vampire in the hotel probably heard me. At the moment, I didn't care. The pleasure was indescribable, and I braced against the pillar with one hand while raking nails from the other down Vlad's thigh until I left scarlet tracks in my wake.

His laughter taunted me not to stop. So did the emotions strafing mine, making me move against him almost as feverishly as his body continued to slice into mine. When rapture eventually broke over me again, it was mine as well as his, and when he laid us back against the cool marble floor, I wanted to roll over and kiss him, but I couldn't move.

It wasn't a supernatural issue or a sign of dawn's imminent approach; I just couldn't summon the strength. My mouth still worked, and when I told him that, laughter puffed onto my back.

"Allow me," he said, rolling me over until I was cradled in his arms, our faces so close they were almost touching.

"Everybody did leave, right?" I asked, only now wondering if we'd given anyone a free, explicit show.

Another laugh. "Yes. I'd kill anyone who stayed to watch."

I smiled before deciding it took too much effort. "My second wedding night," I murmured. "I guess it's your . . . what? Third? Fourth?"

He stiffened slightly, then relaxed when he realized I wasn't jealous. Just curious. "Third human, first vampire," he said, brushing his lips across mine. "And by far the best."

I smiled against his mouth. "No need for flattery. You already got lucky."

"You know me better than to think I would use flattery to get anything I wanted."

No, he wouldn't. He'd consider that lying, and whatever flaws he might have, Vlad was also the most honest person I'd ever met.

"Besides," he continued, his mouth curling down. "My first wedding night was dismal and my second one was spent alone."

"What happened to make the first bad and the other lonely?" My voice was soft while I wondered if he'd tell me. Vlad rarely spoke about this part of his past, and after that tidbit, I was more than a little intrigued.

He didn't say anything for several moments. I'd just decided to change the subject when he spoke.

"My first marriage was arranged by my father when I was a child, a common practice for the time. You know what happened during my boyhood imprisonment and how it affected me, yet I couldn't break the betrothal without losing an important ally." His smile became twisted. "And I couldn't very well admit to my intended, her father, or anyone else that I didn't know if I could stand being close enough to her to father children, as I was expected to do to continue the royal line."

I don't know why this information surprised me. He had told me how his brutal treatment had caused him to hate being touched, even in casual contact. For some reason, I'd just assumed he meant by other men. Vlad was so sensual, insatiable, and dominating in bed; it was hard to reconcile him with what he'd just described.

"Before the wedding, I made sure that I could, in fact, perform as required," he went on, no emotion in his tone now. "It took several unsuccessful visits with whores who knew better than to repeat my difficulties before I could get through the act in its entirety. Then I married Clara and rushed through my husbandly responsibilities with as little contact as possible. I was relieved when she became pregnant because that meant I could finally stop."

My heart broke at how miserable he must have been, unable to talk to anyone because the emotional aftermath from his abuse would have been considered weakness in the fifteenth century.

"I'm so sorry," I breathed.

Now the smile he gave me was jaded. "Don't pity me. Pity Clara, who was forced to marry a traumatized barbarian who couldn't show her any of the gentleness she deserved. Somehow, she didn't hate me for it, and her pregnancy changed things for the better between us. Once I was no longer forced to bed her, I didn't find touching her as repulsive, and feeling my child move in her belly was the first time after my captivity that I put my hand on another person and felt nothing except joy."

My eyes began to sting, but I wouldn't allow the tears to come. The Vlad in front of me wouldn't want me crying for the man he'd been. As stated, he'd take that as pity, and there was nothing pitiful about him overcoming the obstacles he had. I'd had no idea my question would unearth such painful and poignant memories, and the fact that he'd relayed them with his usual unflinching honesty was further proof that his inner strength more than matched his incredible power and abilities.

"Clara loved you," I said, my voice husky. "I felt it in the essence traces she left on you, so whatever guilt you feel over those early days, let it go. You must have made up for it."

His hand was a warm caress on my face, like the first rays of sun after a long winter's night. "I tried, but you of all people know how difficult I can be to live with."

I held his hand against my face. "You might not be the easiest person, but who is? Besides, easy is overrated compared to you in all your spectacular, mercurial, enigmatic glory."

He smiled, a familiar arrogance now shading his expression. "I'll remind you that you said that during our next fight." Then he stretched, the movement making his muscles ripple in a way that claimed my attention long enough to miss the first part of what he said next.

" . . . second marriage was arranged also, but this one by me. The king of Hungary needed someone to marry his pregnant cousin before her condition became obvious, and I needed a new alliance with Hungary to reclaim my throne."

"Wait, Szilagyi was the king of Hungary's uncle, right? So if you married the king's *cousin*, that means Szilagyi–"

"Is technically my father-in-law," he finished, his mouth curling in a mocking way. "Proving yet again that no one has the power to enrage you more than family."

Did that mean I was technically related to Szilagyi, too, as Vlad's wife? Without thinking, my hands tightened into fists. If so, then yes. Sometimes family *sucked*.

"My second wife, Ilona, had little interest in me beyond a name for her unborn son," he went on.

"I had even less interest in her, so our marriage remained unconsummated, though when she became pregnant again, I claimed that child as mine, too."

"Why? Weren't you mad?" Female adultery was a big deal back then and Vlad wasn't the type to share.

He sighed. "Ilona meant nothing to me, as I said. Furthermore, as a vampire, I couldn't give her children and it seemed wrong to deny her another chance at motherhood. She had been discreet with whoever her lover was, so there was no gossip about the babes not being mine. At the time, my firstborn son was the undisputed heir to *my* throne, so I didn't see the boys Ilona bore as a threat." His features tightened. "I was wrong. Szilagyi was behind my first son's assassination, and in addition to personal motives, he also did it to put Ilona's child on my throne after he had mine murdered."

Once again, he wasn't sparing himself in this blunt retelling, and I had to bite my lip to keep from saying that I was sorry. I was, though. He hadn't been much older than me by the time he'd gone through all these atrocities and heartbreaks. I doubted I would've made it with my sanity or soul intact, yet he had, even with hundreds more years of adversity piled on.

I slid closer, wanting to dull the painful memories of his past by giving him something else to concentrate on.

"Thank you for answering my questions, and

now I want to tell you something personal. It's not nearly as deep or important, but . . . I'm glad you're the only man I've ever slept with. For years, my voltage issues kept me a virgin whether I wanted to be or not, but then I met you and it felt like . . . you were the one I'd been waiting for, even when I didn't know it." My voice caught. "Even with all the awful things that happened, if I was thrown back in time, I would still grab that power line because it's what eventually brought me to you."

He kissed me, slow, deep, and with more tenderness than I'd realized he was capable of. Then he drew away, smiling but with a tinge of shadows to it.

"I treasure the gift of your virginity, but if you'd given it to another I would still love you to the same dangerous degree. You are in my soul, and nothing you did before we met or will do in the future can change that. And to answer the question you've never asked me, yes, I do love you more than I loved Clara. If she were alive now, I would still choose you."

Tears filled my eyes and I couldn't speak. How had he known the secret anguish I'd felt wondering if I would ever come close to what he'd felt for her? It was ridiculous at best and selfish at worst to be jealous of a dead woman, but Clara's memory had felt like a wall around Vlad I could never breach, and I hadn't dared to hope that he would tear it down himself.

"I don't know what to say," I choked out, still fighting back the tears.

His smile was slow, challenging, and sensual. Before I registered what was happening, he'd swept me into his arms and was carrying me toward the bedroom.

"You already said it: yes. Now, say it again."

Chapter 25

The instant I came awake, I tensed, expecting my entire body to be engulfed in agony. After a few pain-free seconds, I dared to open my eyes.

Not only was I *not* on fire, we weren't in the bedroom I'd fallen asleep in. Instead of a crystal chandelier, billowy fabric formed a knot of roses in the center of the canopy above me. For a second, I wondered if Vlad had carried me into one of the villa's other bedrooms, but a glance out the window showed unfamiliar buildings and a wide river below.

Definitely not Vegas. The desert didn't have rivers.

"Good evening."

I turned toward Vlad's voice, seeing him emerge from the bathroom. His black hair was damp from showering, but he was dressed in a pair of dark gray pants with a matching charcoal jacket. A pale silvery shirt softened the ensemble and platinum cuff links added a touch of elegance, if one didn't already notice the richness of the fabric and the custom tailoring.

I, on the other hand, was wearing only sheets and my hair was tangled enough for a hairbrush to cringe away from the challenge. What surprised me most was that I was also unchained.

"You left me alone while you showered?" I gestured at the nearby window. "The spell could have made me jump through that!"

"You wouldn't have made it out of bed," a familiar voice said to my right, then Marty's head popped up from the space between the bed and the wall. "Hiya, kid."

Vlad arched a brow as if to say, *You really thought I'd leave you unprotected?* Meanwhile, I snatched at the sheets, which had dipped far too low. No wonder Marty had chosen to lie on the floor instead of sit in the chair opposite the bed.

"H-hi," I stammered. "And thanks."

Marty smiled at me. "No thanks needed. Happy to do it." Then he gave a far more reserved glance at Vlad. "Since you're done, I'll show myself out."

He left, and the coolness between them reminded me of the conversation Marty and I had had right before Szilagyi attacked the castle. With everything else going on, I'd forgotten it. I still intended to address Marty's return to the carnival with Vlad, but now wasn't the time. *Survival first.*

So I started with the obvious. "Where are we?"

"New Orleans," Vlad replied, sitting on the edge of the bed. The fragrance of soap still clung to him, adding a citrusy blend to his natural smoky, cinnamon scent. I found myself sliding closer and inhaling without thinking about it, then almost blushed as his gaze turned knowing.

"We don't have time," he said, though his fingers trailed a warm path from my neck to my collarbone. "You slept later than I anticipated, but your body no doubt needed to recuperate."

At first, I thought he was referring to his sexual prowess since he'd more than exhausted me last night. Then my hands dove beneath the sheets to run over my body.

"I can still feel essence imprints," I said in surprise. "You didn't do it?"

Something dark flitted across his features. "Yes and no. I did burn your skin, but I didn't cover you in my aura after, so all of the imprints you're detecting are mine."

I couldn't have been more relieved that I'd slept through the burning. Maybe exhausting me beforehand had been to my benefit in more ways than one. "Why'd you skip the aura part?"

His sigh was harsh. "Because I will need to burn you again. You didn't sleepwalk this morning, so either preventing you from linking to Szilagyi through his essence trail worked, or destroying your flesh weakened the spell. I believe it's the latter. If I rendered you fireproof with my aura, I'd need to employ different methods to temporarily weaken the spell next time."

My stomach lurched while the macabre saying *There's more than one way to skin a cat* ran through my mind. Yeah, I'd prefer the fire. For one, I'd slept through it. For another, it would be far quicker than any "different methods," and if I woke up during the event, speed would equal mercy. Besides, I never wanted to associate Vlad with the horrible memories I had of my skin being sliced off. Even the thought made me shudder.

Vlad caught it and another shadow flashed across his features. "I don't want to do that, either. Burning you was difficult enough."

Guilt hit me. "I'm sorry. I've been so busy dwelling on how I would deal with this; I didn't give much thought to how rough it would be for you."

"Nor should you," he replied at once. "I'm not the one who's been repeatedly tortured the past few weeks, first by enemies, then by me out of necessity. You need to be focused on your own needs, Leila. You'll lose your mind otherwise."

He had his shields up again, and it hadn't escaped my notice that over the past few days, he'd kept them up unless we were making love. He must not think I could handle what he was feeling when passion wasn't at the forefront.

"You're wrong," I said quietly. "I'm not the only one who's been tortured. Szilagyi used me like a weapon to slice you open, and I know those wounds are still burning. You don't have to hide what you're feeling from me, Vlad. I can take it."

A humorless smile curled his mouth before he brushed it against my ear.

"I'm not hiding my feelings from you." His voice was so low, even at this proximity; I had to strain to hear him. "I'm hiding them from the other vampires I've made. Ever since I realized that the castle was under attack, all I've cared about is your survival. If I have to sacrifice every person in my line to ensure it, I will. That's why I'm blocking off my emotions. If my people knew how little I cared about them now, it would destroy the unity that I've fought so hard to build."

He kissed my ear after he finished speaking, then rose and tugged me up with him. I moved as if on automatic pilot, complying with his directive to shower because we had to leave soon.

He stayed in the bathroom to watch, his aura crackling like it was made of hundreds of Roman candles. If I'd stared at the shower's glass walls too long, he would've melted them. I supposed it was a sign of faith that he hadn't already. Once I was finished, I dressed in one of the outfits he'd packed for me and then followed him out of the hotel, my mind still reeling.

From the moment we'd met, Vlad's concern for his people had been the driving force behind everything he'd done. He'd once told me that he believed in God and the final judgment, yet still wouldn't change his brutal tactics because it was the only way he could ensure the safety of those who belonged to him. I knew he loved me, but to hear him say that he'd sacrifice every one of his people for me didn't just shock me; it rocked me to my core.

I didn't feel worthy of that kind of love, especially from a man like Vlad. He was a centuries-old warrior who'd overcome everything that human and vampire life had thrown at him, and those had been some horrible blows. Furthermore, I knew a little about the members of Vlad's line, and they were heroic people whose feats of bravery made my small accomplishments pale by comparison. Who was I? A ridiculously lucky girl who'd fallen in love with a man miles out of my league, that's who.

In addition to being awed, Vlad's declaration also frightened me, for his sake. For reasons I couldn't fathom, he did love me to that extreme, which meant that Szilagyi's plan had a greater chance of succeeding.

What if what Szilagyi had done to me *did* push Vlad into a reckless pursuit of revenge that would eventually get him killed? Who knew how long this war would last, and it had already gotten nastier and more brutal than we had ever imagined. If things got worse, would it push Vlad to the point where he was willing to do anything—even horrible things—to protect me? I couldn't stand the thought of Vlad losing the best parts of himself over me. He'd been through so much and yet hadn't turned into the monster that Szilagyi was.

On the heels of my fear, determination filled me. I wouldn't let that happen. I'd stop him before he crossed the point of being an avenging husband, and turned into something else. If he loved me so much that I could be the cause of his downfall, I could also be the one to prevent it—or bring him back from it.

I was so consumed by this thought that I didn't ask where we were going until Vlad stopped in front of the iron gates of a cemetery labeled St. Louis Number One. I looked around, seeing ghosts hovering like pale, creepy shadows in and around the many crypts in the cemetery. I shivered. Was it me, or did it feel like the temperature had dropped several degrees since we reached the foreboding-looking cemetery?

"Why are we here?" I asked, also wondering why we were alone. Vlad must have brought his guards with him or he wouldn't have whispered his bombshell when we were alone in our room.

"To see an acquaintance," he replied. At my doubtful look, he smiled sardonically. "Her tomb is where Marie Laveau insists on meeting all of her visitors. And they call me a show hound."

The name sounded familiar, but I couldn't place it. Then the appearance of a large African-American man on the other side of the gates stopped me in mid-ponder.

"Vlad Tepesh," he said, inclining his head in a respectful way. "You are expected and may enter. You," and his gaze barely passed over me, "are not expected and must stay here."

I stiffened, but Vlad only smiled. "My wife goes where I go, as both our laws affirm."

Both our laws. From his lack of heartbeat, I already knew that the large man wasn't human. Vlad's statement narrowed the possibilities down to one: ghoul. I shifted uneasily. The last ghouls I'd met had tried to eat me, and not in the romantic way.

"A mortal ceremony means nothing," the ghoul began, but Vlad pulled out a cell phone and tapped the screen before handing it over. *By my blood*, I heard a replay of his voice say, *I declare that you, Leila Dalton Dracul, are my wife . . .*

I hadn't noticed anyone taping the ceremony last night, but someone must've. The ghoul's brows went up as he watched. Then he handed the phone back, giving me his first full look.

"Congratulations, Leila Dracul," he said formally.

Despite everything that had happened the past several weeks—or perhaps because of it—I couldn't resist.

"Oh, I prefer Leila Dracu*la*," I said, grinning as I felt Vlad's foot trod down on mine.

"You'll pay for that," he muttered, then fixed the ghoul with a harder stare. "As I said, my wife comes with me."

"I will relay this information and return with Majestic's decision," the ghoul stated, melting away into the cemetery.

"Why didn't you tell this Marie person that I was coming with you?" I whispered once I couldn't see the ghoul anymore.

Vlad glanced down at me. "Many reasons."

I didn't know if his vague answer was because he was still pissy about the Dracula quip, or because he didn't want to elaborate in case the large ghoul returned.

"Is she dangerous?" I said in an even softer tone.

Now the glance he shot me was amused in a way that made the hairs stand up on the back of my neck.

"Remember the Remnants? Cat derived that power from Marie, and she's not nearly as good at it as the Ghoul Queen is."

Suddenly, the ghost-filled cemetery seemed as benign as a children's playground. The real danger was our host, and Vlad had insisted that I come with him to see Marie. It was so opposite of his usual overprotectiveness that I couldn't believe it. What was he up to?

I didn't have time to ask. The ghoul returned, opening the gates with another polite inclination of his head.

"Majestic will see you both. Please come with me."

Chapter 26

 I hadn't been inside a cemetery since I visited my mother's grave years before. I was still in the hospital the day she was buried, recovering from the power line accident that would forever change me. Her headstone had been a simple upside-down U, with her name and date inscribed on the front. Marie Laveau had a tall white tomb that was riddled with graffiti, while more junk was piled in front of it. None of the other tombs we'd passed had been desecrated this way, and I didn't understand until a high-school history lesson suddenly popped into my memory as if I'd mentally Googled her.

Marie Laveau wasn't just known as the Ghoul Queen, as Vlad had called her. History had also referred to her as the Voodoo Queen of New Orleans. I took a closer look at her tomb. That wasn't graffiti; those X's were requests for blessings, and what I'd first dismissed as junk actually comprised offerings. Wow. I was about to meet a legendary historical figure.

You married one, dumb ass, came my next thought, and I laughed despite my nervousness.

Vlad cast a sideways glance at me. I waved a hand. "Don't worry about it."

Then I jumped, startled, as the stone slab in front of Marie's tomb began to slide back, revealing an opening. The offerings fell inside and I tried not to think about how it looked like a dark mouth had just swallowed them. Worse, our ghoul guide nodded at the hole in an expectant way. My suspicions were confirmed when Vlad grasped me by the hand and led me to it.

"Put your arms around me and stand on my feet," he instructed.

I figured out why. The hole was too narrow for us to jump into it standing side by side, and I no more wanted to go first than I wanted to be left alone with the large, imposing ghoul. I planted my feet on top of Vlad's and wrapped my arms around his neck. He held me tight and dropped us down into the blackness.

It wasn't a long fall. Only about twenty feet. I didn't like how the opening above us immediately began to close, but Vlad didn't seem worried, so I decided not to be, either. After a few moments of hard blinking, my eyes adjusted and I could see the faint outline of a tunnel ahead. Once again, my imagination wasn't helpful, likening the tunnel to a monster's throat.

Vlad released me from his embrace but held on to my hand, leading me into the tunnel.

"This is all theatrics," he said, probably scenting my unease. "Effective for scaring humans, the newly turned, and the easily manipulated, but no more than smoke and mirrors for the rest of us. Still"—he shot a quick smile my way—"I can't criticize. I keep corpses impaled on poles for the same reason."

A snort of laughter escaped me and my nervousness lessened. "Birds of a feather," I quipped.

His teeth flashed in another grin, but beneath that, I caught a hint of ruthlessness. He might have left his guards at the hotel, yet this clearly wasn't a friendly visit. He intended for something big to go down with Marie, and for some reason, he'd wanted me here when it happened.

I squared my shoulders and found the hard place inside me that would kill if someone I loved was threatened. Especially someone I loved as much as Vlad. Just thinking about the possibility of the voodoo queen trying to harm him made my hand begin to tingle like it was sparking inside the thick rubber glove. When Vlad opened a metal door at the end of the tunnel, I was ready for whatever was on the other side.

Or I thought so. I hadn't expected a small sitting room with three chairs, a bottle of wine, and three glasses. If not for the stone walls that still held the scent of the graveyard, I would've sworn that we'd entered the parlor of a house.

"Vlad Tepesh," the attractive, black-haired

woman said, a heavy Southern accent decorating her voice. "You've surprised me twice today. First with your request for this meeting, and now with the news that congratulations are in order."

It was rude to stare, but I couldn't help it. Marie Laveau didn't match the image my mind had conjured. Her coloring was brown sugar and cream and her manner was more refined cougar than female witch doctor. She was dressed in a cranberry-colored silk blouse and a long black skirt, both pieces giving off a vibe of understated elegance, much as Vlad's clothes did.

"Marie," Vlad said, with a cordial nod. "Allow me to present my wife, Leila Dalton Dracul."

I didn't teasingly change my surname to "Dracula" this time. An undercurrent of tension hummed through the room, even if we were all pretending to be on our best behavior. Since I had my gloves on, I shook Marie's hand. She smiled at me in a friendly way while her eyes raked me with the pitiless assessment I'd grown used to from the undead. Measuring my strengths and looking for my weaknesses.

"Please, sit," she said, all gracious Southern hostess despite that. "You must try the wine. It's one of my favorites."

With those words, a side door opened and our ghoul guide appeared, filling our glasses with a deference that was matched only by his speed. As soon as he was done, he disappeared again.

"To the newlyweds," Marie said, raising her glass.

Vlad touched his glass to hers and so did I. We drank and I let out a small sound of appreciation. The deep red wine had hints of currant, oak, and more than a hint of blood. I'd have to duplicate that mixture in the future.

"So, Vlad, when did we last see each other?" Marie asked, cocking her head as if trying to remember. I wasn't buying her act of forgetfulness, and from his response, neither was he.

"Across a battlefield strewn with the bodies of dead ghouls," he replied in a pleasant tone.

Her gaze narrowed, then she waved a dismissive hand. "Of course. Poor, misguided souls. Those who survived Apollyon's foolish uprising are following me now, to their benefit."

Not modest at all, are you? I thought, with an inner shake of my head. Birds of a feather, indeed.

"Jacques told me you have a recording of your marriage," Marie went on, changing the subject. "May I see it?"

Checking for authenticity? I wondered as Vlad passed his cell phone over. She didn't seem like the type to ask just so she could ooh and aah with feminine appreciation. Marie took it and tapped the screen. Soon, our voices flowed into the small space, repeating our simple, life-altering vows.

"I wonder why I didn't see this video before," she commented as she watched.

If Vlad's shields hadn't cracked, releasing a split second of blistering rage, I wouldn't have noticed her slight emphasis on the word "this." But they did, and after a moment of wondering why, understanding slammed home.

Szilagyi hadn't just sent his tapes of me to Vlad. He must have also released them to the entire undead world. Fury flashed through my veins. Of course he'd want everyone to know how he'd snatched Vlad's wife right out from under him, and then what he'd done to me afterward. To scum like Szilagyi, that would be the same as spiking a football after a touchdown.

"The ceremony was only last night," Vlad replied, his tone daring Marie to elaborate on what she'd alluded to.

I was still boiling in anger, with humiliation clawing close at its heels. Logic said that *I* had nothing to be ashamed of, but the thought of everyone looking at me while a mental image of those tapes played in their minds made me want to run for the nearest exit. If I'd suddenly been stripped naked and staked out in public, I would have felt less exposed.

Marie handed Vlad his phone back, a small smile touching her mouth. "It ends rather abruptly, doesn't it?"

My nails dug into the armrests of my chair. She was making a sex crack now, too?

After Vlad took it, he reached over to clasp my

hand. "I never hesitate when it comes to something I want."

His flesh radiated his usual heat, and the part of me that had fragmented with angry shame soaked it up as if it was the only thing keeping me from shattering into a million pieces.

Marie glanced at our joined hands, at Vlad, and then her brow ticked up. "And what do you want from me?"

Vlad gave her his most charming smile, which was warning enough for me.

"I want to know if you're the necromancer who cast the spell that nearly killed my wife."

Chapter 27

 Marie's expression went danger-ously blank. If the mood in the room had been tense before, it was downright ominous now.

"Why would you suspect me of doing such a thing?" she asked, her Southern accent changing to sugar-coated poison.

Vlad's genial smile never slipped. "The spell is bound in undead flesh, so only someone skilled in necromancy could have cast it. With your exper-tise in grave magic, that makes you the most likely suspect."

My right hand slipped beneath a fold in my long skirt, so Marie couldn't see me work my fingers to slip my glove off. We might have only seconds before she hit us with those hideous, unbeatable Remnants. I hadn't knowingly manifested a whip since my capture, but from the burnt slashes in the villa, the ability was still there. If our lives de-pended on it, I had to do it again. The alternative was unthinkable.

"What if it was me?" Marie's mouth lifted in a challenging quirk. "What would you intend to do about it?"

"Kill you," Vlad replied pleasantly.

I tensed, willing all of my energy into my hand for the imminent attack, but Marie only laughed.

"I never pegged you for a fool, Tepesh. You surprise me a third time today."

With that, a seething gray mass shot up around her before covering the walls of the small room. It took less time for us to be surrounded by the deadly, howling Remnants than it did for me to leap up from my chair, glove off and my hand suffused with glowing, electric white. Vlad remained seated, and to my shock, I saw him regard the Remnants around us with detached amusement.

"Is this supposed to intimidate me?"

He's lost his mind, I thought numbly. Dear God, Szilagyi *had* actually managed to drive him crazy.

"Yes," Marie said, sounding almost as thrown by his response as I was.

He smiled again. "You've shown me yours. Now, let me show you mine."

Fire flooded the room, concealing the Remnants behind bright, destructive bands of crimson, orange, and blue. I only knew that the side door had opened when I heard shouting, but Marie's ghoul bodyguard couldn't make it past the flames that were so hot, they began to eat into the stone walls. If Vlad hadn't held them above the three of us like a gleaming, deadly curtain, only he would have survived.

Just as abruptly, the flames vanished. If not for the smoke and new, charred texture to the walls, no one would have guessed that the room had been a hellish inferno moments ago.

"Now that we've compared the equivalent of our supernatural dicks, why don't you answer my question?" Vlad said, tone as cold as the fire had been hot.

Marie's gaze narrowed and she waved back Jacques, who ran into the room. "You're not afraid of my Remnants. Why?"

Another dangerously charming smile. "Answer my question and I'll tell you."

She glanced at me before a shake of her head dismissed me as insignificant. Okay, compared to Vlad's fire display, the buildup of sparks on my right hand was nothing, but that didn't mean I was helpless, dammit! Anger sent more currents into my hand, but I still hadn't manifested a whip yet. I might only have one shot, so I needed to grow one. Fast.

"If someone had enlisted my help to kill her," Marie said at last, "I wouldn't need to use a spell to do it."

"Not a direct answer. Perhaps you didn't know who the spell was for?" Vlad said, tilting his head in my direction. "She's new to our world, so you might not have recognized her from the pieces of skin used to bind it."

Marie leaned forward, staring at Vlad as if they

were the only two people in the city, let alone the room. "You think I don't make it my business to know every important new person in my most powerful adversaries' lives?"

"You consider me your adversary?" Vlad asked silkily.

"Your race, gender, and kind have been my adversaries for the better part of two hundred years, white male vampire," she said, Southern accent deepening until it was menacingly smooth.

The Remnants surged closer to Vlad, swirling around him like storm clouds in a hurricane. Oddly enough, they kept away from me, but maybe Marie didn't consider me worth their time. *Touch him and I'll show you how wrong you are,* I thought grimly.

"If you are not the necromancer, then swear it by an oath bound in your blood," Vlad said, leaning forward as well.

Marie let out a contemptuous sniff. "You're in no position to make demands."

Vlad didn't glance at the churning, writhing mass mere inches from him. His gaze was all for Marie.

"I'm not afraid of your pets because I have personal experience with them. Their assault is agonizing, yet takes several minutes to be lethal. I, on the other hand, can explode your head off your shoulders in one-point-eight seconds, and once you're dead, they go back where they came from."

At that, I felt ridiculous for standing there, hand poised to strike. Guess my services wouldn't be needed after all!

Marie's candy-coated accent became hard. "You can burn objects and places, but you can't burn people unless you've touched them, and you have never touched me, Impaler."

Vlad laughed, low and insinuating. "Allow me to refresh your memory: you were human and running a liquor store on Dauphine Street. Pure chance that I was in New Orleans at the time. I detest the swamp, but I was traveling with Mencheres and he insisted on seeing Bones, who lived here back then."

"Many people know I ran a liquor store in my early years," Marie said, but from the new rasp to her voice, she was rattled.

Vlad's coppery gaze glinted with green. "How many people know that Gregor was there, too? He and I had the same sire, as you recall, so we were well acquainted with each other. That's why I accompanied him to see the woman he was considering adding to his line as a ghoul, if she proved useful. Took you ten more years to convince him of your worth, though, didn't it?"

Marie's knuckles shone through her skin as she gripped her chair as tightly as I had a few minutes ago.

"If this is true and you don't trust my unbound word that I am not the necromancer, why haven't you tried to kill me?"

Vlad's eyes changed from copper to pure emerald green. "Because while I *will* risk a war with your people if you are, there's no need to start one if you're not."

Marie leaned back, her expression icy even as a smile played about her lips. "I, too, would rather keep you as an adversary than make you or your allies my enemy."

With that, she dragged her palm across her ring, and a tiny point I hadn't noticed before scored a line in her flesh.

"I swear by my blood that I am not the necromancer you seek," she said as the red drops fell. "If my words are a lie, may my own blood turn against me as witness to my deceit."

I almost sucked in a breath, waiting. What would such a thing as someone's blood turning against them look like, anyway? Vlad must've had an idea, because after a tense few moments, he smiled, hoisting his glass and taking a sip as if fire, deadly ghosts, and threats hadn't occurred between his first taste of wine and his last one. I gave him a sharp look, as if to say, *Does this mean we're done threatening to kill her?*

His teeth flashed in a grin that I translated as *For now.*

I finally sat down, yet unease had me sending more currents into my right hand, which now sparked like a child's firework sprinkler. Marie glanced at it with more curiosity than concern.

"They say you can discern someone's worst sin with a single touch, plus read the past and find people in the present through objects they've handled. Is that true?"

"Most of the time," I said in a guarded tone.

Marie held out her hand in challenge. "Then tell me mine."

If I refused, it wouldn't go over well since Vlad had forced Marie to take a blood oath with magical consequences. Good thing he hadn't coated me in his aura this morning or I wouldn't be able to do anything except touch her and guess. I didn't want to know the Voodoo Queen's worst sin, but I took her hand anyway. She jerked from the voltage the contact released into her despite my trying to hold it back. Guess I hadn't tried hard enough. Moments later, I wasn't worried about how I'd electrocuted her.

I was in the hidden cellar beneath my house, glaring at the woman who was cradling her baby while desperately trying to shush it. I'd told her to leave the child upstairs, where it could have been explained as one of the servants' children, but she'd snuck it down here instead. When the child's whimper became louder, one of the runaway slaves moaned.

"They gonna hear us," she whispered. "They gonna kill us!"

"Shh!" I hissed, but she was right.

This patrol was known for their brutality,

and the slaves huddled in the small, dank cellar beneath my house had all fled after a plantation rebellion had left several of their white masters dead. No one would care about the cruelties the slaves had endured before the uprising, or whether or not these runaways had actually participated in the killings. No, their blood would flow because they had been in the vicinity when white blood was spilled, and whoever died fast would be considered lucky.

The child whimpered again and sucked in a breath as if filling up for a full-fledged wail. I looked at the terrified people I'd sworn to protect, several of whom were children, too. All were doomed once that baby's wail reached the patrol's ears, and in that single, frozen second, I made my choice.

I had been born free. They hadn't, and they deserved the same chances I'd had. I forced back the sob that tried to claw out of my throat as I ran toward the baby. If my life would be the only one lost, I'd gladly let the child's forthcoming squall lead the patrol here. But if they found us, everyone would die . . . unless I damned myself by ensuring that all except one lived. My heart felt like it exploded from anguish when I cut off the burgeoning cry the baby made by clamping my hand over the child's mouth . . .

I slammed back into the present, the charred walls of the tomb replacing the packed earth of the underground cellar where Marie had hidden the runaway slaves. I was horrified by what I'd relived even as my heart broke, still feeling the same pain Marie had felt when she did that awful, unimaginable act because she'd lived in an awful, unimaginable time when people of her color didn't even have the right to live, let alone have any expectation of hope, justice, or mercy.

"What did you see?" Her voice vibrated with command.

I didn't repeat her terrible act. Instead, I said the name she'd branded her soul with so she'd never forget the crime that had saved twenty-two lives by forever silencing one.

"Louise," I whispered.

She flinched at the baby's name, the pain in her gaze echoing the one I felt from the remainder of my link to her worst sin. Then, shockingly, her demeanor changed from a woman haunted by her past to a gracious Southern hostess again.

"Well. Since your abilities are real, it seems we each have something the other wants, don't we, Tepesh?"

Vlad's smile was filled with so much deadly intent; I found myself edging away out of pure primal instinct.

"Yes, we do. You can start by giving me the names of sorcerers strong enough to dabble in necromancy, and I'll finish by having Leila psychically read anyone whose darkest secret you simply *must* know."

Chapter 28

When Jacques closed the gates of the cemetery behind us, I was still overwhelmed. Marie had taken a rain check on having me read people for her, but that didn't make me feel better. If she wanted time to think about who she was selecting, then she was really going for the gold, and who knew what the repercussions of that would be? Still, she'd given us valuable information, and if we didn't defeat Szilagyi and get this curse off me, we wouldn't be around to worry about owing Marie a future debt.

We were halfway back to our hotel before I could form questions about the most basic parts of tonight's visit. "Why didn't you tell me *before* we went that you thought Marie might be the necromancer who cast the spell on me?"

Vlad glanced at me with amusement. "Because you're even worse at hiding your emotions than you are at lying."

True, but . . . "If you suspected her, why bring me with you?"

"Backup," he stated. At my questioning expression, he went on. "When Marie grants a meeting, she has specific terms. Only the person requesting it may attend, and that person is guaranteed safe passage to and from the meeting, which is why I didn't bring any of my guards. If, however, Marie was the necromancer, then I was going to kill her, but to do so, I needed you. As my wife, you are the only person allowed to go anywhere that I do, and also the only person who could have withstood Marie."

"Me? You're the one who could kill her in one-point-eight seconds. All I did was stand there and make a light show out of my hand."

He smiled slyly. "I can kill her that quickly now, since we shook hands to conclude our meeting, but before that, I'd never touched her."

I stared at him, some part urging me to close my gaping mouth, but the other too stunned to care.

"You *lied* to her?" I finally got out.

He shrugged. "I inferred. She didn't remember that I'd met her before with Gregor when she was human, which was true. However, I didn't touch her. I am very particular about that, as you know, though it's a fortunate for us that she does not."

"That's not inferring, that's bluffing!"

His grin was almost feral. "About touching her? Yes. About killing her? No. If she'd cast that spell, I would have made it across the room to burn her, Remnant attack or no Remnant attack. On the slight chance that I couldn't, you were there."

The notion almost had me sputtering. "If *you* couldn't withstand a Remnant attack long enough to torch her, I'd have *no* chance against them!"

He ran his hand down my arm, tracing the exact path where my old scar from the power line accident would have been.

"Cat can't control Remnants the way Marie can," he said, a lift of his brow implying, *amateurs, what are you going to do?* "Plus, the abilities she absorbs are temporary, but she's clever, so she thought up a way to keep her grave power, if she needed it in the future. Cat withdrew several vials of her own blood after she drank from Marie and stored them away. When she agreed to help me, she had me swallow one of those vials."

"Why? You can't absorb abilities." Or had he been concealing something else from me, too?

His mouth curled. "No, but their summoner is the only person they won't attack, unless held back by powers Cat hasn't mastered yet. When I drank blood containing grave power, the Remnants were tricked into thinking I was one of their summoners, too. That's why they didn't attack me when I came for you."

Wow. At the time, I'd thought that Cat must have been keeping them off us—"Wait, then why didn't they attack *me*?"

He continued to stroke my arm. "At first, I was so grateful to find you alive that I didn't pause to wonder. Later, the answer seemed simple: you are scorched earth to them."

I didn't understand. Then, I remembered Vlad's cruelly satisfied comment as he watched the Remnants tear into Szilagyi's guards. *They feed from energy and pain.* Ever since my power line accident, I'd had energy running all through me, yet it wasn't normal, organic energy. It was pure, electrified voltage, and apparently, the Remnants wanted no part of it.

"That's why I was your backup." I was stunned and admiring at the same time. "If Marie had called your bluff, the Remnants would've swarmed you but not me, and Marie wouldn't have expected that. Without her best weapon, I could have cut her down with my whip or forced her into contact with you. Either way, she'd be dead."

His expression was cold, yet his touch was anything but. "Yes. I trusted you with my life, Leila, and there is only one other person in this world of whom that statement is true."

Now I *really* felt humbled. He hadn't just trusted me with his life, which was incredible enough. He had also suppressed his fifteenth-century tendency to lock me away at the first sign of danger. Instead, he'd treated me as an equal by believing that both my abilities and my resolve would prove sufficient for the challenge.

Because words wouldn't nearly be enough to describe what that meant to me, I kissed him, trying to tell him with my lips and the arms I wrapped around him that I loved him more than anything in the world. His mouth moved over mine with an intensity that rivaled words, too, but he didn't need them. He dropped his shields and let his emotions spill over mine. The effect weakened my knees while causing my grip to tighten around him as if a thousand-foot chasm had opened up beneath me.

He broke the kiss far too soon, his gaze wary as he glanced around. It was barely eight p.m., so the French Quarter was filled with people, some of whom would be partying until dawn. Most of them felt human to me, but with the crowds, I couldn't be sure.

"Szilagyi would be foolish to attack in the heart of Marie's territory since she'd consider that an assault against her as well, but he's surprised me before," he muttered. "Come. We still have several things to acquire before we leave."

His kiss had roused my body and melted my mind, but at that, I snapped back to mental attention.

"Right, and thanks to the information Marie gave us, we're now in the spell-casting and necromancer-hunting business."

A passerby would have been charmed by his quick smile. I, however, recognized the danger it represented, as if rivulets of invisible blood dripped from his mouth.

"We're not the only ones who can't report the

use of magic to the Law Guardians. After everything Szilagyi has done, it's time we repay him in
kind."

I expected the spell-ingredient treasure hunt,
which consisted of Vlad and me going to various
parts of the city to get items that on the surface
seemed innocuous, but were intended to magically
set Szilagyi back on his ass. That part didn't take
long since Marie had given us an equivalent of a
shopping list plus addresses of where to procure
each specific item. What I didn't expect was where
we went next.

The hospice facility looked like a smaller, pret-
tier version of a hospital. Inside, beneath the heavy
scent of air fresheners, disinfectants, and cleaning
solvents, it smelled of grief and death more than
the cemetery we'd met Marie in.

"Why are we here?" I whispered to Vlad.

"Recruitment," he replied without bothering
to lower his voice. "Szilagyi killed dozens of my
people and more will fall before this is over. I can't
hold off on replenishing my numbers, and while
that includes changing over all the humans I'd been
grooming, I also need people Szilagyi won't recognize as being affiliated with me." Then, to the
receptionist, he said, "Tell me if you have any male
patients between the ages of twenty and fifty."

Since his eyes had been lit up, she didn't ask any
unnecessary questions. Just checked the computer

and then wrote out names and room numbers on a sticky note before passing it over.

Vlad took it, striding to the nearest room. I followed, still a little surprised by where we were, if not by what we were doing. When I thought of Vlad selecting people to join his line, I never expected him to look in places like this.

The first patient was a man who appeared to be in his early thirties, but whose body had aged from the cancer I could smell before we cleared the threshold. Vlad took one look at the pictures around his bedside showing a much healthier version of the man with his wife and children, then walked out.

"Not this guy?" I asked, with a heavy pang as I glanced back at the sleeping man.

"Too many entanglements," he said, holding up a hand at my expression. "What I'm offering is not a way back to their former lives. It's risk, frequent loneliness, and permanent removal from everyone they know. That means I don't choose fathers, or forcing them to abandon their families would make me even crueler than my reputation paints me to be."

"But can't we . . . do something for him?" I said, hanging back.

Vlad sighed. "Even if you distributed pints of your blood to every person here, in their condition, you'd only be adding weeks or months to their lives. Not saving them, as you want to. We're vampires, not God. We can only take a few, solitary people that the world has given up on and offer them another choice."

The coldly logical part of me accepted this even as the rest of me ached for the people we saw, both in this facility and the other three we visited. Out of the four hospices, Vlad found two people that matched his requirements, and out of those, only one wanted what he offered. To that man, Vlad gave a mouthful of his blood before instructing him to wait there until one of his people picked him up. The other got a new memory where he was never visited by strangers who broke the news that vampires were real, let alone the offer to become one.

The next places we went to were homeless shelters, where Vlad used his mind-reading abilities to narrow down recruits. He had a bigger harvest from those stops, eventually netting five guys who were left with instructions to wait for retrieval by Vlad's guards later. Finally, he took me to the last place I expected to look for potential new members of his line.

Death Row.

Chapter 29

The Louisiana State Penitentiary was a huge complex bordered on three sides by the Mississippi River. With guards patrolling on horseback and an entrance that resembled a visitors' welcome center, it looked more like a working ranch than a prison, if you ignored the high fences with layers of razor wire coiled around the tops.

Unlike the other places, Vlad was here for one specific person. "Clergy to see Darryl Meadows," he told the guard, the green in his gaze circumventing any requests for identification or questions since Vlad came off as anything but pious.

"Who's Darryl Meadows?" I asked as we drove to the section of the large compound that housed the Death Row inmates.

"Possibly an innocent man," Vlad replied. "He was imprisoned over twenty years ago on scant evidence and questionable testimony, but since all forensic evidence was lost, he can't request DNA testing to prove his innocence."

"You sound like you know a lot about him."

"I saw a documentary on the death penalty that mentioned him, among other inmates." At my raised brows, he continued almost defensively, "It was late, you were asleep, and there was *nothing* else on."

It was such a normal, human complaint that I laughed, imagining Vlad flipping through channels while muttering under his breath about the lack of decent viewing options. Then I added "secret documentary buff" to the list of things I knew about him. Like, for example, his love of vampire movies. His hatred of Dracula retellings aside, he'd once told me that the varied portrayals of vampirism in film amused him to no end.

"Well, it's easy enough to find out if Darryl is innocent," I said, holding up my right hand.

"Yes," Vlad said, his gaze glinting. "If he is, reading his mind will reveal if decades of unjust imprisonment have ruined him, or hardened him into the kind of man I'm looking for."

We needed more mind control to get through the additional security checkpoints before we were face-to-face with Darryl Meadows, a lean, handsome African-American man whose hazelnut brown gaze regarded us with suspicion when the guard left him alone in the room with us. Some mind control by Vlad ensured our privacy, plus he'd mesmerized the officers who monitored the video feed from the room. Thus, I didn't hesitate to break the first rule of visitation by reaching over the metal table and touching one of Darryl's manacled hands.

"He didn't do it," I said a few minutes later when I was back in my own mind. Darryl's worst sin had been not helping a fellow inmate when the man was jumped and murdered, but since a guard had participated in the crime, I couldn't blame him.

Darryl let out a weary scoff. "I've been saying that for over twenty years, but no one cares. Who're you, anyway? More attorneys? People from the Innocence Project?"

"We're vampires," Vlad said with his usual bluntness.

I let out a small laugh to fill the instant, disbelieving silence. "Bet you didn't expect to meet two of those today."

"Guard," Darryl called out, sounding pissed instead of tired now. "Get these crazy motherfuckers out of—"

His voice cut off abruptly when Vlad's eyes went green and he smiled wide enough to show his fangs.

"I don't have time for a detailed explanation, so understand this," Vlad said, staring into Darryl's eyes. "Vampires are real. We've existed for millennia, and we're not the only supernatural species above humans on the food chain."

Under the powerful effect of his gaze, Darryl had no choice except to believe. I had to give it to Vlad; this way was much faster than going through the usual motions of breaking the news, then dealing with a person's denial, questions, demands for proof, and hysterics, usually in that order.

"What do you want from me?" Darryl asked in a dull voice.

Vlad's smile disappeared as he leaned forward. "What would you do if I made you what I am tonight, giving you more power and abilities than you could ever imagine?"

"I'd leave this place," Darryl replied, still in the monotone that said his answers were compelled by Vlad's gaze.

"Wouldn't you want to kill everyone who put you here?" Vlad almost purred. "The police, judges, lawyers, witnesses?"

"Bernstein," Darryl said after thinking for a moment. "Cop knew I didn't do it, that's why he planted the evidence in my car. Phillips, too. Guard's murdered more people than half the inmates in here."

"Why do you want to know who he'd like to kill?" I asked.

"I want a hardened man, not a mass-murdering, pathologically vengeful one," Vlad said. "There's only room for one of those in my line right now, and that's me." To Darryl, he asked, "And would you give up your humanity to leave this place, knowing you would never see anyone from your former life again?"

"My family gave up on me a long time ago." Not even his monotone could remove all of the pain from that single sentence. "To them, I'm already dead. If I don't get out, I'll be dead for real in two weeks, so if there's a way to live, I want it."

Vlad glanced away from Darryl, gesturing to an upper corner of the room. "See that camera, Leila? Short-circuit it."

"Are we actually about to attempt a prison break from Death Row?" Would vampire mind control be enough to accomplish that without resorting to violence, too?

Vlad's instant laughter made my suggestion seem preposterous. "No. That would cause far too much attention."

Okay, then I didn't know why short-circuiting the camera was necessary, but I did it. By the time I turned around, Vlad was already behind Darryl, his mouth at the other man's neck.

"You're doing it *now*?" I asked in disbelief.

He paused, fangs mere millimeters from Darryl's throat. "You really need me to explain why sending one of my men to pick him up later won't work under these circumstances?"

"But—"

Vlad didn't wait for me to ask more questions. He bit deeply and Darryl shuddered, a harsh grunt escaping him as he tried to jerk away, but the restraints and Vlad's grip kept him immobilized. Only Darryl's eyes were able to move, and when his gaze landed on me, I couldn't look away.

I'd seen many people die through my abilities. Lately, the deaths I'd seen had been in person, sometimes with me wielding the killing blow. This was different, maybe because I'd never seen someone being changed over before. I'd been unconscious during my transformation, and Vlad hadn't drunk me to death as he was now doing with Darryl. I'd bled out from the effects of Cynthiana's spell and a nasty car accident, so all Vlad had done was refill me with his blood before it was too late.

Or, I'd thought that was all he'd done. After Darryl's heart stopped beating and Vlad opened his own jugular with a single hard slice, positioning Darryl's mouth over it, the real work began. I felt it in the surge of energy that seemed to explode from Vlad, sending almost painful vibrations throughout the room. As potent as that was, his dropped shields revealed that the majority of his power was being funneled into Darryl, willing new life into him with far more force than the blood that Vlad forced Darryl to swallow.

Soon, that slack mouth began to seal over Vlad's neck, until Darryl was biting and sucking with a ferocity that made the knife Vlad had used before unnecessary. He held that dark head to his throat and willed more of his power into Darryl, until, with a violent tremor that snapped his restraints free from the table, Darryl went still.

Vlad wiped the blood from Darryl's mouth before he let the man slump forward onto the table. Then he wiped his own neck and rebuttoned his shirt, covering the stray red blotches still dotting his skin. *That's it?* I almost said, but the answer was obvious. From start to finish, the entire process of life, death, and undead transformation had taken only about five minutes.

Vlad looked at me, his mouth curled into a slight smile. "Did you still have a question, Leila?"

"Yeah," I said, still processing what I'd seen. "How do we get him out of here before he wakes up and eats everyone?"

Vlad opened the door, gesturing the guard over with a casual swipe. "This man has suffered a fatal heart attack," he said, his eyes turning green. "Do all of your normal documentation for accidental deaths, but do them quickly. The body will be picked up by the coroner in exactly three hours."

"Yes, sir," the guard replied.

"Coroner, huh?" I said, with a knowing look.

He pulled out his cell phone, texting with his usual blinding speed. "Yes, as well as a few extra passengers."

Vlad mesmerized several more key personnel on our way out, until no one would question his version of Darryl's death or remember that we'd come, let alone question the video disruption in the room during the inmate's "heart attack." By the time he was finished—a mere half hour after leaving Darryl—I was shaking my head in admiration. He was right; a prison break would have been ridiculously splashy by comparison.

When we were back in our car, pulling away from the prison, I said, "I have another question. Why do you only pick men?"

He almost rolled his eyes before glancing at me. "Perhaps because we're recruiting soldiers for a supernatural war."

I wasn't letting him off that easily. "Don't think it's escaped my notice that over eighty percent of the vampires in your line are men, too."

"In my time, nearly every army was exclusively male."

"Don't give me that 'I'm from the fifteenth century' defense," I said with a snort. "Marty told me that all new vampires start out with roughly the same power level, with lineage and character making the difference later as to strength and abilities. Your people come from all cultures, races, and social statuses, yet they're mostly one big sausage fest."

"You want me to subject women to the brutal circumstances of war?" His tone was scornful. "You of all people know what would happen if one of them was captured."

"And you of all people know that being a male

doesn't always shield you from that," I replied, my voice soft. "My point is, when you're recruiting, you should give women the same options you're giving men, and let them decide what they can and can't handle."

He opened his mouth as if to argue further. Then he shut it, flashing me a genial smile.

"Very persuasive points. Therefore, feel free to make as many female vampires as you deem necessary for this war."

"Me?" I exclaimed "No. I mean, I don't know how—"

"You saw: bite, bleed, replenish," he said, ticking the items off on his fingers. "Easier than baking a cake."

I glared at him. "My ass it's easier, and have you forgotten the tiny issue where I electrocute everyone I touch?"

He made a dismissive gesture. "Not to worry, you'll bleed them out long before you electrocute them to death."

But I didn't want to make any new vampires. Transformation issue aside, the responsibilities were weightier than having a child, and I wasn't ready for that. Plus, I was still struggling with some of the aspects of vampirism myself; how could I be the sire of someone who knew even less about it than I did?

I tried again. "We were talking about *your*

sexism, Vlad. My making female vampires has nothing to do with that."

"Oh, but it does," he said, barely controlling the twitch to his lips. "You wanted equality? Here it is. Don't bother to thank me—your expression is gratifying enough."

Chapter 30

 I was getting used to waking up in different places than I'd fallen asleep in. This time, it was Vlad's plane, with him next to me and a thermos of warm blood already waiting.

"Where're we going?" I asked when I finished my breakfast. Or dinner, considering it was dark outside the plane's windows. Vlad must have brought his new recruits with us. Several people were behind the curtain that separated where we were from the seats closer to the cockpit, and from the multiple heartbeats, at least half of them were human.

"Slovenia," he replied. "We're almost there, in fact."

"Back to Europe, huh?"

"It's most likely where Szilagyi is. Both his prior lairs were in Europe and he knows I'll return to my own soil soon. When I do, he'll want to be close enough to take advantage."

That's what I would do, hung unspoken in the air between us. Sometimes, their similarities unnerved me, but where it mattered most, Vlad and Szilagyi were nothing alike. Take, for example, Vlad's inherent nationalism. *My own soil.* Romania would always be his home, no matter how many houses he had elsewhere.

Familiar scents behind the curtain had me inhaling with a single, sharp breath. "My dad and Gretchen are on the plane?"

"Yes." Vlad's expression darkened. "He wanted to speak with you, if you're willing to see him."

He did? As if they'd become sentient, my hands began to fly around my body, smoothing my sleep-tousled hair and brushing imaginary lint from my dress, a soft, long black sheath I hadn't fallen asleep in.

Vlad watched me, but I couldn't read anything from his chiseled, striking features.

"No need for that. You're beautiful, Leila. You always have been, no matter your appearance."

"Doesn't appearance make up the majority of beauty?" I said, trying to mask my nervousness with a quip.

"No." His voice was low, but it vibrated with intensity. "Not in the only way it matters."

He pulled me to him, kissing me with enough passion to muss my hair back to its former, unruly state. By the time he lifted his head, my mouth and other parts of me were tingling and I could care less what I looked like.

Vlad raised his voice and said something in Romanian. I translated the word "father," which was icy water on my libido. Moments later, the curtain separating the two sections of the plane pulled back, revealing Samir and Hugh Dalton.

"*Voivode*," the handsome, black-haired guard said, bowing before letting the curtain drop. My father stood on this side of it, his gaze flicking from me to Vlad and back again. His features might have been schooled into his usual officer's mask, but from his scent, he was more nervous about this than I was.

"Hello, Leila," he said uncomfortably.

"Hugh," Vlad replied before I could say anything, his mouth curling into a hostile smirk. "You've finally summoned the courage to face your daughter. You'll be relieved to know that she recently fed, so you needn't fear that she'll go for your throat if you come any closer."

My gaze slid to him with mild shock. Talk about not trying to smooth things over with small talk!

"Hi, Dad," I said, rising out of habit. Then I didn't know what to do. Go over and shake his hand? Attempt a hug or a peck on the cheek? Neither sounded like a good idea, so I just stood there, feeling the awkwardness creep into my bones.

My father cleared his throat. "You, ah, look good." He sounded surprised, which was more than a little insulting until I remembered the last images he would have seen of me: bald, skinned, and screaming in agony.

The memory brought back a shiver I couldn't suppress. Vlad rose, too, his arm settling almost casually around my shoulders.

"You're unnerved by me, so you wish I'd leave the two of you alone to talk?" Vlad snorted. "Your personal discomfort means nothing to me, Hugh . . . wait, that's not true. I enjoy it."

My father stiffened, either at the words or how Vlad had read his mind.

"Vlad, what are you doing?" I asked in a low voice.

He didn't reply. Just continued to aim his fuck-you smile at my dad, as if daring him to get offended enough to leave. Wow, did he really hate my father that much? If so, why had he brought him on the same plane with us? He hadn't the other times he'd flown my dad and Gretchen to the same places we'd been to . . .

All at once, I realized why Vlad was acting this way. By provoking my father, he was testing his resolve. If Hugh wasn't truly serious about wanting to mend some fences with me, he could use Vlad's taunts as an excuse for walking away. Again.

And so could I, came my next realization. Vlad wasn't just doing this to test my dad. He was also providing a balm for the wound he expected my father to inflict on me. After all, if I was mad at Vlad for supposedly running my father off, then I wasn't hurting as much over my dad rejecting me again.

I slid my arm around Vlad's waist. Even with his aura tamped down and his emotions shuttered, he pulsated with more energy than a live wire. He could decimate the man glaring at him, yet my dad didn't know what I did: that love motivated Vlad, even in his current rudeness. Talk about beauty that defied appearances.

"Dad," I said steadily, "I want to talk to you, too, but Vlad stays. I know you don't like him and he's not being shy about how pissed he is at you, but it's vampire custom that a husband and wife remain together under all circumstances, so you need to get used to us being a package deal."

Vlad's shields cracked and a wave of pleasure rubbed my subconscious. In response, I tightened my grip around him. After everything we'd been through, I meant my declaration of unity, and it covered more than this exchange with my father.

I couldn't read minds, but my father's scent sharpened and his leg muscles tensed as if readying to carry him away. I braced, sad that his impending rejection felt familiar. While I still had the chance, I told him what I needed to say.

"I love you, Dad, and I want a relationship with you, but I don't need one, and that has nothing to do with my changing into a vampire. A long time ago, I learned that I could survive without your approval or your love."

"Leila," he began, taking a step toward me.

"Don't." Briefly, I closed my eyes. "You might

want to forgive me for my telling Mom that you cheated on her, but deep down, you haven't. That's why you keep pushing me away, but here's the truth: I didn't cause Mom to leave you. You did by your actions. I told her about your infidelity out of spite and that's my sin, but she forgave me." My voice strengthened. "She forgave both of us, and she still loves us, too. I felt it when I saw her after I died and before Vlad brought me back."

He took in a harsh breath, his hand trembling so hard that the cane he walked with began to shake. Tears began to trickle in slow trails down my cheeks. Not of sadness this time; of joy at the memory of my glimpse of my mother.

"I'd forgotten the little lines that crinkled around her eyes when she smiled," I said, my voice huskier. "Or how she smelled like rainwater and freesia. And I hadn't realized how much I needed to know that she forgave me until I felt it within every corner of my soul. Maybe you've needed to know that, too."

A tear slipped down his weathered, lined face, and he bowed his head as if embarrassed that I'd seen it.

"Was she . . . where she was, was she happy?" he rasped.

I crossed the short distance to my father, seeing his startled expression as he looked up to find me right in front of him. That's right; my movements would be a blur to him now.

"Yes, she was happy," I said, letting the light out of my eyes. Whatever did or didn't happen in our relationship, I needed him to know that, and if it meant implanting that knowledge with vampire mind control, so be it.

He smiled with a joy I hadn't seen in years, breaking my heart because it momentarily transformed his face into the one I remembered from my childhood. I couldn't stop myself from touching his cheek even as I tried to memorize how he looked.

"I love you, Dad," I whispered, drawing down the power in my gaze. That, he had to choose to believe for himself. Then I left him and walked back over to Vlad. "Why don't you think things over for a little while?" I said in a normal, controlled voice. "Maybe we can talk again in the near future."

He blinked as if surprised to realize that, in effect, he'd been dismissed. Then he swiped his cheek and nodded once.

"Yes. That would be . . . nice." He stumbled over the last word, probably because Vlad was still smiling at him in a way that said he'd enjoy discovering how fast my father could bleed out.

"Take care of yourself," I said, hoping that Vlad didn't air any of those thoughts.

My father turned to go, then paused by the curtain. "I know what you're doing is dangerous, so please, be careful. That video . . . I died a little inside watching it. I won't ever be the father you deserve, but human or vampire, I still love you."

He let the curtain fall behind him, not giving me a chance to respond. Maybe that was for the best. We'd both promised to forget the past before and hadn't been able to, so perhaps it was time we stopped trying to do that and tried instead to accept each other for who we were, flaws, baggage, and all.

Gretchen barged through the curtain moments later. "Tell your goon to back down, he won't listen to me," she said with a wave at Samir, who was right behind her.

The guard said something rapidly in Romanian, and I'd heard versions of the same thing enough before to know that Samir was asking permission to bodily remove my sister.

"Leave her; she's fine," I told him.

Samir hesitated a moment before bowing to me, then going back behind the curtain.

"What happened with Dad?" Gretchen asked at once. "Did you two fight? He looked upset, and he was wiping his face."

"No. We didn't fight, although Vlad might have been a little rough on him," I summarized.

He gave me a sardonic look. "Ask any of my former prisoners if that resembles what I do when I'm being 'a little rough.'"

"Just because you didn't torture him doesn't mean you weren't rough, but I know why you did it." I threaded my fingers through his hair. "Thank you for trying to protect me."

The barest smile touched his mouth. "I prefer simply killing people who hurt you. Much less complicated that way."

"Then you showed a lot of restraint," I said, smiling back because I knew that my dad had been in no danger. "And because I haven't told you this nearly enough, I love you."

His arms encircled me and he bent his head, but before his lips brushed mine, my sister's voice rang out.

"In case Leila hasn't made it clear, you're not allowed to kill my dad," Gretchen said, sounding aggravated.

I rolled my eyes as I turned to look at her. "You really think he'd do that?"

"If Dad pisses him off enough," was Gretchen's instant response. "Killing is kind of your husband's thing, or haven't you bothered to Google 'Vlad Dracul' yet?"

"At least you didn't add an A at the end of the D-word, or I'd be talking him into not killing *you* next," I said irreverently. At her widened gaze, I laughed.

"Gretchen! Vlad isn't going to kill you, Dad, or anyone else who isn't directly threatening him, okay? Stop believing everything you read online."

"Notice how *he* isn't agreeing to that," she pointed out.

I looked at Vlad, whose brows rose in false innocence as if to say, *Who, me?*

"Vlad," I drew out. "Come on. You're scaring her."

His mouth twitched. "Fear *is* the beginning of wisdom, and your sister needs to start somewhere."

I made an exasperated noise. "He already promised not to hurt my family back when we started dating," I told Gretchen. "You don't have anything to worry about and neither does Dad."

At that, her frown cleared. "Oh, okay. He'd do anything for you. That much I figured out."

"Then you're not as simple-minded as you appear," Vlad murmured, but thankfully, Gretchen didn't catch that. She was onto the next subject already.

"When do we land? The homeless guys you picked up ate all the food hours ago and I'm starving."

As if on cue, the plane began to descend, dropping a little more abruptly than normal, but maybe we'd hit an air pocket.

"Looks like now—"

I didn't finish my sentence. The plane went from a steeper-than-usual slant to a full nose dive, all so fast I would have slammed into the ceiling like Gretchen did, if not for Vlad's grip on me. Gretchen screamed, hitting the seats next as the plane's trajectory briefly made her bounce from the ceiling to the floor. My stomach lurched nauseatingly as I grabbed her, gripping her so hard she screamed in pain this time.

"*Ce faci?*" Samir's shout rose above the other

passengers' screams. Some part of my mind translated it as "What are you doing?" but the rest of me was too shocked to care what he was saying. All I could focus on was what was happening. Moments ago, I hadn't seen any lights outside the windows. Now, I did, and they looked like they were rushing toward us.

We weren't landing. We were crashing.

Chapter 31

 Everything that happened next happened so fast, it reminded me of the first time I'd seen Marty move with inhuman speed: I couldn't do anything except stare, struck stupid by what my eyes were processing, yet my mind still refused to believe.

Vlad's grip on me turned to steel, then he was flying us toward the front of the plane with me yanked against him and Gretchen clutched in my arms. We didn't even reach the curtain before we were bombarded by bodies hurtling at us from the plane's downward velocity. The horrible sound of overstressed metal mixed with screams, forming a deafening screech. Then the rapid changes in cabin pressure hit me with almost as much force as the multiple limbs that struck us as Vlad forced his way through the living barriers between him and the front of the plane.

"*Este prea tarziu*! *Ne vom prabusi*!" someone screamed. "We're going to hit!"

Vlad shouted something back and whipped me around until I was facing him. "Grab my neck," he ordered. "I have Gretchen."

I must have done it, because the next thing I knew, Vlad snatched my father from the writhing, screaming mass of people. Then we were sucked sideways with such force, I felt like an ant that had gotten swept up in a vacuum. Darkness and light flashed around us, too fast to pick one point to focus on, followed by a bright orange glow below and a *boom* I felt more than heard.

We landed hard a few moments later, the orange glow about a mile away, but the stench of burning fuel already reaching us. Vlad set Gretchen and my dad down, and another odor made me realize that Gretchen had pissed herself, either from terror or the voltage she'd absorbed when I first grabbed her. Before I could check to see if she was okay, Vlad gently pushed me down next to my father.

"Leila," he said in a calm tone, "you need to shock your father's chest now. His heart has stopped."

That snapped me out of whatever stunned inertia that had gripped me since I realized the plane was crashing. With a strangled sob, I ripped open my father's shirt, exposing his chest. Then I laid both palms against it and released a current that made his body spasm. When I pressed my ear against his chest afterward, panic filled me.

No breathing, no heartbeat. Nothing.

"You need to give him mouth-to-mouth while I keep trying," I said in a gasp, tears making everything blurry. Then I began to push on my father's chest the way I'd seen people do in the movies, pausing to let Vlad blow air into his lungs between compressions. After several seconds, I said "Clear!" out of senseless desperation, and shocked him again.

This time, I heard a few faint *buh-bumps* before things went ominously silent once more. I began chest compressions again, blowing into his mouth myself because I couldn't stand even those brief seconds of not *doing* something. Then, I shocked him again, using enough current to raise his back all the way off the ground for a few moments. When his body returned to its prone position, I pressed my ear to his chest again, praying.

Buh-boom . . . buh-boom . . . buh-boom . . .

Now that his heart had finally started beating, I laid my head on the ground next to him and cried from relief.

"I don't understand." Samir sounded as dazed as I felt. Maybe that's why he was speaking in English. He usually had to be reminded to do that around me.

Relief over my father had turned to sorrow when we met up with the rest of our group and saw how few of us there were. Aside from me, Vlad, Gretchen, and my dad, only Samir, Petre, and two of the new human recruits had made it. Everyone else perished when the plane slammed into the ground after a near vertical dive. Not even vampires could survive that kind of impact, let alone the resulting fireball that had lit up the sky, and Vlad and Samir were the only vampires who could fly away before the doomed plane crashed.

Vlad had saved me and my family, and Samir had grabbed Petre and the nearest two humans in the frantic seconds before he'd flown out the exit door Vlad had torn open. To my everlasting gratitude, Marty hadn't been on this flight. His dislike of Vlad had caused him to elect to stay behind with Darryl while the new vampire overcame his hunger.

"Claude and Erin looked right through me," Samir went on. "I've known them both for over two hundred years, yet they were like strangers when I tried to wrestle them off the controls to save the plane."

Vlad's head snapped up. "Did they do anything else odd?"

"You mean aside from killing themselves along with several other people?" I asked in disbelief.

Vlad didn't respond to that, only continued to stare at Samir. "Well?" he prodded.

"They didn't seem angry," Samir said slowly, as if trying to remember. "Or afraid, or sorry, or anything I would have expected based on what they were doing. Claude and Erin were just . . . blank, aside from their determination to crash the plane."

Vlad muttered a particularly foul course in Romanian. "When we were in Vegas, did they ever leave the hotel to feed?"

Samir looked startled. "Of course. It was Vegas."

Another ear-scorching curse later, I understood. "I acted that way when I tried to kill myself, didn't I? So you think the necromancer found a way to spell the pilots, too."

God knows I'd felt blank beyond a single-minded need to take my own head off. I hadn't cared about anything else, and I'm sure I'd looked right through Vlad when he stopped me, just as Claude and Erin had looked right through Samir when he tried to stop them from forcing the plane into a fatal dive.

"It would explain why people loyal to me for nearly three hundred years suddenly attempted to kill me," Vlad ground out. "Or at least, kill my wife and the remainder of my most-trusted men, since Szilagyi would know that's who I'm traveling with."

Szilagyi. Even when we thought we were going on the offensive against him, we turned out to be fighting for our lives again. How were we expected to take him down if we had to give a wary eye to the people around us, wondering which one of them might have been magically motivated to kill us next?

On the heels of despair, the solution popped into my mind.

"Everyone needs to drink the potion I did," I told Vlad. "If it's a lesser spell, it'll cure them. If it's the same one, it'll temporarily turn them blue. Either way, we'll know who Szilagyi's necromancer has gotten to and who he hasn't."

Vlad pulled out his cell phone, dialing. "Mencheres," he said moments later. "I need the ingredients for your cure."

Chapter 32

 We'd crashed in Slovenia, but we didn't go to Vlad's house there. No surprise, he no longer trusted whoever might be waiting for him. We trusted Samir and Petre because they'd tried to save the plane, which meant that they weren't spelled, and the two surviving men from the homeless shelter were human, so the necromancer wouldn't bother with them.

Instead, we went to Lake Misurina, in Italy. On the outside, the small hotel Vlad pulled up to struck me as a formerly grand structure that time and progress had left behind. It also had a supremely gothic feel, with mountains that towered like dark giants behind it, while the lake in front reflected the hotel and backdrop as if it were a huge, glassy mirror.

Inside, the hotel appeared spotless and renovated with all the latest amenities. It also wasn't occupied, which became obvious when Vlad walked us right past the empty reception desk.

"Is this place empty?" I asked, my voice echoing off the high ceilings in the grand entryway.

"Most of the time," he replied. "This is a safe house for members of my line, so it's kept up by locals, but they don't remember why it hasn't been reopened as a business."

"Whatever, please tell me there's a hospital nearby," Gretchen said, helping our dad keep his balance since his cane had blown up with the plane. "He needs a doctor."

I also didn't like the grayish tone to my father's skin, but his heartbeat had been steady the entire way here, which consisted of driving and flying via Vlad Air. That might have given my father another heart attack, if Vlad hadn't mesmerized him beforehand into thinking that we drove the whole way.

"I'm fine," my father gritted out. "I just need to lie down for a little while."

"No doctors," Vlad stated. "We can't have our presence exposed to more people than absolutely necessary. Besides, what I have will heal you faster and more thoroughly."

At that, my father whitened. "I will *not* drink your blood."

"And I will *not* let you die after I soiled my mouth with yours breathing air into your lungs," Vlad replied at once. "Leila loves you and she's been through enough without dealing with the loss of her father, so you don't get to refuse, Hugh."

I didn't know which appeared to shock my dad more: discovering that Vlad had given him mouth-to-mouth, or hearing that he had no choice about drinking Vlad's blood. I was still very concerned about my dad's health, but I didn't want him to be forced to do something against his will. Maybe if I talked to him, he'd see that this was his best choice, and it could be my blood instead of Vlad's, too.

"Dad, I think you should—"

"Open wide," Vlad interrupted, then slashed his wrist with a fang and clapped it over my father's mouth.

My dad's eyes bugged, but with Vlad gripping him from behind, he couldn't dislodge the red-smeared wrist from his open mouth. He could only attempt to kick Vlad in silent, furious protest, but with one leg crippled, he was having a hard time doing that, too.

"I'll get to that next," Vlad muttered.

I watched this, torn. On one hand, I hated seeing my father manhandled. On the other, this was for his own good and it beat the hell out of seeing him dead, which I briefly had.

"This won't be a regular occurrence, Dad," I said, trying to make the best out of a bad situation for him. "When it's safe, we'll get you to a doctor and you won't have to drink vampire blood again."

"Of course not," Vlad said, shocking me by dragging my dad down onto the floor next. "At least, not after this."

With that, his hand crushed my father's bad knee before I could scream at him to stop. Then he bit his wrist again, willing out such a spurt of blood into my dad's mouth that it overflowed on both sides. My father coughed and gagged, his shout of anguish cut off by that crimson flow.

Gretchen gasped. "Look!"

I didn't need to because I hadn't taken my eyes off my father's knee. A split second after seeing Vlad crush it into pulp, I realized what he was doing. Months ago, he'd said he could heal my dad's knee. My father must have remembered that, too, because his disbelief turned to understanding as the bloody, misshapen lump began to knit itself back together.

If Vlad hadn't crushed it first, the healing properties of vampire blood wouldn't have caused new bone, tissue, and tendons to replace the old, damaged ones. I didn't need to see my dad bend his leg in a way that he hadn't been able to do in years to know that the "irreparable" injury from the roadside bomb that had crippled him was now gone.

Vlad forced him to swallow one final gulp, then he released him, giving him a charming smile as he stood over him.

"If you think this is unforgivable, wait until you see what I'm going to do to my *other* father-in-law."

At that, Gretchen finally found her voice. "You're a bigamist? Leila, did you know this?"

"That wife died over five hundred years ago," I said, watching my father's expression to judge if he was going to lose it. "Dad, I know you're upset . . ."

"Don't coddle him; if nothing else, he's a soldier," Vlad said, drilling my father with a hard stare. "You've seen my abilities, yet if the vampire who sired me were still alive today, I would be considered weak compared to him. That's how powerful he was, and when I first realized it, I was terrified, but I surrendered my humanity to him because it was the best way I could protect my country and my family."

He glanced at me next, his stare no less hard, but the emotions that spilled over mine when he dropped his shields were wave after wave of raw, unadulterated love.

"She is my family and my country now, so there is nothing I won't do for her, including healing a man who keeps failing her. You're angry that I gave you blood, strengthening you and repairing the damage you'd suffered from a previous battle?" His tone became matter-of-fact. "You should have begged me to, just like hundreds of years ago, I begged someone far more frightening than me to do the same."

Once he finished speaking, he held out his arm to me. I stared at it, my emotions in a maelstrom. Part of me was upset at Vlad for his complete disregard of my father's wishes. Even if my dad was wrong, he was a grown man who was entitled to be. The

other part of me—vampire? survivalist?—agreed
with what he'd done. My dad was letting stubborn-
ness dictate his actions, and in a war where both
his daughters could become collateral damage, he
shouldn't. Vlad had made sure that Dad's health or
former injury wouldn't be a weakness our enemies
could exploit, and a career military man like my
father would know that they would, if he stopped
being so angry about his circumstances.

So, after only a second's hesitation, I took Vlad's
arm. Like I'd told my father earlier, we were a package deal now, which meant whatever issues we had
would be worked out together.

Samir coughed to get our attention as he came
over to us, Petre and the other crash survivors
behind him. "I've been here before, so I can show
you where to go to get cleaned up."

"Great," Gretchen said, tearing her gaze away
from Dad's newly healed knee at last. "I need a
shower like I've never needed one before."

We'd lost all our spell ingredients in the plane
crash, so our plan to make magical versions of grenades was put on hold. Instead, Vlad took me with
him to get what we needed for the "cure," which I
now referred to as the spell-detector test.

"Maybe I should stay with my family, see if Dad
can be reasoned with," I'd suggested.

"Not a chance," had been his reply. "If the spell
on you reactivates, you'll slaughter them and your-

self. Only I am strong enough to stop you, so we stay together."

Selfishly, I preferred that anyway. The fastest way to travel was to have him fly us, and with the cover of darkness, it was the least conspicuous, too. Still, it took the remainder of the night to get everything we needed. The last thing I saw before passing out in Vlad's arms was light breaking over the mountains behind the hotel, the lake reflecting the image as though I were seeing double.

The next thing I saw was Gretchen, peering at me curiously from her crouched position a few feet away.

"If she bites you, it's your own fault," Samir said in an exasperated tone. "You should never get that close to a new vampire who's just waking up."

"'S going on?" I mumbled, looking around. I was in a small, windowless room that I recognized as a vampire holding cell. My hands were manacled together, but my right hand was also covered in about a foot of rubber, which had been taped onto it like a cartoon-sized boxing glove.

"Where's Vlad?" I asked, coming fully awake at the realization that only Gretchen and Samir were with me.

"Sleeping," Samir said, shaking his head. "Had to force him to, but he can't keep running on hate and blood alone. That's why you're trussed up like this. He keeps burning your skin off while you sleep, which seems to keep the spell at bay, but if it kicks in again, he'd hear you by the time you worked yourself free to hurt yourself."

"You look dead when you sleep," Gretchen added, as if I'd ever want to know that. "It's kind of freaky."

"Thanks," I muttered, sitting up. As soon as I was vertical, Samir shoved a covered thermos at me.

"Courtesy of one of the tourists at the next hotel, not that he remembers," he said, smiling.

The blood was no longer warm, but I drank it to the last drop, my glare daring Gretchen to comment. She didn't, just watched with her mouth curled in repugnance. Right. As if this was grosser than how she always ordered her steaks cooked rare.

"I'd totally do the vampire thing if I could skip the drinking blood part," she stated when I was done.

Samir let out a strangled noise, as if he'd almost swallowed his tongue. The former Janissary who'd so impressed Vlad with his fighting skills that Vlad had made Samir part of his line, even when Vlad had hated "Turks," apparently couldn't handle the thought of Gretchen as a vampire. Guess there were some things that were too frightening even for a five-hundred-year-old vampire who'd captained the Sultan's guard as well as Vlad the Impaler's.

"We have to drink it all the time," Samir said, emphasizing those last three words. "Sometimes, buckets and buckets of it."

I stifled my laugh at the look on Gretchen's face. She'd deserved that fallacy.

"Since I'm awake and not suffering from any homicidal impulses, can I get out of these?" I asked, rattling my chains.

Samir glanced up at the ceiling. "Five hours, that's a decent rest," he said, almost to himself.

"Vlad's only slept five hours?" I winced. "Never mind. I'll stay down here like this."

Samir went over to the corner of the room, pressing numbers into a keypad. "It's dusk, so he might be awake now anyway. I'll check. If he is, there's no need for you to stay down here."

"Gretchen, go with him," I said at once.

She wouldn't have noticed his shudder, not with how fast he suppressed it. "I'll be *right* back," Samir promised. "Gretchen, Leila's chain is three feet long, so stay back at least three feet and you'll be safe."

"She said she's fine, go," my sister replied. Once Samir left, the solid rock door closed behind him. Gretchen rolled her eyes. "You have *no* idea how irritating he can be."

"You don't say?" I replied dryly.

She missed the inference. "Seriously, Samir was more restrictive than Dad while we were in Vegas, and in New Orleans, I wasn't even allowed to leave the hotel. I mean, we were right in the French Quarter, but Samir wouldn't even let me take one of those Haunted History tours . . . which reminds me, did you send me a weird text the other day?"

"A text? No," I said, not adding that I didn't

text because my electricity issues short-circuited all but the most elaborately protected cell phones.

She grunted. "Huh, thought it had to be you since it was a link to an article about an underground Dracula dungeon being found—"

"What?" I interrupted, alarmed. "Someone sent you a link about Dracula stuff?"

Was this Szilagyi's way of taunting us that he'd found my family? It couldn't be random spam; what were the odds of someone *accidentally* texting Vlad's only living sister-in-law with an article about Dracula?

"What phone number did it come from?" I pressed. Maybe we could trace it back to the source.

"It was an out-of-country number, but when I called it, it was disconnected," Gretchen said, not catching the fear in my voice. "You don't think your husband did it, do you?"

"Not a chance," I said grimly. "Vlad would sooner stab himself in the heart with silver than advertise any new Dracula hype . . ."

"Leila?" Gretchen prodded when my voice trailed off and I didn't say anything for several moments.

"You say that the article was about an underground dungeon?" I said, an idea forming in my mind.

Gretchen sighed. "Yeah, guess historians or something think they've found the place where he was imprisoned as a child—"

"Where?" I interrupted more urgently.

"I don't know, somewhere." Gretchen shrugged.

I resisted my urge to shake her. "What about numbers? Were there any numbers after the link to the article?"

She gave me an irritable look. "That was two countries and a plane crash ago, so I don't remember. I didn't know I'd have to study the thing because there would be a quiz."

"Give me your phone and let me see it," I demanded.

"I can't, it blew up in the plane crash, remember?"

Right. I was now so wired that I'd forgotten that. "Doesn't matter, I'll look up the articles to get the location myself," I said, then yelled, "Samir, let me out of here!"

Chapter 33

Vlad glanced at what I typed into his default search engine page and annoyance grated along my subconscious.

"This is why you needed to use my laptop? If this is a joke, Leila, I'm not amused."

"I know, you hate anything to do with the word Dracula," I said, clicking on the first link that came up. "That's why you'd never look at these on your own and why none of your people would mention them to you, either. It's also why Szilagyi's first lair was under the castle you lived in when you were human. He knew you wouldn't be caught dead near that tourist trap."

"Your point?" Vlad said, sounding no less irritated.

I found what I was looking for, then nearly shoved the laptop toward him. "Read this."

Vlad glanced at the article, a frown darkening his brow. "As usual, lies. Mehmed didn't relocate his palace to Tokat until years after I was released, so I was never there—"

"Vlad," I interrupted. "Say you're Maximus. You're watched all the time because Szilagyi still doesn't quite trust you, so you can't leave any written messages at the drop points. You also can't risk contacting any of your old allies because you don't know who Szilagyi's necromancer has bespelled. So, how do you relay information about where Szilagyi is without getting caught?" I tapped the screen for emphasis. "Maybe by texting an article link like this to Gretchen. She's someone Szilagyi's necromancer wouldn't bother with because she's human, yet she's also in regular contact with me, and thus by extension, you."

He looked at the article again, rage sweeping across my emotions when he pieced together what I hadn't said yet.

"If so, then my boyhood prison is where Szilagyi has been hiding." The words were coated with so much scorching wrath, I was surprised smoke didn't pour from his mouth. "He chose it because the site of my torture and rape would be the very *last* place I'd ever return to."

And with Szilagyi's sick sense of irony, he'd enjoy plotting against Vlad in the same setting where his old enemy had experienced the worst years of his life.

"So if it's not in Tokat where the archeologists think it is," I said very softly. "Where is it?"

* * *

Two nights later, I viewed Edirne, Turkey, from over a mile above it while clasped in Vlad's arms. With my enhanced vision, I could make out a mix of modern and ancient structures below, with rivers and empty patches of land cushioning the city. A lot had changed in the almost six hundred years since Vlad had been brought here as a child prisoner, so much that Vlad had needed to look up Edirne on Google Maps to acquaint himself with a bird's-eye view of the city so he'd know where to go.

Even with the changes, being back here had to hurt. Every ruin that had survived since the fourteen hundreds must be filled with memories for Vlad, not that he was letting on. Even with my body pressed along his, I couldn't detect his aura. He'd tamped it down to undetectable levels and his emotions were just as securely locked up.

For a few seconds, we hovered in the air, Vlad checking the images on his satellite phone to verify that we were in the right section of the city. The brief delay gave Samir a chance to catch up. He had Petre clasped in his arms, and the two vampires looked as grimly determined as I felt. The four of us made up the entirety of our forces tonight, but a larger presence might have alerted Szilagyi to our arrival. Even if Szilagyi did have security systems scanning the skies over his hideout, we could easily be mistaken for a small flock of birds.

"There," Vlad said, pointing to one of the city's

many bridges. Then he angled his body to swoop us toward it.

We landed at the beginning of a stone bridge that ended at a smallish island. On the island, a tall triangular tower rose at least sixty feet in the air. The tower was illuminated by exterior lighting so that it drew the eye, but that wasn't what held Vlad's attention. He let me go and stared at the bridge, his hands clasped behind his back and his entire body rigid.

I wanted to take one of his hands and squeeze it in silent support. Or wrap my arms around him, yet I remained where I was. He'd told me what he needed from me tonight, and it hadn't been handholding or hugs. Besides, he didn't want comfort. What he wanted—needed—right now was bloody, fiery revenge.

And so did I, but we had a problem.

"Is this the place?" I asked quietly. "There are people on that island. Humans."

His mouth curled with a coldness I'd rarely seen from him. "Yes, on the other side of that bridge is where the former imperial palace used to be, so it's a tourist attraction."

"Maybe we should wait until later." It was only an hour after dark. The site was bound to empty out soon—

"No."

The vehemence in that single word had Samir and Petre taking off their backpacks and unloading their contents. I stared at Vlad, momentarily speechless. He couldn't mean to take out a bunch of innocent people along with Szilagyi, could he?

"I want him dead, too, but not over the bodies of people whose only crime is being in the wrong place at the wrong time."

"Do you know what tourists do very, very well?" Vlad asked, the new silkiness in his voice more frightening than his previous granite tone. "Run at the first sign of danger."

Then he started striding down the bridge, ignoring the backpack that was meant for him, his only weapons the two silver swords that he had in sheaths crisscrossed on his back.

"Time to give them something to run away from," he muttered. Fire shot out in front of him, which had me, Samir, and Petre exchanging stunned looks. We had agreed that we would approach Szilagyi's base quietly. When had that changed?

"New plan," Vlad called out, as if in answer to that. "Keep Leila on this side of the island. I'm going in alone."

The people on the island saw the streaks of fire lighting up the bridge and began to murmur in concern. Those murmurs turned to screams when large creatures seemed to form out of the flames, surging ahead of Vlad and rushing onto the island. Then the fiery creations howled, the sound channeling the ominous roars of an inferno. More and more of them formed, until it appeared as though the island were being overrun by wolves made entirely of fire.

That's when the stampede started, proving that Vlad was right. Tourists ran away *very* fast at the sign of danger. Samir, Petre, and I were almost trampled by their mad scramble over the bridge to the mainland, which was now the only place that wasn't swarmed by fire creatures. Vlad was already a hundred yards ahead of us, his hands lit up by orange and blue flames. Suddenly, a pack of the fire creatures merged into one large, whirling ball that shot into the air before rocketing back down with an impact that made the ground shudder as if gripped by an earthquake. When the fireball cleared away, a tunnel was revealed in the ground to the right of the triangular tower. Vlad dropped into it and disappeared.

Samir finished unloading the weapons that his backpack contained. "We hold the line here," he said crisply. "If Szilagyi manages to run from Vlad, we will stop him."

"No, we won't, because he could fly out," I argued. "Or swim, or jump, or whatever! Vlad made a mistake by going off-plan, but we shouldn't compound that mistake by complying."

"He is the *voivode*," Samir said, as if that settled it.

My jaw clenched from the effort it took to keep from screaming at them. "That means 'prince,' not God, so he isn't above making a mistake."

They continued to stare at me as if I were speaking a strange language. I cast a frustrated glance at the island. It was rapidly emptying of people, but Vlad was there, and in all likelihood, so was his worst enemy and the most dangerous kind of sorcerer: a necromancer. I wasn't about to just wait here, cross my fingers and hope for the best.

"Fine. Don't disobey Vlad by going in there to help him. Do it to protect me, because I am *not* staying here."

"You can't, you could be a danger to yourself," Samir said, grabbing my upper arm.

"Believe me, I'm the farthest thing from suicidal right now," I snapped, yanking away. "But Vlad's acting like *he* is, so we're going to do what we planned when we were all thinking clearly. One of us stays at the bridge while the rest of us go to back up Vlad."

I didn't wait for him to reply, but spun away and ran across the bridge. Once on the island, I went for the nearest bright object that wasn't on fire. That turned out to be the exterior lighting around the tower, and I ripped my glove off before plunging my hand through one of the bulbs.

The surge of electricity hit me with sudden, delirious force. I'd relived cocaine highs through other people that didn't feel this good. Just like what had happened when I was escaping my old cell, I found myself not only absorbing the energy, but also pulling it into my body by force. All too soon, the lights around the tower shorted out and went dark.

I whirled, going for the next source of electricity. That was a small power grid next to a modern-looking stadium, and the far higher voltage shook me with its potency. By the time the stadium went black, taking out the rest of the power to the small island, I was shuddering with near-ecstatic bliss.

But I hadn't siphoned all that electricity for a cheap high. I re-channeled it into my right hand, where a cord of dazzling white began to grow. A few seconds of intense concentration later, and I had a sizzling whip that coiled and snapped like a snake chasing after prey. I forced back the almost irresistible urge to look for more electricity and ran over to the hole that Vlad had blasted into the earth.

I paused before jumping into the opening that led to the labyrinth of tunnels beneath the ruins of the former palace. The overload of voltage made my vision a little blurry. That, combined with the fearsome fire display still ravaging the island, made it impossible for me to see if Petre or Samir were still at the bridge, or if one of them had entered the tunnels while I was powering up. I decided not to go back to the bridge to find out. Too much time had been wasted already.

I dropped down into the tunnel, glancing around at the rough stone walls. The narrow, barren structure gave no indicators on whether I should go to my right or to my left. Which way had Vlad chosen?

A faint orange glow to my left answered that, and I ran in the direction of the ebbing light from his flames.

Chapter 34

 After about fifty yards, I began to see modern touches in the ancient structure that backed up our notion that this was someone's secret lair. The cameras stuck to the ceiling in several places of the stone tunnel certainly hadn't been standard in the sultan's time, and I blasted each one I passed with electricity, killing their feed. Vlad could have done the same with fire, but he hadn't, and that worried me. Was he so consumed with rage that he didn't care about Szilagyi knowing where he was?

Concern for Vlad plus desire for vengeance, all fueled by an electric high, had me charging ahead like the proverbial cavalry, and made me almost oblivious to the faint noises behind me. Once I heard them, I tensed, but didn't turn around. It couldn't be Petre or Samir. They weren't stupid; they would never sneak up on me in enemy territory without saying anything. Nor slink behind me while trying to mask all sounds of their presence.

I paused as if confused, trying to hide my whip as much as possible. That wasn't easy since the glow from it lit up my section of the tunnel. Despite that, with luck, whoever this person was might think that an unarmed vampire was an easy catch. Still, the tunnel was so narrow that I wouldn't be able to get a decent strike on whoever was behind me. I hadn't brought any other weapons, so I couldn't afford to let the walls take the brunt of my whip. Maybe if I made it to one of the cells, I'd have room enough to swing a full, lethal arc at my stalker. They had to be down here somewhere.

Decision made, I started running again, listening hard to determine if my stalker was keeping up. He was, from the faint footfalls, but much slower. The tunnel began to slope downward, taking me deeper belowground. Fear started to chew its way up my spine because the only light I now saw came from my whip. The glow from Vlad's flames was gone, and there was no sight or sound from him. It was as if the dungeon had swallowed him.

The thought made me run faster, bringing me to the open door at the end of the tunnel. I dashed through it—and then stopped in surprise. Vlad was still nowhere in sight, but a five-thousand-foot antechamber spread before me, with multiple entrances to other passages showing that this wasn't the end of the dungeon. It was the beginning.

Survival mode kicked in and I darted away from the entrance. I wasn't about to make myself a stationary target for my stalker, who, from the barely perceptible sounds, was still coming down the tunnel after me. Aside from the staggering size of the dungeon, I was also surprised by the hundreds of small holes that dotted the right side of the antechamber. They extended all the way to the ceiling, which had to be thirty feet high. The layout reminded me of an odd stone honeycomb and I figured they had been storage compartments until I saw the rotted wood and bones that lined them. Then I understood.

These weren't storage compartments. They were cells, and the tiny, cramped spaces made the worst cells in Vlad's dungeon look like suites by comparison. I shuddered, keeping my right hand close to my side. What those poor prisoners went through might break my mind if I touched an essence trail down here.

Footsteps sounded outside the tunnel entrance. I crouched down, coiling my whip in readiness. I snapped it as soon as my mysterious stalker walked into the antechamber, but he leapt back with exceptional speed, avoiding its entire deadly length.

"Wait," he said when I raised my hand again.

I did, more to repower the whip than to be obedient. He'd moved faster than anticipated, so I'd need a longer reach.

The glow my whip gave off cast a soft white light on the stranger's face, making him easy to recognize. He was the passenger from my earlier glimpse of Szilagyi in the car, but that glimpse hadn't done him justice. In fact, it was a toss-up as to which was more striking: his youth or his looks. He couldn't have been much older than eighteen when he was changed. Curly black hair framed a face that would send Abercrombie and Fitch advertisers running for their checkbooks, and full yet masculine lips turned up in a smile that accented sky-high cheekbones. The only other person I'd seen with such flawless, beautiful features was Bones, the vampire Vlad disliked so much.

I stared at him to buy time while my whip recharged, but the stranger obviously thought I did it out of admiration. Copper-colored eyes regarded me with amusement.

"Don't worry, this happens all the time," he said, waving a hand with a *think nothing of it* gesture. "Leila, isn't it?"

His accent wasn't just Romanian; it was ancient Romanian, like Vlad's. That alone had me pegging him to be at least a few hundred years old, and the powerful vibes from his aura confirmed that. No matter how young and pretty he looked, this was no pushover in the vampire world.

"Leila," I agreed, moving closer. "And you are?"

He smiled almost impishly. "Don't you know who I am?"

Scraping sounds filled the right side of the antechamber. My first instinct was to look, but I forced myself not to take my eyes off the boy. He wasn't going to trick me into missing my shot at him. If I could just get him to move a couple feet closer . . .

Countless forms suddenly appeared in my peripheral vision and made me jerk my head to the right. I intended it to only be a quick look, but then I couldn't stop myself from staring and I instinctively recoiled until my back was pressed against the wall.

Fully formed walking skeletons filled the side of the antechamber. Right before my stunned gaze, more continued to form from the piles of bones in the honeycomb cells before jumping down to join the rest of the horde. I blinked to clear my vision, but the impossible sight didn't change. Had I accidentally touched something with my right hand? Was I reliving a hallucination from one of the dungeon's insane former prisoners?

No, I decided as those horrible skeletons began to smash into me with more force than any pile of bones should have. This was real.

Don't you know who I am? the grinning boy had asked.

I did now. He was the necromancer, and to prove it, the master of the dead was showing off some of his skills.

The skeletons swarmed me en masse, dragging me onto the floor with bony fingers that stabbed at me like dull knives. They hemmed me in so much that I didn't have room to strike with my whip, so I began to punch, kick, and head-butt them as I tried to get away. Bones smashed and flew from my assault, but what the skeletons lacked in durability, they made up for in numbers, and I was grimly aware of the other danger they posed.

Distraction.

I couldn't see the necromancer anymore. For all I knew, he was climbing up one of the rows of cells to drop down on me like a lethal spider. Worse, if I was fighting skeletons, then I wasn't helping Vlad. Where was he? Was he dealing with other supernatural tricks from the necromancer? Or had Szilagyi and whoever else he had down here proved to be a greater danger?

"You have more lives than a cat, you know."

The necromancer raised his voice to be heard above the sounds of multiple bones smashing. From it, I gauged that he was still near the tunnel we'd used to enter the antechamber. I wanted to keep him talking, so I yelled out, "How so?"

"No one has survived two of my spells before, though to be fair, Cynthiana cast the first one. Such an eager student. I was sorry to lose her."

"We should have known she had a teacher," I shouted. "She went from ineffective love spells with flowers to killing a baby for a fireproofing spell."

My last word was cut off when one of the skeletons scored a direct head shot. Solid, regenerated bone made it feel like a bowling ball had just smashed into my cranium. A few more blows like that could knock me out, then they'd probably rip my head off before I regained consciousness. I switched tactics and quit trying to make it back onto my feet. Instead, I streamlined my body and kicked off the wall, cutting through a forest of bony legs with my whip as I slid across the stone floor.

"That fireproofing spell was yours, too, wasn't it?" I yelled as I continued to clear a path with my whip.

"Of course," the necromancer replied. "The only reason I didn't cast it myself was to avoid you using your abilities to find out about me the same way you did with Cynthiana."

Speed and the chainsaw-like effect of my whip had me almost to the other side of the antechamber, where there were the fewest skeletons. I was battered and bruised, but that would fade as soon as I quit getting new injuries. If I quit getting new injuries, that was.

Why hadn't the necromancer taken advantage of the skeleton attack to charge me? Was he that wary of my whip? Or was he gearing up for something worse? He'd bound his suicide-compelling spell into my very flesh. What if his delay was because he was doing something to reactivate it?

I lashed at the skeletal horde with more desperation. I hadn't brought any weapons with me because I hadn't wanted to risk using one on myself, but this whip was more than enough to do the job. If I wrapped it around my neck and pulled hard enough, my head would come off.

Twin flashes of green briefly shone through the skeletons that raced over to continue their attack on me. I recognized it as the glow from the necromancer's eyes. He was coming closer.

I sought to find a way out, but my options were grim. I wasn't naïve enough to expect someone to appear and rescue me, so I couldn't wait this out. Even if I made it to one of the many tunnel entrances around the antechamber, the skeletons would chase me. Then I'd be trying to fight them off in a narrow space instead of a large one, which would give them the advantage. If the tunnel I chose led to a dead end or a prison cell, then the necromancer wouldn't have to bother with reactivating the spell. I'd be trapped, so the skeletons could rip me to pieces at their leisure.

No, I realized with a surge of determination, if I wanted to leave this antechamber alive, I had to find a way to kill the necromancer first.

Chapter 35

 Decision made, I stopped using my whip to slash at the skeletons. Doing so was only draining my energy and either the antechamber had an endless supply of bones or the necromancer kept regenerating the skeletons I cut down. Instead, I curled my whip back into my hand, hoping the necromancer would think I'd used up my electrical defenses. Then I focused on protecting myself while using the walls as springboards to slide away from the skeletons. That only afforded me a few seconds' respite until they swarmed me again, but maybe that would be enough.

Without my whip lighting up the room, the emerald glow from the necromancer's eyes was easier to spot. He seemed to be circling me, not getting too close, but obviously up to something or he could have picked a comfy spot somewhere to sit and watch. The skeletons parted around him wherever he went, reminding me of how the Remnants had acted with Cat. *Come on, get close enough to make your move*, I silently urged him. Then I could make mine.

When minutes went by but he did nothing except continue to circle me, I decided to make myself look like more of an appealing target. With that, my head snapped back as if I'd been struck by a skeleton's skull with one those brain-bashing blows. I sold it so well that the movement caused me to smash the back of my head against the bony cranium of one of my nearest attackers. Despite the instant sear of pain, it wasn't enough to knock me unconscious, but I pretended that it was, going limp on the stone floor.

I braced for sudden, urgent defense if one of the skeletons grabbed my head with decapitation intentions. None of them did. In fact, the entire attack stopped, which struck me as odd until I heard the scrape of bones on rock and realized that they were parting to let the necromancer through. I kept my eyes closed and my mouth slack, but every cell in my body felt like it vibrated as I forced electricity into my hand while still keeping the whip beneath my skin. With vampire healing, the necromancer would expect me to regain consciousness in a few seconds, giving me only between now and then to make my move.

Please, let him be close enough, I found myself praying.

When I felt the tingling power of his aura, I

opened my eyes and snapped my wrist. The whip
shot out, the energy I'd willed into it making sparks
fly from it as it arced toward the necromancer. He
leapt back with incredible speed, avoiding the killing strike it should have been. Instead of cleaving
his upper body in half, the whip sliced him from
throat to chest in a long, shallow cut.

The scream that escaped me wasn't just of dis-
appointment. Pain flared along my upper body in
a sizzling arc. My left hand instinctively flew to
cover the wound, but when I touched my chest, expecting to feel a knife or other weapon protruding,
nothing was there. A glance down didn't reveal the
source of the injury, either. It just showed a bloody
slice from neck to breast, as though I'd been hacked
at by an invisible machete . . .

I looked at the necromancer. In the unguarded
instant when his eyes met mine and I read the
strangest sort of terror in their coppery-hued
depths, an explanation flashed through my mind.
It can't be, I immediately thought, rejecting the
notion. Then I remembered Mencheres explaining
why he couldn't break the spell that had caused me
to nearly kill myself.

*Whoever cast it must have bound it flesh to
flesh and blood to blood. Since you are a vampire,
that is more than magic; it's necromancy . . . The
spell was set with your flesh and blood as well as
the necromancer's . . .*

We'd considered that to be a good thing because

then the death of the necromancer could break it, too, but what if there was another ramification to our flesh and blood being supernaturally bound together?

Before the necromancer could guess my intention, I grabbed one of bones I'd knocked off a reanimated skeleton and raked the ragged end across my face. The necromancer yelped as his cheek opened up in exactly same spot.

"Oh, shit," I breathed, and the truth was so mind-bending that I couldn't stop myself from testing it again.

"Stop it," he said curtly when I sliced open my arm and his skin split to the bone as though I'd done it to him, too.

"So *this* is why you didn't kill me during your B-movie attack with the skeletons!" I said in amazement. "You wanted me too distracted to help Vlad, but not really hurt because whatever happened to me would happen to you, too! But then *why* would you cast a spell that did this if it was also supposed to make me commit suicide?"

"Because you shouldn't have lived long enough for it to bind us together this way," he snapped. "I was protected from the first destruction of your flesh, which was supposed to be the last because *no one's* survived this spell before. Then you kept destroying and regenerating your flesh, making the part that was meant to protect me bind us tighter together instead. Now, I feel it every morning when that crazy fucker you married burns you!"

I couldn't help it—I laughed with demented amusement. After all the backfiring I'd experienced with my abilities, the necromancer's spell biting him in the ass in such a stupendous way was the most hilarious thing I'd heard all month.

"You think that's funny?" he said, his tone scathing. "Let's see how amused you are when you have to beg your revenge-obsessed husband for my life. Do you think he loves you enough not to kill me? I don't, so we both need to leave here, now."

Then again, maybe it wasn't so funny, I reflected, my laughter fading away. We'd counted on the necromancer's death to break the spell over me, but if every wound on him was mirrored on me, then he was right. Killing him would mean my death, too. Frustration filled me. What were we supposed to do? Resign ourselves to battling my suicide attempts for the rest of my life? Tell the necromancer to take care of himself while escorting him safely out of the underground dungeon?

The walls suddenly shook with a violent tremor and the scent of smoke filled the antechamber. *Bombs,* I thought, the pitching ground and charred stench nauseatingly reminiscent of Szilagyi's attack on the castle. Had they rigged the underground dungeon with the same kind of explosives, too?

The necromancer's scowl vanished. "So Vlad has reached the section where Szilagyi is. If he blasts through it to get to him, he'll find out how many other surprises we have in store."

As if to punctuate that, a roar echoed through the dungeon, followed by the scald of agony and rage across my emotions. Vlad wasn't close, but he was still down here, and whatever had caused the walls to shake had hurt him, too. More pain was coming, if the necromancer was correct, and Vlad had already suffered too much in this underground nightmare.

Vice versa, I reminded myself, my gaze glinting as I stared at the sorcerer. If I was forced to make sure that he stayed alive, he was forced to do the same with me, which meant that I had a large bargaining chip to use.

"You're going to tell Vlad how to avoid your traps," I told the necromancer.

He looked at me as if he couldn't have heard me correctly, and then he laughed. "No, I'm not."

"Yes, you are," I said, coiling my electrical whip around my own throat. "Or I'm going to do something that will make you really, *really* sorry."

Chapter 36

 I followed the necromancer down the tunnel, holding the end of the whip in my left hand. My right hand was still resting on my collarbone, and the glowing whip circled my neck like a large dazzling piece of jewelry. The necromancer walked in front of me, the boomeranged effects from my whip showing in the red welts around his throat. My flesh might be immune to the effects of electricity, but his wasn't. He kept tugging his shirt collar down, as if it that would alleviate the burning constriction around his throat.

"Stop this foolishness," he said, speaking for the first time in several minutes. "You won't kill yourself, Leila. You don't want to die any more than I do."

"Ready to bet your life on that?" I said evenly. "Then prepare to be amazed at what I'll do to protect Vlad. Don't worry, if you do what I told you to, you'll be fine . . . unless the suicidal urge you embedded into this spell rears its head and causes me to do something unfortunate to both of us."

"I already dulled that aspect of it days ago," he snapped, then stopped as if realizing that he'd revealed too much.

Good to know, I thought coolly. "Well, we'll just stick to the part where I'll take myself out to kill you if one of your evil little booby traps ends up murdering my husband."

Vlad was still alive at the moment. I knew it from the geysers of rage blasting across my subconscious, with worrying amounts of pain thrown in with increasing frequency. When an orange glow began to light the tunnel ahead of us and I could feel Vlad's power spilling over my skin in invisible waves, I kicked the necromancer to get him to move him faster.

"Stop it," he growled.

"Or what, you'll kill me?" Impatience made me snippy. "Been there, tried that, remember?"

He muttered something in a language I didn't understand. It could have been harmless comments about what a bitch I was, but I didn't want to run the risk of it being a new spell.

"English only," I said, tightening the whip around my neck in warning. A fresh red line appeared on his throat.

He turned around to glare at me. "Want it in English? Fine. You're the bastard daughter of a diseased whore."

I snorted. "Have to give it to you older vamps. Your insults are much more colorful than my generation's variations on 'fuck you, you fucking fuck.'"

"Oh, you like that?" he purred. "How about this? I laughed when I saw those videos of you being fucked and skinned. I only wondered why Mihaly didn't have both happen at the same time."

The horrifying thought almost made me miss a step. The necromancer whirled around and lunged at me, but I recovered and jumped backward, missing his swipe at my arms. Once out of his reach, I wound another length of whip around my throat, feeling vicious delight at seeing the new welt appear on him.

"Nice try," I said evenly, "but fuck you, you fucking fuck."

Might not be as colorful, but it was straight to the point. My generation got that right.

He gave me a look filled with hatred. "We're almost there. How do you intend to fight off Szilagyi's men, if you don't remove that from your neck?"

I'd already thought of that, and I smiled at him. "You're going to say you captured me and compelled me to wrap this around my neck. Kind of like holding a gun to my head, but more magical."

"You're insane," he breathed.

"I don't think so," I shot back. "I'm even willing to bet my life that you haven't admitted the ramification of your spell's backfiring to anyone, right? That would be too embarrassing for you, and man, would that piss Szilagyi off. The spell he had you cast that was supposed to guarantee my death now has you protecting me."

"He doesn't command me," the necromancer all but snarled. "I outgrew him in power a century ago!"

That was frightening information, but I didn't let him see how it rattled me.

"All the more reason for everyone to believe that I'm a prisoner," I said. "Hell, everyone probably thinks I'm a captivity magnet already, but what they don't know is that I freed myself two out of the four times by single-handedly killing my captors. So, I'll play the helpless victim, you'll play the triumphant captor, and we'll both walk out of here alive afterward—"

The tunnel shaking with sudden, violent force cut me off. Cracks appeared in the stone around us, and the layer of ground rock that coated us was an ominous sign of things to come.

"How much farther again?" I asked.

His smile did nothing to quell my unease. "We're almost there."

A few turns later, we reached another open area. At least a dozen bodies were strewn around this new antechamber, each one burned so badly that little more than charred bones remained.

"So much for the captor/captive charade," the necromancer said, barely glancing at the ones we passed. I didn't pause to stare at them, either, but that was because I couldn't risk him trying to wrest the whip away from my neck again.

"These are your people dead at your feet, and you could care less. You're a real prize of a leader."

He glanced at me, his mouth curled in scorn. "No, they were Szilagyi's people. Not mine."

I kept sneaking wary glances as I followed him to the only exit to this chamber aside from the tunnel we'd entered it by.

"Oh? I thought Szilagyi didn't command you, so if these were *his* people, then aren't you here under his authority?"

"You're not going to get me to reveal any more information than I already have," he replied shortly.

Maybe, maybe not. He was arrogant enough to have given me a couple important tidbits already. If I kept poking at his pride, maybe I could get another nugget out of him that we could use.

As we entered the new tunnel, a deafening noise combined with the ground heaving as if shaken by an invisible fist threw me forward. I used my left arm to steady myself, but kept the right one to my throat. Even still, the brutal jolting cut the whip deeper into my neck than I would have liked.

"Let go, you'll kill us both!" the necromancer shouted, clutching his neck while blood seeped out between his fingers.

My throat burned, too. Not from the electricity, which I was immune to, but the cut. Still, I wouldn't unwind the whip. If I did, Vlad was as good as dead.

"Not gonna happen," I spat.

The necromancer stared at me as if measuring my resolve. "Then hurry up, he's progressing faster than I thought him capable of."

The tunnel shook again while more thunderous crashes sounded, followed by countless booms and an ominous cloud that rushed into the tunnel. I knew what that meant, and I ran after the necromancer, who had quickened his pace without prompting this time. The cave-in blocked the exit behind us, but after a few seconds of running, we were free from falling debris and the cloud of ground stone.

"He's already blasted through the three outer barriers around Mihaly," the necromancer muttered, almost to himself. "If he breaches the door, he'll kill himself and us."

"How?" I demanded.

He gave me an irritated look. "Because Mihaly destabilized every part of the dungeon except the room where he is. The door to that part is rigged so that if it goes down, the floor outside of it blows up, then the rest of the dungeon piles on top of the remains."

And thousands of pounds of rock coming down onto whoever was trapped below would be lethal, even to someone as strong as Vlad. I ran faster,

turning the corner almost in unison with the
necromancer—and then nearly plowed into him
because he stopped so abruptly, I thought he was
making a play for my whip again.

"If you," I began, not finishing the threat when
I saw what was right in front of him.

Flames blocked the tunnel. Since he wasn't
trying to scare tourists anymore, Vlad hadn't bothered to form the fire into wolflike creatures. It was
just a solid wall that burned so hot, the heat made
my skin start to blister even from several feet away.

"Vlad!" I shouted, fear rising when he didn't
respond. Was he too far away? Or did the continuing sounds from the cave-in plus the roar of the
fire drown me out so he couldn't hear me? "Vlad,
listen to me!" I tried again, shoving the necromancer behind me and going as close to the flames as
I dared.

That didn't work, so in desperation, I switched
my wedding ring from my left hand to my right,
fingers rubbing over the wide, flat stone until I
found the essence trail Vlad had left when he put it
on my hand again.

Vlad, I shouted with all my mind when I followed it and saw him amidst an inferno. Shattered rock littered the ground and his hands were
stretched out toward a wall of black stone in front
of him. *Vlad, don't do it! I'm here!*

He didn't lower his hands, but his head cocked.
"Leila?"

I could only hear him through the link, so he must not be able to hear me the other way, either. I responded with an instant, mental roar of *Yes, it's me. Let me through the fire, quickly!*

His emotions were still entwined with mine, so I felt it when his surprise turned to angry concern.

"Get out of here," he said, returning his gaze to the charred wall. "You won't survive what I'm about to do."

Neither will you! I yelled back, hoping he could hear everything I said. He hadn't been able to the last time I tried this. *Szilagyi rigged the door. If it comes down, so will the floor beneath you and the entire prison will dump on your head.*

Not sure if he'd gotten all that, I repeated the word *trap* over and over, hoping that did the trick. The necromancer watched me, not making any move at the whip around my neck. That, plus his grim expression, let me know that he hadn't been lying or exaggerating the seriousness of the situation. If Vlad ignored me and blasted through that last door, we were all dead.

The wall of fire abruptly pulled back as if yanked, until the long, empty tunnel was revealed. I ran ahead, not checking to see if the necromancer followed me. He had no choice. The way behind us was blocked by a cave-in.

When I reached the end of the tunnel, I had to step over piles of charred rocks. Vlad was in the clearing beyond. I couldn't call it a room because I don't think that's what it originally was. Instead, it looked like it had been wall after wall of fortifications, which had been blasted into an open space from the power of Vlad's fire assault. The final door that the necromancer referenced was easily discernable from the rest of the rock. That was a dull, grayish-brown color, like the tunnel walls had been. The door was black, smooth like slate, and as inviting as a welcome sign to the vampire who wanted nothing more than to kill his enemy hiding behind it.

Vlad remained exactly as he was when I'd glimpsed him through the link: legs braced in a wide stance, arms extended to the door, and fire flowing from him as if his entire body was sweating flames. His emotions felt more explosive than the damage he'd done to this room, which was why I didn't run over to him. I stayed by the entrance to the tunnel, not wanting to exacerbate his already volatile state.

"Don't touch that door. It's rigged to trigger a detonation that will take down the rest of the dungeon," I said in as calm a voice as I could manage, and just in case he hadn't heard that from my mind.

He didn't ask me how I knew that. He didn't even look away from the black rectangle, as if doing so would allow Szilagyi to escape him once again. "Just the door? Or the walls around it, too?"

I glanced down the tunnel at the necromancer, who, as anticipated, had followed after me.

"Just the door? Or the walls, too?" I pressed him.

"Door only," he replied, crossing his arms and cocking his head as if curious to see how Vlad got around that.

Vlad stared at the smooth black slate and smiled. Then his power began to blast through the room in ever-increasing shockwaves, until it felt like he was manipulating gravity into a weapon that kept hammering me with full-body punches. I sucked in a breath to try and balance the awful squeezing sensation, as if my guts were being pureed by the violent pummeling. Behind me, I heard the necromancer moan, and then a thump that might have been his legs giving out when the awful sensations continued.

"What are you doing?" I managed to gasp.

Vlad ignored me. From the virulent emotions scalding mine, I wondered if he even heard me. He felt lost to the hate that he allowed to consume him, until those pulses of power coming from him became so punishing that I fell to my knees, too.

With sudden, shocking swiftness, it felt like he sucked all the power back into himself. All the air seemed to leave the room, too, in a *whoosh* that popped my ears and made my head throb like it was about to explode. He centered that incredible power and then hurled it at the walls, with a blast of heat that made my skin feel like it was going to melt off.

It didn't, but as I watched, amazement replaced my fear. The stone walls around that black door shined with pure, white heat. After a few moments, they began to waver, then concaved in places like candle wax. Then holes appeared, growing and stretching, until what looked like molten rock puddles began to form.

I couldn't believe it. Vlad was melting the stone. It was one thing to do that to thin glass shower doors, but this rock wall had to be a foot thick at least. *What kind of temperature would that take?* I found myself wondering almost dazedly. Two thousand degrees Fahrenheit? Three thousand? The only thing more incredible than Vlad channeling fire into that kind of heat was how he contained it to the walls in front of him. I should be in a puddle on the floor. So should the black door. Yet the only things dissolving were the walls.

With another blast of power, they shuddered and began to fall, collapsing into slowly moving pools of dark brown lava as the room beyond the black door was revealed. And in that room, staring in disbelief at the stone walls that continued to puddle into piles on the floor, was Mihaly Szilagyi.

Vlad looked at him and smiled with wolfish anticipation. "Hello, old friend."

Chapter 37

Szilagyi lunged for the weapons on the other side of the room, which was surprisingly modernized. I didn't have a chance to glimpse more than the wall of computer screens that funneled feed from the still working cameras before he had a machine gun in his hands. Before the barrel finished its upward swing, the metal went from black to glowing orange. Szilagyi screamed as the metal melted, coating his hands in the scalding remains of his weapon.

"How?" he almost croaked.

Vlad's smile turned cruel. "You wanted to drive me into recklessness by what you did to Leila. Instead, you drove me into the next level of my power. When I burned my castle down, my near-insane rage caused my abilities to overload until I began to melt stone. Once I knew I *could* do that, it was only a matter of focusing my power to improve upon it."

He'd said something similar to me the first time

he'd goaded me into turning my electrical whip into a weapon. Wow, had he followed his own advice.

"The last time we were face-to-face, I intended to capture you so that I could torture you for a long, long time," Vlad went on, his smile dissolving from his face. "This time, what I want more than anything is your agonizing, screaming death, and I want it now."

Then he grabbed Szilagyi by the shoulders. The necromancer sighed deeply and looked away. I tightened the whip around my neck in warning, but the necromancer seemed more resigned than vengeful. Maybe, after seeing Vlad melt the walls right off Szilagyi's version of a panic room, the necromancer had reconsidered his role in Szilagyi's plan to take Vlad down.

Fire spilled from Vlad's hands to cover Szilagyi like a bright, full-body halo. Yet nothing burned under those orange and blue flames.

"You coated yourself in another fireproofing spell?" I didn't understand the wave of savage pleasure across my emotions until I heard Vlad's next words, spoken in a chillingly genial tone. "Spells, no matter how powerful, wear off."

Szilagyi began to fight with the only weapon he had left: himself. Punches, kicks, head-butts, and brutally aimed knees bashed into Vlad, who absorbed the blows without trying to protect himself. Instead, he kept his hands planted on Szilagyi's shoulders while more power spilled out of him, intensifying the heat from the fire.

After a few minutes, Szilagyi began to scream as first his clothing began to burn. Then his hair went up with a stench that would've made me gag if I still breathed. His struggles became more frantic when his skin began to blacken, and when it cracked and split, revealing raw, red flesh that quickly turned dark, he wasn't just screaming. He was pleading in between agonized shrieks that caused me to do something I didn't think I was capable of.

I pitied him.

Szilagyi had been behind my kidnapping and torture a few times. He'd intended to rape me himself before passing that off to Maximus under the auspices that it would be more brutal for Vlad that way. He'd murdered my friends, tormented my husband, tortured my best friend, and would have gleefully tortured and killed my family if he could, yet listening to him scream from the kind of pain that made his pleas incomprehensible and his body violently contract made me wish that his suffering was over. I'd thought I would be glad to see him in awful, extended pain. Instead, I couldn't even look anymore. His high-pitched, agonizing screams would already haunt my nightmares.

"Please," I said to Vlad, not knowing if he could hear me through the horrible sounds Szilagyi made, let alone his own near-consuming need for revenge. "*Please*, Vlad. End it."

Out of the corner of my eye, I saw the necromancer jerk his head as if surprised to hear me
plead for mercy on Szilagyi's behalf. I didn't look
at the necromancer, though. I stared at Vlad, silently willing him not to drag this out. With how
vampires healed, he could, and though he wouldn't
bring Szilagyi back as a prisoner to torture him
over weeks or months, he could make his death
last for hours, at least.

Vlad didn't respond and he didn't look away
from Szilagyi's charred form, which was only still
upright because Vlad hadn't released his iron grip
on his shoulders. Yet I knew he'd heard me when I
felt the strangest emotion thread through mine. It
wasn't frustration, or annoyance, or admiration,
but a blended version of all three. When the flames
covering Szilagyi went from orange and blue to a
shimmering, white haze, I almost sagged against
the tunnel entrance in relief.

I'd thought myself incapable of pity for Szilagyi
and been proved wrong. Now, I was proved wrong
again. I hadn't really believed that Vlad would
show mercy to his oldest, worst foe, but as that
white haze increased, Szilagyi's screams were cut
off. Then his body shrank with the suddenness of
a balloon being popped, and in seconds, Vlad had
nothing left to hold on to.

A charred skeleton dropped to the stone floor,
where it began to stick in the still-cooling rock.
Vlad knelt, holding his hands over the bones. That

white sheen over them brightened, and with an almost imperceptible noise, the bones burst into a powdery substance that Vlad burned until nothing but faint smears on the rock remained.

A door at the back of the small room opened. I jumped, startled into almost yanking my whip off to confront this new threat. Maximus walked out of a closet lined with electrical panels, like the switchboard for a large fuse box. The lights on the tabs flashed in a sequence of colors before going dark, one by one, until they were all off.

Vlad's emotions flared with an intensity that almost matched the fire he'd just manifested. Then a wall of blankness slammed into me as he raised those impenetrable shields to cut off what he was feeling from me and the other vampire he'd sired. Maximus.

"As soon as he saw you on camera, he had me go in here to start the self-destruct sequence," Maximus said, his tone oddly flat. I couldn't read anything from his expression, either. Those striking, rugged features were as closed off as Vlad's emotions. "Unless the cancel code was entered in time, the bombs beneath the floor would have detonated and started the cave-in. It was his backup plan in case you killed him."

At that, my gaze swung to the necromancer. "Looks like you forget to mention something *really* important, huh?"

He gave an oblique shrug, but his eyes were all for the vampire over my shoulder. "Mihaly hid some final contingencies from even me, it seems. And it also seems that his early mistrust of Maximus was well-founded."

"Who's that?" Vlad asked sharply, just now noticing that I wasn't alone in the tunnel.

"Meet the infamous necromancer," I said, and moved aside to let him enter the room, although I tapped the whip around my neck in warning as I did so.

When he emerged from the tunnel, Vlad got his first look at the vampire who was now bound to me in a frightening way. Even if I hadn't felt the instant shock icing my emotions as his shields cracked, I would have realized that Vlad knew him, because he stared at him as though thunderstruck.

"Radu," he whispered.

Chapter 38

 I stiffened in disbelief. That was the name of Vlad's brother, who had died back in the fifteenth century. Good Lord, what if he hadn't?

All at once, I remembered the deep copper color of the necromancer's eyes. Add a ring of emerald around the irises, and they would be identical to Vlad's.

The necromancer's laugh was cold. "No, though Mihaly often said that I favored my father a great deal. That would have caused serious problems for my mother if you hadn't stayed away for the entirety of my childhood, but she knew others would notice the resemblance. That's why she sent me off to Oradea."

Now the look Vlad gave him was calculating, if no less amazed.

"Mircea." A single, humorless laugh escaped him. "Ilona's lover was my own brother. No wonder Szilagyi pushed so hard to have me marry her. The irony of me claiming Radu's children as my own would have delighted him."

"And would have put one of Mehmed's loyal subjects on Wallachia's throne, eventually," Mircea concurred with a shrug. Then his gaze gleamed. "But while Mihaly groomed my brother to replace your son as prince, he had other plans for me."

"Yes. He turned you into a vampire and then turned you against me," Vlad stated, his tone now emotionless.

"Mihaly didn't need to do that," Mircea said instantly, his scent sharpening with hatred. "You did it yourself. Until I was turned, I didn't know that you weren't my father. All through my childhood, I loved you, yet you cared nothing for me. You didn't even visit me enough to notice that I was the spitting image of the brother you hated and hounded to his death!"

"Yes, I left you and your brother in your mother's care," Vlad said in a toneless voice. "Is that why you plotted against me with Szilagyi for centuries?"

"Yes," Mircea hissed. "He was a cold, cruel substitute for a father, and yet more of one to me than you ever were."

I'd stayed quiet, mostly from surprise at the revelation that the sorcerer was Vlad's stepson and nephew all rolled into one, but I couldn't any more at that.

"Don't you dare use bad-daddy syndrome as an

excuse for what you've done," I snapped. "I was pushed aside by my father, too, yet you don't see me casting evil spells, crashing planes, and committing God-knows-how-many other acts of mass murder!"

"Then you're not as strong or driven as I am," Mircea said curtly.

Vlad's hands became engulfed with flames, signaling that he was done discussing the necromancer's motives. I yelled "Stop!" at the same time that Mircea said something very fast in Romanian.

"He's tied to me now, Vlad," I confirmed, feeling his suspicion sweep over me. "The spell did it. Look."

I dragged a fang over my palm and Mircea held up his hand, showing the bloody slice that appeared in the same place. Then he pulled out a small, silver dagger from a concealed sheath on his back and laid open his cheek to the bone.

I fought the urge to grab my cheek at the instant, white-hot pain. Silver hurt worse than any metal for vampires, and I didn't think it had been an accident that Mircea had gone for that knife instead of using his fangs like I had. No, I realized as I saw the malevolent gleam in his eyes, he'd wanted to hurt me, and he'd wanted Vlad to see him do it.

"You can't kill him without killing me, too," I said before Vlad could respond in the violent way he wanted to. "So we need to let him go."

"I will do no such thing." Each word fell like a

hammer. "I can keep him alive without leaving him free to wreak more havoc on you, me or mine."

"That's where you're wrong," Mircea said, his beautiful features twisting with hatred. "I would rather be dead than your prisoner, not that you could ever hold me."

At that, Vlad smiled, as charming as if he was trying to sweep Mircea off his feet. Then a wall of fire blocked the tunnel, cutting off Mircea's only means of escape.

"Is that a dare?"

Oh, shit, I thought, bracing myself, but Mircea smiled back with equal charm.

"I only stayed to save her life since it's currently tied to mine. Now that that's done, so is my work here. Good-bye for now, Uncle, but don't worry. We *will* see each other again."

Vlad lunged at him and Mircea made no move to sidestep him. He just . . . disappeared, causing Vlad to grasp only thin, smoky air where the necromancer had just been.

"Spread out, this is a trick. He's still somewhere in this room," Vlad said at once.

"No, he's not," Maximus replied in a low voice. "He's really gone."

"Impossible," was Vlad's flat reply.

Maximus sighed. "Szilagyi didn't trust me enough to tell me about Mircea until he thought I'd raped Leila. Then he took me here and I met him. The things Mircea can do . . . That's why

Szilagyi wasn't afraid to come after you. He just waited until the boy had grown powerful enough because he needed Mircea's abilities to build his army. Otherwise, your allies and even some of your enemies would have been too afraid of you to side with Szilagyi."

Vlad's bark of laughter startled me. It was hard, ugly, and foreboding, all at the same time.

"If that's true, then what you're telling me is that I've finally killed my worst enemy, but the threat against me is still very much alive."

"Yes," Maximus said steadily.

The two men stared at each other, and a new kind of tension filled the air. Maximus had saved my life, kept me from being raped, enabled me to escape, gave Vlad the location to Szilagyi's lair . . . and yet everyone in the vampire world thought he'd betrayed Vlad in the worst way possible. Even if he wanted to, could Vlad let Maximus go without it looking like an act of extreme weakness? With the precarious position we were still in, would Vlad risk that, knowing that his enemies would use it as a rallying cry against him?

"Vlad," Maximus began.

"Don't." The single word was edged. "I can never forget what I saw on that video. Despite Leila's assurances, every time I look at you, I will see a replay of you raping my wife."

Maximus bowed his head in resignation, and Vlad's hands slowly began to fill with flames.

"Don't," I said with a gasp. "Vlad, you can't!"

He ignored that and grabbed Maximus. Not by the shoulders, as he had with Szilagyi, but by the head. As soon as he touched Maximus, the flames extinguished, and he brought their faces close together.

"Aside from Mencheres, you are the truest friend I have ever had." Vlad's voice was so thick from emotion, it was almost choked. "And yet I meant what I said. A good man could forget, but I can't, and so I cannot reward your loyalty with what I promised. You have no place in my line, Maximus, and you never will."

A harsh sigh escaped Maximus and my heart broke as his shoulders began to shake with suppressed sobs.

"I didn't do this for a place back in your line." Each word was a rasp. "I did it for you."

Vlad kissed him, once on each cheek. Maximus bent his head until their foreheads touched.

"You are my friend forever, *voivode meu*," Maximus murmured.

"Princes don't have friends, they have subjects," Vlad said in an equally low voice. "You are no longer my subject, but even though I will not see you again, you will forever be my friend."

He kissed Maximus one more time on the forehead, and then released him. "Go," he said, the word as ragged as the regret strafing my feelings.

Maximus bowed, turned . . . and paused. "I

can't. The floor's molten rock and you caved in the only way out."

The barest smile twitched Vlad's lips. "Rather ruins the moment, doesn't it?"

Maximus's mouth curled faintly as well. "Good thing neither of us is sentimental."

As I watched them, I felt a flicker of hope that was uniquely mine. Vlad thought he could never get over the illusion that had so devastated him; it had pushed his powers to a new level. Yet I believed that, with time, he could look at Maximus and see the true friend he loved, not the painful images of deception. After all, Vlad's powers weren't the only thing that had grown under our horrible circumstances recently. So had his capacity for love and perhaps most surprisingly, for mercy.

"Leila, were you the only one who followed me down here?" Vlad asked, bringing me back to our present issues. "Or did Petre and Samir ignore my commands to stay at the bridge, too?"

"I don't know," I started to say, but Maximus turned and, sidestepping some slowly spreading puddles of steaming rock, went to the cameras lining the walls.

"Petre's still at the bridge," he said after a moment. "Samir isn't. I don't see him on the other cameras in the tunnels, but over half of them aren't working anymore."

"Find him," Vlad said to me.

I was confused for a moment until the obvious

dawned. "How did you know that Samir grabbed me when I told him I was going after you?" I asked as I ran my right hand over my upper arm.

Vlad grunted. "If he didn't, then he didn't try hard enough to stop you."

Samir's essence imprint flared beneath my fingers. Good thing he'd been sufficiently mad at me when I wrenched away from him. I followed the link and saw him in the antechamber, trying to remove the rocks blocking the tunnel, piece of stone by piece of stone.

"He's in the antechamber with the honeycomb cells," I said.

Vlad glanced upward. At first, I thought he was thinking, but then I felt that painful, crushing sensation as his power began to swell and contract in ever-increasing rotations.

It took far longer than it had for him to melt the stone walls, but I was still awestruck when he flew me through the hole he'd created all the way back up to the surface. Maximus flew himself out, and then the three of us went around to the original hole that Vlad had blasted into the tunnels to get Samir. That was easy since the way to the antechamber hadn't caved in. Just the way leading deeper into the dungeons had, and Samir—loyal friend that he was—hadn't been willing to leave until he knew that Vlad and I were safe.

Samir had also tried to kill Maximus on sight,

proving that we had a lot of work to do before people knew what had really happened. I intended for that to be sooner rather than later. Maximus deserved to be recognized for his bravery and loyalty. Not reviled for crimes he hadn't committed.

But first . . . "Now what?" I asked as we crossed over to the bridge.

Vlad scanned the island, which looked deserted since Petre had been making sure that tourists left while also keeping police and any other interested parties away.

"Now I do what I should have done many years ago," he said, closing his eyes. "Destroy the past."

From our distance, the subsequent explosions felt like a series of percussion grenades going off. I couldn't see the flames that Vlad ravaged the former dungeon with, but from the power pouring off him, he was converting all of the awful memories this place held for him into fierce, destructive fire. It was obvious when those explosions set off the bombs that Szilagyi had lined beneath the tunnels. The ground shook so hard that the tall, triangular tower fell, landing in the first of many deep impressions that began to snake across the ruins. Soon, the rest of the few remaining monuments crumbled into the deep, sunken patches of earth around them, until not a single structure from the former palace remained standing.

I waited until the flames extinguished from his

hands, signaling that he finally was done with this dark, brutal chapter from his past, before I took his hand.

"Now what?" I said once more, very softly.

His smile was faint, but after everything that had happened tonight, I was grateful that it was genuine.

"We return to Romania. What has been destroyed can never be resurrected, but it can be rebuilt, so that is what we will do, Leila. Rebuild."

I squeezed his hand, tears of happiness stinging my eyes. "Then let's go home and get started."

Epilogue

 We returned to Romania, but our first stop wasn't the castle we'd lived in that Vlad had burned to the ground. It was another castle he'd destroyed, only we didn't go up to the top of the mountain to see the crumbled ruins of Vlad's former home when he was a human prince. We walked along the banks of the Arges River instead.

I didn't notice the small stone cross in the tree line along a sharp curve in the river until Vlad pulled back the brush to reveal it. The inscription had weathered off until it was unreadable, which was a good thing. Otherwise, Clara Dracul's grave would have been desecrated decades ago, her remains on display for tourists along with all the other pieces of "authenticated" Dracula history.

Vlad traced his hand over the stone and a myriad of feelings began to interweave with mine. Regret, as well as a wave of remembered love that was as poignant as it was difficult for both of us to feel.

I braced myself for what I'd see once I touched her bones, which was why we were here. I didn't know which would be worse for Vlad to discover from what I found: if Szilagyi had told the truth and murdered Clara? Or if she had jumped to her death of her own free will, as he'd believed for so long?

"You don't have to be the one to dig her up," I said quietly. "I can do it."

He looked at me, a rueful, almost self-deprecating smile curling his mouth.

"Neither of us is digging her up. Back at the island, I decided to let Clara rest in peace. If she jumped of her own free will, I forgave her for it long ago. If Szilagyi pushed her, she's been avenged. However her death occurred, much like my time in those dungeons, it needs to remain in the past."

I was so relieved to hear that, and not just for selfish reasons. Yes, it would have been hard for me to relive parts of Clara's life through her bones, which would have been necessary for me to find the events of her death. I didn't want to see Vlad through her eyes, whether she'd loved him unconditionally or had been driven by inner demons to commit suicide. The Vlad she knew wasn't the man I loved. Our pasts might shape us, but they weren't the end sum of us.

Most of all, I was glad Vlad's decision meant that he was letting go of pain that had haunted him for too long.

"If Clara could whisper through eternity, I bet she'd tell you she was happy that you're letting her go," I said, wishing the inadequate words could express how proud I was of him.

He let out a short laugh. "Probably, though she'd also tell me that I had taken far too long to do it."

"Wives are usually right," I said with a smile.

He laughed more naturally this time, touching the headstone once more before turning and briskly walking away. I followed him, not saying anything. The sounds of the forest and the winding river were the only noises around us, and they were as soothing as whispered reassurances in the dark. This place deserved a little peace after its long, bloody history, as did the man striding by my side.

After several minutes of walking in silence, Vlad's emotions became tinged with steely resolve, as though he were bracing himself to do something truly painful.

"I didn't only bring you out here to witness my saying goodbye to Clara for the last time," he said. "There's something I need to tell you, and this is a remote enough area that it won't be overheard by anyone else."

I cast a glance at the seemingly endless forest and river. No, no one could overhear us out here. We were the only two people around for miles.

"So . . . what did you want to tell me?" I asked tentatively.

He closed his eyes and cut off our emotional connection, which concerned me. Was it so bad that he didn't want me to know what he was feeling?

"Over a hundred years ago," he said quietly, "I swore that I would never repeat this to another soul, yet now I am going to break that oath because you deserve to know."

"What is it?" I asked, a fearful alarm snaking through my veins like fast-acting poison.

Vlad opened his eyes, torment reflecting in his coppery green depths. "I am responsible for the Dracula hype."

I stared at him, certain that I must have briefly gone insane and misheard him. "*What?*"

His jaw clenched with such force that I could almost hear his teeth grinding together.

"In the late eighteen hundreds, I was in a . . . dark mental state, which probably doesn't surprise you, and I did something incredibly stupid. I procured a substance known as Red Dragon, which is blood tainted with the equivalent of a vampire narcotic. Either I overestimated my tolerance to its effects or the dose was stronger than advertised, because it rendered me in a state of inebriation the likes of which I hadn't experienced in over four hundred years."

My gaze continued to widen, until it probably looked as though my eyes were about to pop out of my head. "And?" I managed.

He shot me an irritated glance. "I did what all drunken fools do: something I regretted. At a bar, I met a writer who was looking for a nasty historical figure to base his new novel on. In my intoxicated state, I thought it was the height of hilarity to relay the most horrid lies about my past to this stranger. I never touched Red Dragon again, which should have been the end of it. Then, years later, the damn writer's book came out. I was mortified when I read it, but I thought it would fade into obscurity as most literary works did. Instead, it kept growing in popularity and growing until over a century later, it's infected every form of media ever invented—"

I burst out laughing, which part of me felt bad about since this was a huge reveal for him, yet I couldn't hold it back any more than I could stop the glower Vlad leveled at me.

"Th-that's why you can't s-stand to hear th-that word!" I crowed, laughing so hard that I could barely speak. "It reminds you of when you did a s-stupid, totally humanlike move. Oh, Vlad, I love you even more knowing this!"

"I'm warmed to my soul," he said in an icy voice.

I ignored that and threw my arms around him, still laughing. "I'm warmed to *my* soul, truly. Now I'll never doubt that you love me. You proved it beyond words or deeds by telling me this."

"And I'm already regretting it."

Muttered with no less rancor, yet the arms that settled around me were possessive, and the feelings that he once more allowed to flow into mine were anything but angry or cold.

"Don't worry, I won't tell," I said, finally getting my laughter under control. "Your darkest secret is safe with me."

The strangest look crossed his features. If he were any other man, I'd say it was sheepishness over his former misdeed.

"It had better be. We have a necromancer spell to get off you, and I would hate to search for the solution while you were locked away in the new dungeon I'm going to build."

I snorted at the empty threat. "Don't we need to build a new house first?"

That brief hint of sheepishness vanished as he smiled. His smile was so like him: sensual yet predatory, hard and yet filled with humor. "The best-laid houses *and* plans start from the ground up."

Vlad and Leila will return in 2016
for the conclusion to
the Night Prince series

For now, continue reading for a peek
into the Night Huntress world
and discover why
#1 *New York Times* bestselling author
Charlaine Harris raves,
"Cat and Bones are
combustible together."

HALFWAY TO THE GRAVE

Half-vampire Catherine Crawfield is going after the undead with a vengeance . . . until she's captured by Bones, a vampire bounty hunter, and is forced into an unholy partnership. She's amazed she doesn't end up as his dinner—are there actually good vampires? And Bones is turning out to be as tempting as any man with a heartbeat.

"*Halfway to the Grave* has breathless action, a roller-coaster plot . . . and a love story that will leave you screaming for more. I devoured it in a single sitting."

ILONA ANDREWS

 "Beautiful ladies should never drink alone," a voice said next to me.

Turning to give a rebuff, I stopped short when I saw my admirer was as dead as Elvis. Blond hair about four shades darker than the other one's, with turquoise-colored eyes. Hell's bells, it was my lucky night.

"I hate to drink alone, in fact."

He smiled, showing lovely squared teeth. *All the better to bite you with, my dear.*

"Are you here by yourself?"

"Do you want me to be?" Coyly, I fluttered my lashes at him. This one wasn't going to get away, by God.

"I very much want you to be." His voice was lower now, his smile deeper. God, but they had great intonation. Most of them could double as phone-sex operators.

"Well, then I was. Except now I'm with you."

I let my head tilt to the side in a flirtatious

manner that also bared my neck. His eyes followed the movement, and he licked his lips. *Oh good, a hungry one.*

"What's your name, lovely lady?"

"Cat Raven." An abbreviation of Catherine, and the hair color of the first man who tried to kill me. See? Sentimental.

His smile broadened. "Such an unusual name."

His name was Kevin. He was twenty-eight and an architect, or so he claimed. Kevin was recently engaged, but his fiancée had dumped him and now he just wanted to find a nice girl and settle down. Listening to this, I managed not to choke on my drink in amusement. What a load of crap. Next he'd be pulling out pictures of a house with a white picket fence. Of course, he couldn't let me call a cab, and how inconsiderate that my fictitious friends left without me. How kind of him to drive me home, and oh, by the way, he had something to show me. Well, that made two of us.

Experience had taught me it was much easier to dispose of a car that hadn't been the scene of a killing. Therefore, I managed to open the passenger door of his Volkswagen and run screaming out of it with feigned horror when he made his move. He'd picked a deserted area, most of them did, so I didn't worry about a Good Samaritan hearing my cries.

He followed me with measured steps, delighted with my sloppy staggering. Pretending to trip, I whimpered for effect as he loomed over me. His face had transformed to reflect his true nature. A sinister smile revealed upper fangs where none had been before, and his previously blue eyes now glowed with a terrible green light.

I scrabbled around, concealing my hand slipping into my pocket. "Don't hurt me!"

He knelt, grasping the back of my neck.

"It will only hurt for a moment."

Just then, I struck. My hand whipped out in a practiced movement and the weapon it held pierced his heart. I twisted repeatedly until his mouth went slack and the light faded from his eyes. With a last wrenching shove, I pushed him off and wiped my bloody hands on my pants.

"You were right." I was out of breath from my exertions. "It only hurt for a moment."

ONE FOOT IN THE GRAVE

Cat Crawfield is now a special agent, working for the government to rid the world of the rogue undead. But when she's targeted for assassination she turns to her ex, the sexy and dangerous vampire Bones to help her.

"Witty dialogue, a strong heroine,
a delicious hero, and enough action
to make a reader forget to sleep."

MELISSA MARR

"Hallo, Kitten."

I was so preoccupied with my breakdown that I didn't hear Bones come in. His voice was as smooth as I'd remembered, that English accent just as enticing. I snapped my head up, and in the midst of my carefully constructed life crashing around me, found the most absurd thing to worry about.

"God, Bones, this is the ladies' room! What if someone sees?"

He laughed, a low, seductive ripple of the air. Noah had kissed me with less effect.

"Still a prude? Don't fret—I locked the door behind me."

If that was supposed to ease my tension, it had the opposite result. I sprang to my feet, but there was nowhere to run. He blocked the only exit.

"Look at you, luv. Can't say I prefer the brown hair, but as for the rest of you . . . you're luscious."

Bones traced the inside of his lower lip with

his tongue as his eyes slid all over me. Their heat seemed to rub my skin. When he took a step closer, I flattened back against the wall.

"Stay where you are."

He leaned nonchalantly against the countertop. "What are you all lathered about? Think I'm here to kill you?"

"No. If you were going to kill me, you wouldn't have bothered with the altar ambush. You obviously know what name I'm going under, so you would have just gone for me one night when I came home."

He whistled appreciatively. "That's right, pet. You haven't forgotten how I work. Do you know I was offered a contract on the mysterious Red Reaper at least three times before? One bloke had half-a-million bounty for your dead body."

Well, not a surprise. After all, Lazarus had tried to cash a check on my ass for the same reason. "What did you say, since you've just confirmed you're not here for that?"

Bones straightened, and the bantering went out of him. "Oh, I said yes, of course. Then I hunted the sods down and played ball with their heads. The calls quit coming after that."

I swallowed at the image he described. Knowing him, it was exactly what he'd done.

"So, then, why *are* you here?"

He smiled and came nearer, ignoring my previous order.

AT GRAVE'S END

Caught in the crosshairs of a vengeful vampire, Cat is about to learn the true meaning of bad blood—just as she and Bones need to stop a lethal magic from being unleashed. Will Cat be able to fully embrace her vampire instincts to save them all from a fate worse than the grave?

"A can't-put-down masterpiece that's sexy-hot and a thrill-ride on every page. I'm officially addicted to the series. Marry me, Bones!"

GENA SHOWALTER

I was sitting at my desk, staring off into space, when my cell phone rang. A glance at it showed my mother's number, and I hesitated. I so wasn't in the mood to deal with her. But it was unusual for her to be up this late, so I answered.

"Hi Mom."

"Catherine." She paused. I waited, tapping my finger on my desk. Then she spoke words that had me almost falling out of my chair. "I've decided to come to your wedding."

I actually glanced at my phone again to see if I'd been mistaken and it was someone else who'd called me.

"Are you drunk?" I got out when I could speak.

She sighed. "I wish you wouldn't marry that vampire, but I'm tired of him coming between us."

Aliens replaced her with a pod person, I found myself thinking. *That's the only explanation.*

"So . . . you're coming to my wedding?" I couldn't help but repeat.

"That's what I said, isn't it?" she replied with some of her usual annoyance.

"Um. Great." Hell if I knew what to say. I was floored.

"I don't suppose you'd want any of my help planning it?" my mother asked, sounding both defiant and uncertain.

If my jaw hung any lower, it would fall off. "I'd love some," I managed.

"Good. Can you make it for dinner later?"

I was about to say, *Sorry, there was no way*, when I paused. Tate didn't even want me watching the video of him dealing with his bloodlust. Bones was leaving this afternoon to pick Annette up from the airport. I could swing by my mom's when he went to get Annette, and then meet him back here afterward.

"How about a late lunch instead of dinner? Say, around four o'clock?"

"That's fine, Catherine." She paused again, seeming to want to say something more. I half expected her to yell, *April Fool's!* but it was November, so that would be way early. "I'll see you at four."

When Bones came into my office at dawn, since Dave was taking the next twelve-hour shift with Tate, I was still dumbfounded. First Tate turning into a vampire, then my mother softening over my marrying one. Today really was a day to remember.

Bones offered to drop me off on his way to the airport, then pick me up on his way back to the compound, but I declined. I didn't want to be without a car if my mother's mood turned foul—always a possibility—or risk ruining our first decent mother-daughter chat by Bones showing up with a strange vampire. There were only so many sets of fangs I thought my mother could handle at the same time, and Annette got on my nerves even on the best of days.

Besides, I could just see me explaining who Annette was to my mother. *Mom, this is Annette. Back in the seventeen hundreds when Bones was a gigolo, she used to pay him to fuck her, but after more than two hundred years of banging him, now they're just good friends.*

Yeah, I'd introduce Annette to my mother—right after I performed a lobotomy on myself.

"I still can't believe she wants to talk about the wedding," I marveled to Bones as I climbed into my car.

He gave me a serious look. "She'll never abandon her relationship with you. You could marry Satan himself and that still wouldn't get rid of her. She loves you, Kitten, though she does a right poor job of showing it most days." Then he gave me a wicked grin. "Shall I ring your cell in an hour, so you can pretend there's an emergency if she gets natty with you?"

"What if there *is* an emergency with Tate?" I wondered. "Maybe I shouldn't leave."

"Your bloke's fine. Nothing can harm him now

short of a silver stake through the heart. Go see your mum. Ring me if you need me to come bite her."

There really was nothing for me to do at the compound. Tate would be a few more days at least in lockdown, and we didn't have any jobs scheduled, for obvious reasons. This was as good a time as any to see if my mom meant what she said about wanting to end our estrangement.

"Keep your cell handy," I joked to Bones. Then I pulled away.

My mother lived thirty minutes from the compound. She was still in Richmond, but in a more rural area. Her quaint neighborhood was reminiscent of where we grew up in Ohio, without being too far away from Don if things got hairy. I pulled up to her house, parked, and noticed that her shutters needed a fresh coat of paint. Did they look like that the last time I was here? God, how long *had* it been since I'd come to see her?

As soon as I got out of the car, however, I froze. Shock crept up my spine, and it had nothing to do with the realization that I hadn't been here since Bones came back into my life months ago.

From the feel of the energy leaking off the house, my mother wasn't alone inside, but whoever was with her didn't have a heartbeat. I started to slide my hand toward my purse, where I always had some silver knives tucked away, when a cold laugh made me stop.

"I wouldn't do that if I were you, little girl," a voice I hated said from behind me.

My mother's front door opened. She was framed in it, with a dark-haired vampire who looked vaguely familiar cradling her neck almost lovingly in his hands.

And I didn't need to turn around to know the vampire at my back was my father.

DESTINED FOR AN EARLY GRAVE

They've fought against the rogue undead, battled a vengeful Master vampire and pledged their devotion with a blood bond. Now it's time for Cat and Bones to go on a vacation. But Cat is having terrifying dreams of a vampire named Gregor who's more powerful than Bones . . . and has ties to her past that even Cat herself doesn't know about.

"Frost's dazzling blend of urban fantasy action and passionate relationships make her a true phenomenon."

Romantic Times BOOKreviews

"Who is Gregor, why am I dreaming about him, and why is he called the Dreamsnatcher?"

"More importantly, why has he surfaced now to seek *her* out?" Bones's voice was cold as ice. "Gregor hasn't been seen or heard from in over a decade. I thought he might be dead."

"He's not dead," Mencheres said a trifle grimly. "Like me, Gregor has visions of the future. He intended to alter the future based on one of these visions. When I found out about it, I imprisoned him as punishment."

"And what does he want with *my wife*?"

Bones emphasized the words while arching a brow at me, as if daring me to argue. I didn't.

"He saw Cat in one of his visions and decided he had to have her," Mencheres stated in a flat tone. "Then he discovered she'd be blood-bound to you. Around the time of Cat's sixteenth birthday, Gregor intended to find her and take her away. His plan was very simple—if Cat had never met you, then she'd be his, not yours."

"Bloody sneaking bastard," Bones ground out, even as my jaw dropped. "I'll congratulate him on his cleverness—while I'm ripping silver through his heart."

"Don't underestimate Gregor," Mencheres said. "He managed to escape my prison a month ago, and I still don't know how. Gregor seems to be more interested in Cat than in getting revenge against me. She's the only person I know whom Gregor's contacted through dreams since he's been out."

Why do these crazy vampires keep trying to collect me? My being one of the only known half-breeds had been more of a pain than it was worth. Gregor wasn't the first vampire who thought it would be neat to keep me as some sort of exotic toy, but he did win points for cooking up the most original plan to do it.

"And you locked Gregor up for a dozen years just to keep him from altering my future with Bones?" I asked, my skepticism plain. "Why? You didn't do much to stop Bones's sire, Ian, when he tried the same thing."

Mencheres's steel-colored eyes flicked from me to Bones. "There was more at stake," he said at last. "If you'd never met Bones, he might have stayed under Ian's rule longer, not taking Mastership of his own line, and then not being co-Master of mine when I needed him. I couldn't risk that."

So it hadn't been about preserving true love at all. Figures. Vampires seldom did anything with purely altruistic motives.

"What happens if Gregor touches me in my dreams?" I asked, moving on. "What then?"

Bones answered me, and the burning intensity in his gaze could have seared my face.

"If Gregor takes ahold of you in your dreams, when you wake, you'll be wherever he is. That's why he's called the Dreamsnatcher. He can steal people away in their dreams."

This Side of the Grave

Cat and Bones have fought for their lives as well as their relationship. Just as they've triumphed over the latest battle, Cat's new and unexpected abilities are making them a target. And help from a dangerous "ally" may prove more treacherous than they've ever imagined.

"Cat and Bones are combustible together."

Charlaine Harris

 The vampire pulled on the chains restraining him to the cave wall. His eyes were bright green, their glow illuminating the darkness surrounding us.

"Do you really think these will hold me?" he asked, an English accent caressing the challenge.

"Sure do," I replied. Those manacles were installed and tested by a Master vampire, so they were strong enough. I should know. I'd once been stuck in them myself.

The vampire's smile revealed fangs in his white upper teeth. They hadn't been there several minutes ago, when he'd still looked human to the untrained eye.

"Right, then. What do you want, now that you have me helpless?"

He didn't sound like he felt helpless in the least. I pursed my lips and considered the question, letting my gaze sweep over him. Nothing interrupted my view, either, since he was naked. I'd long ago learned that weapons could be stored in various clothing items, but bare skin hid nothing.

Except now, it was also very distracting. The vampire's body was a pale, beautiful expanse of muscle, bone, and lean, elegant lines, all topped off by a gorgeous face with cheekbones so finely chiseled they could cut butter. Clothed or unclothed, the vampire was stunning, something he was obviously aware of. Those glowing green eyes looked into mine with a knowing stare.

"Need me to repeat the question?" he asked with a hint of wickedness.

I strove for nonchalance. "Who do you work for?"

His grin widened, letting me know my aloof act wasn't as convincing as I'd meant it to be. He even stretched as much as the chains allowed, his muscles rippling like waves on a pond.

"No one."

"Liar." I pulled out a silver knife and traced its tip lightly down his chest, not breaking his skin, just leaving a faint pink line that faded in seconds. Vampires might be able to heal with lightning quickness, but silver through the heart was lethal. Only a few inches of bone and muscle stood between this vampire's heart and my blade.

He glanced at the path my knife had traced. "Is that supposed to frighten me?"

I pretended to consider the question. "Well, I've cut a bloody swath through the undead world ever since I was sixteen. Even earned myself the nickname of the Red Reaper, so if I've got a knife next to your heart, then *yes*, you should be afraid."

His expression was still amused. "Right nasty wench you sound like, but I wager I could get free and have you on your back before you could stop me."

Cocky bastard. "Talk is cheap. Prove it."

His legs flashed out, knocking me off-balance. I sprang forward at once, but a hard, cool body flattened me to the cave floor in the next instant. An iron grip closed around my wrist, preventing me from raising the knife.

"Always pride before a fall," he murmured in satisfaction.

ONE GRAVE AT A TIME

Cat's "gift" from New Orleans's voodoo queen just keeps on giving, and now a personal favor has led to doing battle against a villainous spirit. But how do you send a killer to the grave when he's already dead?

"Every time I think I know all there is to know about Cat and Bones, Ms. Frost creates new layers of depth. . . . Prepare yourself for blood and gore galore, interspersed with tons of dark, witty humor, fierce fighting, and one-of-a-kind romance."

Joyfully Reviewed

"We summon you into our presence. Heed our call, Heinrich Kramer. Come to us now. We summon through the veil the spirit of Heinrich Kramer—"

Dexter let out a sharp noise that was part whine, part bark. Tyler quit speaking. I tensed, feeling the grate of invisible icicles across my skin again. Bones's gaze narrowed at a point over my right shoulder. Slowly, I turned my head in that direction.

All I saw was a swirl of darkness before the Ouija board flew across the room—and the point of the little wooden planchette buried in Tyler's throat.

I sprang up and tried to grab Tyler, only to be knocked backward like I'd been hit with a sledgehammer. Stunned, it took me a second to register that I was pinned to the wall by *the desk,* that dark cloud on the other side of it.

The ghost had successfully managed to use the desk

as a weapon against me. If it hadn't been still jabbed in my stomach, I wouldn't even have believed it.

Bones threw the desk aside before I could, flinging it so hard that it split down the center when it hit the other wall. Dexter barked and jumped around, trying to bite the charcoal-colored cloud that was forming into the shape of a tall man. Tyler made a horrible gurgling noise, clutching his throat. Blood leaked out between his fingers.

"Bones, fix him. I'll deal with this asshole."

Dexter's barks drowned out the sounds Tyler made as Bones slashed his palm with his fangs, then slapped it over Tyler's mouth, ripping out the planchette at the same time.

Pieces of the desk suddenly became missiles that pelted the three of us. Bones spun around to take their brunt, shielding Tyler, while I jumped to cover the dog. A pained yelp let me know at least one had nailed Dexter before I got to him. Tyler's gurgles became wrenching coughs.

"Boy, did you make a colossal fucking mistake," I snarled, grabbing a piece of the ruined desk. Then I stood up, still blocking the dog from any more objects the ghost could lob at him. He'd materialized enough for me to see white hair swirling around a craggy, wrinkled face. The ghost hadn't been young when he died, but the shoulders underneath his dark tunic weren't bowed from age. They were squared in arrogance, and the green eyes boring into mine held nothing but contempt.

"*Hure,*" the ghost muttered before thrusting his hand into my neck and squeezing like he was about to choke me. I felt a stronger than normal pins-and-needles sensation but didn't flinch. If this schmuck thought to terrify me with a cheap parlor trick like that, wait until he saw *my* first abracadabra.

"Heinrich Kramer?" I asked almost as an after-thought. Didn't matter if it wasn't him, he would regret what he did, but I wanted to know whose ass I was about to kick.

Up From the Grave

Cat and Bones should have known better than to relax their guard. A rogue CIA agent is involved in horrifying secret activities that threaten to cause an all-out war between humans and the undead. As Cat and Bones race against time to save their friends from a fate worse than death, their lives—and those of everyone they hold dear—will be hovering on the edge of the grave.

"Featuring superior writing as well as a thoughtfully structured plot, Cat and Bones's final adventure is appropriately splendid and satisfying."

Publishers Weekly (★Starred Review★)

 "I want their bodies."

Madigan showed more surprise than he had when I lunged at him. "What?"

"Their bodies," Bones repeated, his tone hardening. "Now."

"Why? You didn't even like Tate," Madigan muttered.

My murderous haze cleared. He was stalling, which meant in all likelihood, he was lying about their deaths. I tapped Bones's arm. He released me, but one hand remained on my waist.

"My feelings are irrelevant," Bones answered. "I sired them so they're mine, and if they're dead, then you have no further use for them."

"What possible use would *you* have?" Madigan demanded.

A dark brow rose. "Not your concern. I'm waiting."

"Then it's a good thing you don't age," Madigan snapped as he rose from his chair. "Their bodies were cremated and their ashes disposed of, so there's nothing left to give you."

If Madigan wanted us to believe they were dead, then they must be in serious trouble. Even if Madigan wasn't behind it, he clearly intended to leave them to their fates.

I wasn't about to.

Something in my stare must have alarmed him because he glanced left and right before flinging a hand in Bones's direction.

"If you're not intending to let her complete her term of service, then both of you can get out. Before I have her jailed for dereliction of duty, desertion, and trying to attack me."

I expected Bones to tell him where to go, which was why I was stunned when he merely nodded.

"Until next time."

"What?" I burst out. "We're not leaving without more answers!"

His hand tightened on my waist.

"We are, Kitten. There's nothing for us here."

I glared at Bones before turning my attention to the thin, older man. Madigan's face had paled, but underneath the heavy scent of cologne, he didn't smell like fear. Instead, his blue gaze was defiant. Almost . . . daring.

Once more, Bones's grip tightened. Something else was going on. I didn't know what, but I trusted

Bones enough not to grab Madigan and start biting the truth out of him like I wanted to. Instead, I smiled enough to bare my fangs.

"Sorry, but I don't think you and I would have a healthy working relationship, so I'll have to decline the job offer."

Multiple footsteps sounded in the hall. Moments later, heavily armed, helmeted guards appeared in the doorway. At some point, Madigan must have pushed a silent alarm—an upgrade he'd installed since my previous visit to his office.

"Get out," Madigan repeated.

I didn't bother with any threats, but the single look I gave him said that this wasn't over.

*G*ive in to your Impulses!

**These unforgettable stories only take a second
to buy and give you hours of reading pleasure!**

Go to *www.AvonImpulse.com* and see what we
have to offer.

Available wherever e-books are sold.

AVONIMPULSE

IMP 0811